THE COPPER EGG

What Reviewers Say
About Catherine Friend's Work

The Spanish Pearl

"A fresh new author...has penned an exciting story...told with the right amount of humor and romance. Friend has done a wonderful job..."—*Lambda Book Review*

"The author does a terrific job with characterization, lush setting, action scenes, and droll commentary. This is one of those well-paced, exciting books that you just can't quite put down. ...This is one of the very best books I've read in many months, so I give it my highest recommendation! Don't miss this one."—*Midwest Fiction Review*

The Crown of Valencia

"Her storytelling talent is superb and her plot twists continually keep the reader in suspense..."—*Just About Write*

Hit By a Farm

"*Hit By a Farm* goes beyond funny, through poignant, sad and angry, to redemptive: all the things that make a farm—and a relationship—successful."—*Lavender Magazine*

"A sweet and funny book in the classic 'Hardy Girls Go Farming' genre, elegantly told, from the first two pages, which are particularly riveting for the male reader, through the astonishing revelation that chickens have belly-buttons and on to the end, which comes much too soon. It has dogs, sheep, a pickup truck, women's underwear, electric fences, the works."—*Garrison Keillor*

Sheepish: Two Women, Fifty Sheep, and Enough Wool
to Save the Planet

"As provocative as her reflections are, it is Friend's acerbic wit that keeps the reader turning pages. A perfect choice for book groups, this is a look at the road not taken with a guide who pokes as much fun at herself as she does at the world around her."—*Booklist*

"Friend details the challenges of balancing a writing career with sheep farming in southeastern Minnesota....Her voice is wry and funny; she's self-deprecating and thoughtful, and strikes a balance between teasing and kindness, whether her subject is pregnant sheep, yarn-loving 'fiber freaks,' or spirituality and nature."—*Publishers Weekly*

Visit us at www.boldstrokesbooks.com

By the Author

Bold Strokes Novels

The Spanish Pearl

The Crown of Valencia

A Pirate's Heart

The Copper Egg

Nonfiction

Sheepish: Two Women, Fifty Sheep,
and Enough Wool to Save the Planet

The Compassionate Carnivore, Or, How to Keep
Animals Happy, Save Old MacDonald's Farm,
Reduce Your Hoofprint, and Still Eat Meat

Hit By a Farm: How I Learned to
Stop Worrying and Love the Barn

Children's

Barn Boot Blues

The Perfect Nest

Eddie the Raccoon

Silly Ruby

Funny Ruby

The Sawfin Stickleback

My Head is Full of Colors

THE COPPER EGG

by

Catherine Friend

2016

THE COPPER EGG

ISBN 13: 978-1-62639-613-5

THIS TRADE PAPERBACK ORIGINAL IS PUBLISHED BY
BOLD STROKES BOOKS, INC.
P.O. BOX 249
VALLEY FALLS, NY 12185

FIRST EDITION: MAY 2016

CREDITS
EDITOR: CINDY CRESAP
PRODUCTION DESIGN: SUSAN RAMUNDO
COVER DESIGN BY JEANINE HENNING

Acknowledgments

When we slip into a fictional world, we'd like everything in it to be real. It's not, however, since authors enjoy making stuff up. We even mess with reality now and then. In *The Copper Egg* I messed with the heavens, so please don't use my location of the Carina Nebula as a tool for finding your way in Peru!

My beta readers Kathy Connelly, Carolyn Sampson, Ann Etter, Mary Casanova, and Irene Friend (my mom!) gave me valuable, thoughtful feedback. As always, my editor, Cindy Cresap, gently nudged me toward a stronger story. A special thanks to the late Sandra Moran for reading an early draft and sharing her thoughts on archaeology, Peru, and the Quechua language.

The looting of Peruvian tombs continues to be an enormous problem, but there are many people working hard to stop it. I admire their continued perseverance in the face of such difficult odds.

Dedication

For Melissa, who still makes me laugh every day

CHAPTER ONE

Claire
Wednesday, March 15

Claire Adams had just poured herself a glass of Cabernet to celebrate surviving another Wednesday when the doorbell rang.

It was the UPS guy. As Claire signed the screen, she said, "You're working late today."

He rolled his eyes. "Delivering packages is my life."

She chuckled, then accepted the smallish package. "Hell of a life."

"Don't I know it."

Claire closed the door with a wave, then froze at the postmark on the box.

Peru.

Claire and that country had parted on less than friendly terms. She'd left three years ago, humiliated and professionally embarrassed.

She peered closer at the box. Not just Peru, but *Trujillo*, Peru.

Claire's heart did some impressive acrobatics, ending up lodged halfway up her throat until she realized it wasn't *that* woman's handwriting. Relieved, Claire's heart slid back down where it belonged.

That woman. Sochi Castillo. The woman who'd earned Claire's trust and captured her heart, then betrayed her to the whole world. Claire could weather lots of crap—she liked to think not much ruffled her thirty-two-year-old feathers—but Sochi's actions had knocked

Claire on her butt. Took her these three years to recover. And if pressed—which Claire's mom sometimes enjoyed doing—Claire perhaps wasn't yet entirely over the whole thing, since she'd gained ten pounds this year alone. Agitated, Claire pulled her long hair back in a ponytail.

Sochi wouldn't have sent this box. If not Sochi, then Hudson? For the four years Claire lived in Peru, she'd been the youngest ever subdirector of excavation at Chan Chan, the ruins of the largest adobe city in the world. Hudson had been her assistant. But the thread of their friendship wound all the way back to the doctorate program at Brown. When Claire left Peru in shame, Hudson had been given her job. He deserved it, and she was pleased he'd kept up the programs she'd started. She loved that job, spending her days working hard to preserve and explore an amazing adobe city that was over one thousand years old.

Claire dug out her phone and thumbed a text to Hudson. *Did you send me a package?*

Her phone chimed less than a minute later. *No. Did I miss your birthday?*

No, just wondering.

Even though it was the same time in Trujillo, Hudson would still be at work. She could easily imagine him sitting in his office, since the office had once been hers, only now its walls would be covered with Japanese woodcuts, Hudson's Firefly T-shirt collection, and there'd probably be a few surfboards leaning in the far corner. The two windows would be open, and a ceiling fan would be circulating the dry air.

She and Hudson had had some good times in that office. Since Hudson's office looked out over the trash bins and was too full of junk to actually use, he often worked in Claire's office for part of each day.

When their boss, Silvio Flores, would praise Claire for her clean office, Hudson would lean back in the extra chair, hands laced behind his head, and say, "She gets it from me." Claire would laugh so hard she'd snort.

A pang of longing stabbed her, but she ignored it. Claire Adams didn't do nostalgia.

How are you? Haven't heard from you in ages.

She ignored Hudson's jab. He could have texted her at any time as well, but it had been months since they'd connected. *Fine. You?*

Just had another fight with Sochi over my backflap. She still won't return it.

The week after Claire left Peru, Hudson had accepted the subdirector job at Chan Chan. Two months later he'd been digging by himself—something archaeologists rarely did—in an area long believed to have been exhausted of all artifacts. But he'd uncovered a small treasure of flattened gold panels, high quality pots, and a solid gold backflap weighing almost two pounds. The backflap was a flat, ceremonial gold piece warriors hung from a waist cord at the small of the back.

But she stole it, Claire keyed.

Damn right.

Claire knew the story by heart. Sochi had claimed the backflap in the name of the country's antiquities organization, El Centro Nacional de Tesoros Peruano, or CNTP, and Hudson had been fighting ever since for its return to Chan Chan.

Sorry, Hud. Wish I could help, but Sochi is ancient history for me.

She is daily nightmare for me. Gotta go.

Claire considered the box. She could never turn down a treasure hunt, no matter her age. Whether it was searching for Easter eggs when she was eight, or trying to get into Amanda Blakeley's boxer shorts when she was eighteen, she could never resist searching for the hidden.

Part of the joy of a treasure hunt was anticipation, when you imagined finding the X-marked spot on the sand under which some crazy pirate had buried his treasure. She sipped her wine, wondering what could be in a box sent from Peru without a return address.

She savored the anticipation for a full twenty seconds, then cut open the box and removed a wad of packing paper. She peered inside. A nest?

Claire carefully lifted out a bird's nest made of slender twigs. Nestled into this fragile structure were three small eggs, each half the length of her thumb: one made of gold, one made of silver, and the last one copper. Each egg was banded around its middle with a deeply etched design.

Etched seals circled the gold egg. The silver egg was adorned with etched birds. The copper egg seemed the heaviest of all, which made no sense because gold weighed two and a half times more than silver or copper. The gold egg should have been the heaviest, but it was the copper egg that sank deeply into her palm as if it'd come home.

Fish swam around the copper egg. Verdigris had obviously been cleaned from it because there was green still embedded in the etching. The verdigris helped Claire see that in addition to the deep etchings, a few lighter scratches wandered randomly across the copper egg. She checked the other eggs, and they were scratched as well.

Claire had never really appreciated how small her kitchen was until she started pacing it. Three eggs—gold, silver, and copper—could only mean one culture: the Chimú. They'd lived along the northern coast of Peru from about 900 to 1450 and were the ones who'd built Chan Chan, a city of towering twenty-foot adobe walls carved with gorgeous seals, birds, and fish.

The Chimú had a charming origin myth. They believed that God laid three eggs for them. Out of the gold egg hatched members of the elite ruling class. Out of the silver egg hatched the women who married these rulers. Out of the copper egg hatched everyone else—artisans, farmers, laborers—the people who kept the "gold" and "silver" fed, clean, and safe. If these eggs were Chimú, they were extremely valuable.

No way would Sochi have sent these, since she lived by only two rules. One, it was fine to betray the woman you loved, and two, Peruvian artifacts belonged only in Peru.

If Hudson had found the eggs, he would have made sure the entire archaeological world knew about it. It couldn't have been him.

One more search of the box yielded a note in the bottom. The messy handwriting was the same as on the package. *Dearest Claire Adams, Please accept my gift to you of these three Chimú eggs. They are from King Chacochutl's tomb.*

Claire actually gasped. King Chacochutl's tomb was the Holy Grail for which everyone searched but no one found. Most modern archaeologists now dismissed it as a legend. She'd never considered it to be real, even though she loved to fantasize just as much as the next scientist about that one incredible discovery, the one that would set you apart from all the others in your field. The person who found King Chaco's tomb, if it actually existed, would become part of the history books.

The note continued:

Looters approach the King's glorious tomb and will soon steal its wealth and history. The King wishes you to find him first. This way his treasures—and his story—will be preserved for all the world to know. You can hear the voices, so you're the only one who can find the tomb... " She stopped.

Crap. Not this again.

The King calls out to you. Come listen. Sincerely, Your humble servant, a loyal subject of King Chaco...

Claire fought the urge to do something destructive, but lost the battle and flung the box across the room. Whoever sent the eggs and the note knew why she'd left Peru. This person thought Claire could walk back into the country and lead everyone to King Chaco's tomb.

Forget it. Claire retrieved the box and replaced the nest and eggs, planning to send them straight back to Peru, to the CNTP. She opened another bottle of wine, then laughed, which felt like a weird thing to do when you're alone. A chuckle, fine, but this was a deep-throated belly laugh.

King Chacochutl's tomb? *Seriously?*

She did a quick search on her phone to refresh her memory and found an excerpt from a book written by a Spanish missionary who'd accompanied Pizarro when he conquered the Incas in the early 1500s.

Fifty years before that event, the Incas had conquered the Chimú people and marched them to Cuzco to be slaves. Once the Spaniards arrived, some of the surviving Chimú talked of King Chacochutl to the Spanish missionaries. Considered a god by some, the deceased Chaco was entombed in an underground chamber filled with gold and silver and copper, valuable gemstones, shells, and ceremonial gear like backflaps, masks, shields, and Tumi knives.

Twenty women and twenty llamas were sacrificed to accompany Chaco on his journey to the next world. But when the missionaries eagerly asked these Chimú for the location of this treasure, none of them knew. Chaco had been buried two hundred years earlier, and the knowledge of the secret location had died not long after. Only the myth remained.

Claire drank another glass of wine, forced to admit that this box had her a little agitated.

Would she return to Peru to search for Chaco's tomb? Return to the country that held the memory of being loved more deeply than she'd ever thought possible? Return to the memory of a betrayal so deep the scar would never heal?

She emptied her glass.

The answer was clear: No freaking way.

But then, damn it, hunting for treasure was like mainlining a drug—once you've done it, your desire only grew. Her fingers itched to buy a plane ticket, since her "people"—geocachers, those treasure hunters who used GPS to find hidden caches—loved to be the first to find a new cache. FTF was the proud claim: First to Find.

Part of her wanted to return to Peru and find King Chaco's tomb. Then she could say to the media, "Yes, you made fun of me. Yes, you disparagingly called me the Tomb Whisperer, but now look what I've done for your country." Claire stared at the box, knowing her thoughts were small-minded.

"But a small mind's all I have to work with these days," she muttered. Maybe another glass of wine would help her decide.

Life was okay. It wasn't the greatest, certainly not where she'd expected to be by this point, but she had a job with good people. She lived in a nice condo near the Metro, went out with a few friends now and then, and she'd been working hard to see the positives in her life. She didn't need a stressful treasure hunt. She didn't need to be on the same continent as Sochi Castillo.

She liked Washington, DC. She'd even learned to blend in, staring at her phone all the time when she wasn't working, and sometimes when she was. Most of the time she was watching a video or playing a game instead of communicating with others, but no one knew that because they were too focused on their own phones. Claire felt an odd sense of connectedness when everyone around her was doing the same thing. It was like the communal experience of seeing a movie in a theater instead of at home—everyone hyper-focused alone, but together.

Claire checked her phone and read a few social media entries from people she didn't know, and a few from people she knew but didn't care about, and tried not to feel lonely. She tossed the phone onto the cushion beside her and looked around the room, which was done in grays with splashes of turquoise. She had a lovely home.

No. She wasn't going to Peru. If the eggs truly came from King Chaco's long-lost tomb, then someone else already knew where it was. They didn't need her.

CHAPTER TWO

Claire
Thursday, March 16

The DC skies were heavy and gray, not helping Claire's mood. Absolutely *nothing* interesting happened at work, which was usual. As a result of the messy way she'd left Peru, the great job Claire had hoped for at the Smithsonian in DC disappeared faster than a puff of smoke. She ended up as a mid-level manager for a new Smithsonian venture—moving priceless museum art and artifacts for other museums. This way the museum administration didn't have to be embarrassed that they'd hired the Tomb Whisperer.

So instead of searching for treasures as an archaeologist, Claire supervised the transport of treasures, a job that was just as exciting as it sounded. The closest she came to the actual artifacts was reading their descriptions on work orders. The only hunting she'd been able to do was the day Bob misplaced the necklace of Hapiankhtifi, 12th dynasty, as it was being transported from New York's Metropolitan Museum of Art. Hunting down that impressive necklace proved to be the most fun she'd had in months.

But today Bob didn't lose anything, and the morning dragged on. Nothing broke in transit. All the clients were happy with their work. Claire's training session for new employees nearly put her to sleep. They laughed when she shared their internal motto: *If you don't break it, you don't have to fix it.* It wasn't a joke, just a daily truth everyone seemed to forget.

She didn't even have any outstanding invoices to try to collect. By noon, her boss Mac, a round, bald guy always chewing on a toothpick to help him stop snacking, said she was doing a bang-up job. Claire rolled her eyes and let him see it. How could Mac not see the phrase "bored to death" tattooed all over her face?

Mac had brought his black lab, Roger, to work because the dog needed medication four times a day for an infection. After lunch, Claire kidnapped Roger and took him to her office. She sat on the floor, her back against the wall, with Roger's head on her lap. She played with his soft ears, rolling and unrolling them until Roger grunted with pleasure. She played with his big feet, amazed to learn that dog feet smelled oddly comforting, and vaguely like toast.

Claire wanted to be the type of person who shared her life with a dog. The dog owners she knew just seemed better grounded, less likely to float up and away from their life's pathway. But the time had never been right—college, grad school, then the move to Peru. She'd been in DC now for three years, plenty of time to settle down and get a dog. But she hadn't done it. Maybe she was like those writers who enjoyed talking and thinking about writing, but who disliked actually writing. Maybe she was a wannabe dog owner, doomed to only talk about it.

Mid-afternoon, Claire returned Roger to Mac for his pill, then closed her office door and made a personal phone call.

"Hey, Mom."

"Claire Bear! How's my absolutely most favorite daughter?"

"I'm your only daughter."

"And my absolutely most favorite daughter!"

Maybe instead of going on a stupid treasure hunt, what she really needed was to go home for a few days. She could curl up on the faded brown sofa and have a *Lord of the Rings* movie marathon with her parents. During the tense moments Mom would cry, while Dad and Claire would fire popcorn at each other. Unlike many people, she'd had a childhood filled with love and support.

"Mom, I think I need an early spring vacation. Are you and Dad around?"

"Actually, no. We're packing for a white water rafting trip in Mexico. We leave tomorrow."

"I've heard the rivers down there are really swollen from all the rain."

"Precisely why we're going. It's an opportunity for some extreme rafting that we can't miss. Your dad and I don't want to get old until we're actually old. Hey, come with us!"

"Thanks, Mom, but that's not the kind of vacation I was looking for."

"I know. What you really need is to visit Peru one more time."

Claire snorted, unnerved that Mom would bring up Peru. "Mom, you can't be—"

"I am totally serious. You left before you had time to figure things out, to process everything. And you dumped Sochi, whom we adored."

"Mom—"

"And you've practically abandoned poor Hudson."

"I have not. We just texted yesterday."

"When's the last time you've seen him?"

Claire hesitated.

"Every time he comes back to Virginia to visit his parents, you find an excuse to be gone."

"No, that's—"

"When was the last time you actually spoke?"

She opened her mouth then closed it again. She couldn't remember. No wonder their texts had started to feel stilted.

"You've not been a good friend to Hudson. In fact, sweetie, you haven't been a good *anything* these last three years."

"That's harsh, Mom."

"Claire, you're stuck. You've been stuck since all that ghastly publicity about you finding tombs by hearing voices of the dead, which is totally unfair. Speaking with the dead is a perfectly legitimate way to work." Only her parents would think the paranormal was normal. "You've been stuck since you left Peru. Don't you think it's time to go back there and get closure?"

"What sort of closure?"

"I don't know, babe. It depends on what you need."

Claire hated it when Mom made sense, which she almost always did.

"Your father's yelling at me from the garage. Gotta go. I'll text you when we're off the river."

Claire moaned softly at the phone. It was freaking exhausting to have parents who were younger than she was.

The workday still hadn't ended, so Claire did some research on the current state of archaeology in Peru and was horrified by what she found. The looting of Peruvian tombs had really gotten out of hand. Two dominant looting gangs were on the verge of declaring war on each other. One was purportedly run by Carlos Higuchi, a Japanese-Peruvian with his manicured fingers in every business possible—legit and illegit. The other was run by a woman, which captured Claire's attention. This woman was called *La Bruja sin Corazon*—the witch without a heart. If Claire'd been in any other line of work, she would have admired La Bruja for taking on this Higuchi. But looting Peru of its treasures? Unforgiveable. Disgusting. Between the two of them, unprotected sites were being raided and the treasures smuggled out of Peru.

She cheered herself with the idea of bringing back the delightful practice of mounting heads on spikes as a deterrent to crime. Now *that* would be something worth traveling to Peru for—the sight of two heads mounted in Lima's main square: Higuchi's and La Bruja's.

The longer she researched, the harder it was to convince herself that she wasn't going back to Peru. She felt as powerless as a gambler trying to avoid Las Vegas, or a mountain climber trying to avoid Everest. Claire sat there, making a list of all the metaphors that applied until she finally accepted that the hunt was going to lure her back. Nothing she could do about it.

Claire poked her head through her boss's open door. His office smelled of microwave popcorn cooked a few seconds too long. "Hey," she said.

"Hey." Mac nodded toward the open bag of popcorn on his desk.

She took a few kernels and tossed them to Roger. "How many vacations have I taken in the three years I've been here?"

"None."

"Do you think the company would survive if I took off for two or three weeks?"

"We'd probably teeter on the brink of disaster, but I think we could hang on by our fingertips until your return."

"What about four weeks?"

"Hmm. That might be pushing it, but a few weeks is fine, unless, of course, your assistant has his head too far up his ass to do your job."

"Only partially up there. He'll be fine."

"Then get out of here. Don't want to see your face for a few weeks, or at least until Bob loses something."

That evening she stared at her half-packed suitcase. This was insane. Why leave so quickly? Why not take some time to think about this? The plane ticket would certainly be cheaper if she waited a few weeks instead of buying one at the last minute.

Five minutes later, she zipped the faded rose suitcase shut. She knew why she was going now. You never put off a treasure hunt. If you did, someone else might get there first. And when it came to King Chaco's tomb—if it actually existed—Claire was determined to be FTF. First to find.

The next day Claire texted a few friends to cancel plans, then texted her rafting parents. She tucked the gold, silver, and copper eggs into her pocket and flew to Peru.

CHAPTER THREE

Claire
Friday, March 17

Las Dulces was Claire's favorite outdoor café in Trujillo, Peru. Located on the large central plaza, it was perfect for people watching. She gazed across the huge square to the Cathedral, which rose up yellow and white like a marzipan creation. The bright blue building next to the cathedral created an optical illusion, looking as if it were a lake curled around the Cathedral. She shook her head a few times to turn the "lake" back to a building.

Maybe she'd make time to visit the city's historic churches during her stay. While she was as far from religious as one could get, Claire did find it calming to sit inside the old buildings that smelled of smoke and candle wax. Even when the doors were thrown wide open, as they often were, the sounds of the city magically stopped at the entrance, as if chaos knew it wasn't welcome there.

True to its name, Las Dulces—the sweets—boasted everything sweet—pastries glazed with honey and toasted almonds, *orejitas de chancho*, crème caramel, and *tres leches*—a sponge cake soaked in sweetened milk. Claire used to come for the people watching and stay for the sweets. She couldn't resist anything sweet, which was why her attraction to Sochi had never made sense. Sochi had been fiery, passionate, obstinate, intense, but never sweet.

But today, as Claire nibbled on a heart-shaped *orejitas* and enjoyed the occasional crunch of caramelized sugar, she began to feel like an idiot. What sane person dropped out of her life and flew to South America?

And even worse? The CNTP office was only three blocks away, straight down Ayacucho Avenue. Trujillo was one of the largest cities in northern Peru, but you could easily run into people you knew. She scanned every blonde who passed. How could she sit here, on the city's busiest pedestrian sidewalk, and *not* see Sochi Castillo? Claire had come back for a treasure hunt, and if she were to listen to her mother, perhaps some closure with Sochi, but now she lacked the courage to face her. Perhaps that afternoon she'd walk over to the Cathedral, slip inside, and meditate on why she was such a coward.

Claire adjusted her chair so the sunshine hit more of her body. Summer in Trujillo was perfect—blue skies, temperatures between sixty-five and seventy, and hardly any rain, given that the city was located in the Sechura Desert.

A black dog with flecks of white in his face nudged Claire's elbow. He rested his chin on her knee and gave her one of those irresistible looks dogs were famous for. "I'm immune," Claire said. The dog just blinked. Weak as a newborn lamb, Claire broke off a piece of *orejitas* and fed it to him. After a quick lick of her hand in gratitude, the dog trotted away to the next occupied table. Now that was a practical dog—too focused on eating to get wrapped up in sentimentality. Yes, she definitely needed a dog. A dog could pull her out of the hole she seemed to have fallen into. Getting a dog would be easier—and more pleasant—than seeking closure with Sochi.

She took another gulp of Coca Cola Lite. Why hadn't she stayed at one of the hotels farther out? Instead, she'd chosen La Casa del Sol, a converted colonial mansion built in the late eighteenth century near the center of the old city. Her parents had stayed here when they'd come to visit. Her friends, back when she'd had them, had done the same.

Claire chewed the inside of her cheek. If Sochi heard Claire was in Trujillo, she'd know right where to find her.

Cars honked in traffic, and a jackhammer blasted concrete a few blocks away. Flowers were blooming nearby, perfuming the salty air. Then a new thought brought panic—Sochi could have changed her hair color or grown it out. What if Sochi suddenly appeared and Claire didn't recognize her?

She finished the pastry and licked her fingers clean, resolving to come up with a plan. If she found herself face-to-face with Sochi, what would she do? She inhaled slowly for calm, enjoying the heat of the sun on her head.

Okay, here's what she'd do: She would stand and meet Sochi's five foot seven with her own five foot eight. She would simply say, "You betrayed me." Then she'd watch guilt and shame spread over Sochi's perfect face.

Sochi would say, "It was a mistake. I see that now."

Claire would flare her nostrils as haughtily as she could. "No, the mistake was mine…in trusting you." Then she'd freeze Sochi's very soul with her gaze. Only when Sochi was immobile, frozen to the ground, would Claire turn her back and walk away, listening to the sound of her ex-girlfriend crumpling to the ground in despair.

Well, maybe not. Sochi would never fall to the ground, overcome. Whenever she was upset, her backbone hardened to a steel rod. Okay, no crumpling, but perhaps she would reach out a trembling hand while a strangled sob escaped from her throat. Good. Claire *wanted* her to be devastated. And if Sochi was overcome with regret for what she'd done, Claire could live with that.

A native woman in her bowler hat bartered at her stand with two tourists. Those hats never failed to crack Claire up. In the 1920s, a shipment of bowler hats was sent from Europe to Peru and Bolivia for the European workers building railroads. The hats, too small for the men, somehow ended up in the hands of the native women, and it became their thing.

No, Claire wouldn't go for shame the first time she saw Sochi. Instead, her wit would be as cutting as a knife. She'd say, "You look great, which is no surprise since they say 'a betrayal a day keeps the doctor away.'"

Well, okay, perhaps the wit was more butter-knife sharp than steak-knife sharp, but she had time to work on it.

"Mrs. Claire? Mrs. Claire?"

"Nancho!" Claire rose to her feet and hugged the man who'd approached. "It's so good to see you."

She hadn't seen Nancho Quiroga for three years, but he was dressed exactly the same: baggy shorts, T-shirt, dark blue blazer, and a gray, battered fedora wrapped with colorful cords.

"Mrs. Claire, I am so glad you called me. My car is yours for as long as you need me." Nancho had the warmest smile, one that reached every plane of his broad, brown face, and created in others the need to smile just as widely, even her. He'd been her driver for the four years she'd worked at Chan Chan. She'd tried biking, and buses, and even driving herself, but she'd been so hyper-focused on work that she'd nearly been hit dozens of times. Since she was transportationally challenged, someone had given her Nancho's name, and she gladly put herself in his backseat.

He strode toward a gleaming but very old Buick, water still dripping from its freshly-washed back fender.

"Nancho, you have a different car."

"Thanks to you, Mrs. Claire." He held the back door open. When she'd left so suddenly, she knew Nancho would have to find all new clients because she'd been his sole customer for so long. When they'd reached the airport, Claire had jammed a huge tip into his jacket pocket, then grabbed her suitcase and fled into the small, one-story terminal, fighting back tears. Leaving him had been an unexpected hurt.

"So, Mrs. Claire, where we go today?" She'd tried to shift him from Mrs. Claire to Ms. Adams or just Claire, but he always reverted to Mrs. Claire, his way of showing respect. And he insisted on speaking English, even though her Spanish was better than his English.

Claire slid across the worn but pristine seat. "I thought we'd take a drive up the Pan American, if that's okay."

"We will have lovely drive," Nancho said as he wedged his considerable bulk behind the wheel. Nancho wasn't fat, just a large man whose size sometimes made her feel like a Barbie doll. Yet he was one of the gentlest men she knew.

Claire leaned back and sighed happily. Having a driver felt so bourgeois, but it reminded her of being safely cocooned in the backseat with her little brother, Nick, while her parents talked quietly in the front seat.

"Nancho, how is your family?"

He smoothly merged into traffic. "Anna is eight. Pedro five. They good kids...and bad kids!" They easily slipped back into their comfortable relationship. Claire enjoyed watching Nancho's face in his rearview mirror as he talked about his family. His features were more native than Spanish, of which he was very proud. No sense of native inferiority for Nancho. As they talked, Claire rolled the eggs around in her pocket, her fingers easily picking out the copper egg because of its weight.

Nancho was one of Peru's indigenous natives, derisively called "indios" by some. Most of the natives spoke Quechua, the language of the Incas. Dozens of other languages died out when the Spaniards arrived, so many natives later adopted Quechua as their language. Claire only knew enough Quechua to recognize it, but not to speak or understand it.

As they neared the entrance to Chan Chan, Claire's body tightened. Even though the voices had finally faded in DC, she expected they would start up again now that she was back in Peru. She quickly downed two aspirin, since the voices were always worse at the edges of cities and in the rural areas, the sites of many as-yet undisturbed tombs. You didn't have to dig very deep to find an ancient skeleton in Peru. Literally—sometimes less than half a meter would uncover bones or pottery sherds. She clenched her fists and closed her eyes. First the voices would come, then the pounding headache would follow.

But nothing happened. Claire finally cracked her eyes open to see they'd passed the entrance to Chan Chan and were well on their way out of Trujillo. Huh. Perhaps she needed to get farther out into the countryside to hear the voices.

Claire loved this part of Peru. The ocean and the Andes were so close together you could turn in a circle and experience both. This early in the day, the foothills were indistinct blue shadows, deeply curved, as if a dozen denim-clad women had laid down to rest. But this afternoon, the sun would highlight every crag and crevasse on the mountains. While Claire loved the summers, she did miss the funky fog collectors set up only in the winter. The large poly nets sparkled with condensed fog, to be collected for drinking water. Thanks to the breezes off the ocean, the nets would dance with light.

Twenty minutes later, Claire still had no voices clamoring to be heard. "Nancho, could you take me back to Chan Chan?" The voices were often worse there, since over the centuries thousands and thousands of people had lived in that huge city.

"You gots it, Mrs. Claire." He quickly found a place to turn around.

Soon he pulled into the long street that led to the Chan Chan Visitors Center and Museum. Surprised to feel a lump in her throat, Claire squeezed her hands together until the damned nostalgia passed. Yes, she had enjoyed working here, but that was part of her past. People who dragged their pasts with them into the future were as burdened as pack llamas.

Nancho parked in the lot.

"I'll just be a few minutes."

At eight square miles, Chan Chan had been the largest city in the Americas, and the largest adobe city on earth. Over ten thousand structures, some with walls nearly thirty feet high, were connected with mazes of passageways and streets. Some Chan Chan streets were over twenty-five feet wide. By the time the city was overrun by the Incas, Chan Chan held 60,000 people.

The parking lot was at the edge of Chan Chan's nine adobe compounds, each of which had been governed by its own Chimú monarch. A ruler built his compound and filled it with pyramidal temples, gardens, reservoirs, rooms for the royal family, and administrative rooms where the Chimú from other cities would pay their tributes. There were doors of silver and walls of gold. When the ruler died, he was buried in a tomb within his palace.

The new ruler would then build his own complex of plazas, gardens, and rooms, displacing city residents so the city kept spreading out. Outside of these palatial compounds lived everyone else who went about the business of supporting city residents. To find water in an area that received less than one-tenth of an inch of water per year, they dug sunken fields, stopping only when they reached the water table. Some fields were planted nearly twenty feet below ground level.

King Chaco hadn't been one of the rulers of Chan Chan. His city had been somewhere else, its location lost to history. A lost city meant a lost tomb.

Claire headed down the path leading to the Tschudi compound, which was now called Nik An. Years ago, the compounds had been given mostly Spanish names, or named for archaeologists. One of her last triumphs as subdirector of excavation was to convince her boss, Silvio Flores, to rename the compounds with native names.

The restored, towering walls of the Nik An complex glowed bronze in the morning sun. The walls of the other compounds, however, were barely a meter high and looked like they'd melted in the sun, thanks to centuries of rain beating down on the adobe. The city had been abandoned when the Incas forced the Chimú to become their slaves and marched them all to Cuzco. The city had been stripped of all its gold and silver by the conquering Spaniards fifty years later.

Since then, centuries of El Niño rainy seasons had nearly destroyed the city. Only a small portion of the walls were now protected with awnings. Chan Chan employees all worked hard to slow the destruction, but there was little work more futile than this. Claire's heart went out to the devoted employees and volunteers who raced against nature to slow the decline.

As she walked, she probed her brain for voices. Where were they? Waves crashed against the beach to the west. A few seagulls called as they swooped over the sugarcane fields surrounding Chan Chan. Bits of sand blew down the path.

She passed a well-preserved section of fishnet wall. Instead of being solid, the thick walls were carved in a series of deep Xs, like a net. Archaeologists believed these were to improve airflow within the walled compounds.

A group of tourists approached from Nik An, so she veered off to the north. Workers stood around a van, so she avoided them as well. It looked like Hudson was making progress on Fechech An, a small compound with well-preserved carvings, although, sadly, most of the walls were disfigured stumps.

Claire followed the path through Fechech An until she reached the ancient city's northern edge. To the north, a long ridge of sand rose above the crops. Her favorite spot in Peru had been at the top of that ridge. She and Sochi had called it "our hill," and they would hike there after work with a bottle of wine and a picnic supper.

Footsteps grated against the rocky path.

"Silvio." Claire recognized the bowlegged gait of Chan Chan's director.

"Claire." The man came to a halt, ignoring her outstretched hand. "Why are you here? There are no job openings." He licked his lips.

She blinked. "Seriously? Wow. It's good to see you as well, Silvio." He was as agitated as the last time she'd seen him, the day the papers had gloated over the ridiculous Chan Chan subdirector who claimed to have found tombs by listening to dead people. The day he'd fired her.

"Silvio, relax. I'm not looking for a job." She should smile to put him at ease, but she didn't really smile. It wasn't her thing. People who smiled too much made her nervous, except for Sochi, whose face just naturally fell into a smile. She already had great crinkles in the corners of her eyes, and would have a beautiful face when she was older.

Silvio scanned the horizon. "We can't afford any more bad press. Are there reporters with you?" He was tall and gaunt, with hair that had begun receding in primary school. His personality had begun receding in utero.

"I've come back to Peru for a few days. There's nothing illegal about that, is there?"

"No, of course not." He had the good grace to blush. "I'm sorry. Looting in the surrounding area has gotten worse, so I thought you might be a looter scoping out the compounds. I am sorry to have accused you, Claire." This time he offered his hand and she took it. Then, with an embarrassed wave, he left her alone.

Weird man. But she'd always be grateful to him. Even though she'd had her PhD and lots of excavation experience in Turkey and Guatemala, she'd been shockingly underqualified for the subdirector position. Yet Silvio had offered her the job anyway.

She faced north again. The long, sandy ridge sent Claire's heart into a weird thumping act. That pile of sand and rocks and tired bushes had been *their* place, hers and Sochi's. To her left, the ocean was a perfect, thin blue horizon. Far off to the right, foothills to the Andes bumped along to form a more ragged, but quite distinctive, horizon.

In between lay the desert, home to Moche and Chimú civilizations. The Andes Mountains effectively created the desert, since the prevailing winds blew westward from Brazil to Peru. The mountains blocked the moisture so it fell as rain on the Brazilian side of the Andes. By the time the wind topped the mountains and rushed down into Peru, the air was dry as a desiccated mummy. Despite this, the land was highly cultivated in sugarcane and avocados, fields and groves so lush you could easily forget they'd been planted in sand until you saw the irrigation pipes. The Moche and Chimú had brought the desert to life centuries ago, also by irrigating.

Yet popping up now and then were sandy hills with erosion-cut rivulets running down their sides. Many of these hills were actually tombs that time and wind had disguised. Looters left them alone because they were too big to safely excavate without being buried in an avalanche, or being caught by the authorities as the work went on night after night.

Claire left the boundaries of Chan Chan and followed the path she and Sochi would take, lunch basket in hand, circling around the sugarcane field. Twenty minutes later, she stood up on the ridge.

Shivers ran through her. "No nostalgia," she snapped. But as usual, she refused to listen to herself. She began hearing voices, but it wasn't the voices of the dead. It was her voice, and Sochi's, three years ago...

...Claire stood under the Visitor Center awning, ignoring the chaos of two busloads of tourists disembarking. She focused only on the woman she loved approaching from the parking lot. Today might be the most important day of her life. For the hour they had together, Claire was determined to ignore the endless voices pounding against her skull.

"Ready?" Sochi called. Her languid smile shot warm tingles down Claire's arms. She had a good feeling about today, and about Sochi's answer. She was ready for some quiet time with her, since the accolades had been coming fast and furious now that Claire had been declared Peru's most successful archaeologist. She'd found five new tombs in the two months since the voices had started.

Twenty minutes later, they reached the scruffy hill north of Chan Chan. Just then, the sun pierced the gray blanket overhead like a dagger slicing through fabric. The sun gave off no warmth, but when a shaft of radiant light hit the dull gray ocean, the water exploded into iridescent sparkles. Claire and Sochi stood in awe as the light danced for them. Claire took this as a sign Peru was blessing this day.

She dropped to the sandy ground, sighing with relief. At her back, to the east, foothills rose up in a distinctive formation. Claire opened the basket, and Sochi spread out a towel to keep the sand out of the food. Claire leaned close, kissing her lightly. "Baby, I need to talk to you about something."

Sochi reached for Claire's hands. "And I want to talk to you about something. But I have to go first. If I don't, I'm going to pop."

"But—"

"Please." Fingers shaking, Sochi opened a flat package and slid out a wooden box with intricate Chimú designs painted on the top and sides.

She handed the box to Claire, who lifted the lid to discover sand with a tiny shovel on top. "Oh, thank you. Sand. Just what I need."

"Funny you. C'mon, you're an archaeologist," Sochi said. "Excavate."

Intrigued by what was clearly a treasure hunt, Claire picked up the two-inch shovel by its tiny handle and began to move the sand around. After she found two small clay figures, one with short, white-blond hair, the other with long brown hair, she met Sochi's gaze. "Love you," Claire whispered.

Sochi inhaled shakily. "Keep going."

"There's nothing left in here. Oh, wait. Look. Here's a teeny tiny key." She brushed off the sand. "Is this the key to your heart?"

Sochi laughed. "No, that's way too mushy. It's the key to that drawer beneath the sand compartment."

"Hidden treasure," Claire whispered. The lock clicked and she slid the drawer open. "More sand?"

Sochi just smiled.

It didn't take her long to find the only item in the sand. She gasped, then held up the ring. "Oh, my." Claire's heart thumped harder than a dog's tail.

"I had it custom made," Sochi said softly. A series of stones circled the platinum band: diamond, gold ball, diamond, silver ball, diamond, copper ball. The pattern circled around the ring until it met itself. Chimú—gold, silver, and copper. Its beauty sucked the oxygen out of Claire's lungs.

Sochi licked her lips. "I know that in America we could legally marry, but I'm hoping this ring, and a ceremony with friends, will be enough for you. From the moment we met at Huanchaco Beach, I knew you were my other half, my soul mate. No, more than soul mate. I have never loved anyone in my life as deeply as I love you. I want to spend all my life with you."

"Stop." Laughter bubbled up Claire's throat, but she needed to have her say before she let it go.

"What?"

Claire reached into her pack and pulled out a black velvet box. "This is for you."

Sochi flipped open the box to find a single marquise diamond, stark in its beauty. They looked at each other and broke up laughing. "What happens when both of us propose?"

Claire kissed her tenderly. "We both say 'yes.'" Then she handed Sochi a thick envelope.

Inside were pages of job listings. "Washington, DC?" Sochi asked.

Claire leaned forward, unable to contain her excitement. "I've applied for four jobs at the Smithsonian. Any of them will be a huge move forward for my career. But I'll have to move back to DC, so I want us to move there together. As you can see, there are oodles of jobs you are qualified for, and we might even be able to get you into the Peruvian embassy."

Sochi stared at the listings. "But I thought you understood...I thought we would live in Peru. There is so much work to be done here. I can't abandon my country now."

Claire had been afraid of this, but was confident Sochi would see reason. She bit her lip. "I need to tell you something that might make a difference." She set her ring back into the sand and slid the drawer closed. "Over two months ago, Hudson and I took San Pedro. It was his idea, not mine, and a stupid one. I started hearing voices... voices babbling in Quechua. The voices speak even faster than your grandmother, so I can't understand them any better than I can understand Mima. They return every day. Whenever I hear voices, I know there's a tomb nearby."

Sochi rubbed her face with both hands. "You hear voices. Of the dead? I am not surprised that someone hears them, but that it's you is unexpected."

"I know. Nancho has been driving me up and down the Pan American, and I have him stop whenever the voices start. I tramp through the brush until the voices are at their loudest. Most of the time, I find a looted tomb, broken pottery, and skeletal remains scattered across the ground."

"Gods, I hate looters."

"But if the ground is undisturbed, I mark the location and send out a team from Chan Chan. They've been excavating the sites."

"Those were the five tombs you found?"

She watched Sochi struggle to reconcile such a fantastical story with down-to-earth Claire. Balanced Claire. Organized Claire. Why hadn't she told Sochi about the afternoon with Hudson and the San Pedro earlier? The freaking drug had really messed her up, and she'd been ashamed to admit it.

"Something happened to me, something that opened a door in my mind, and I can't shut it."

"No, that's impossible. Let me research this. I'm sure—"

"Sochi, don't you think I've already done that? There's nothing out there on this problem."

"Do you hear voices here, at Chan Chan?"

Claire nodded.

"But this is an abandoned city. There were only a few tombs here."

"The voices scream all day long. Do you believe me?"

"Of course I believe you. The voices give you headaches?"

Claire nodded again.

"Okay, we'll move south along the coast. Or inland. We can—"

"I don't want to live in Peru. It's time for me to move to the next level. It's time for us to move on together."

Her heart plunged at the look on Sochi's face. "But I can't leave Peru. People are raping the land, stealing our heritage right from under us."

"Come to DC with me. You can help Peru from there."

Sochi pressed her lips together and squeezed her eyes shut for a second. "Claire, I can't leave Peru. My heritage won't survive if all the people who can help just abandon her. We can find you a great job in Lima. We don't have to stay in Trujillo."

"But I need a Smithsonian job to further my career."

Unable to look at each other, they stared at the cooler, the sandwiches inside forgotten. If Claire put even one bit of food in her mouth, she'd be sick.

Sochi pulled in a huge breath. "We love each other, right? You've been dealing with this for months—thanks, by the way, for waiting so long to share it with me. But I've only had ten minutes. Give me more time. We'll figure this out. I know we will. We can stay in Peru and you can still advance your career."

Why didn't Sochi understand how important this was? A deep blanket of certainty fell over Claire. They weren't going to work this out. It was impossible. She'd been deluding herself. She reached over and took back her velvet box, snapping it shut so emphatically that Sochi jumped. "Soch, you can't leave Peru. I hear you. But I don't want to stay. There's nothing more to discuss."

As they stared at each other, Claire's head throbbed with pain. She would not remain in Peru. She couldn't.

The day's heat was suddenly unbearable. Sweat stung Claire's eyes, but she refused to wipe them. Instead, she kept her gaze on Sochi, giving her one last chance to change her mind, to see that they had to move to DC.

But Sochi grabbed her wooden box and stood, fury sharpening her features. Without a word, she staggered toward the path. The wedding ring Claire had rejected rattled inside the box…

Claire shook her head and looked around, forcing herself back to the present. Crap. This was one reason why she'd avoided coming back to Peru. The memories were just too painful. The evening of that horrible fight, Claire had slid a letter under Sochi's door. A letter of apology. The very next day, Sochi destroyed their relationship by betraying Claire. End of story.

Claire stood, brushed the sand off her palms, and arched her back as she surveyed the land around the ridge. She'd spent enough time this afternoon away from Trujillo to know that the voices had probably faded for good. Why had she expected them to return?

Claire grunted in frustration. Without the voices, she had no way to track down King Chaco's tomb.

What had she been thinking? That she would simply drive through the Peruvian countryside, listening intently until the voice of King Chaco's ghost called out to her, *I'm over here. Dig down half a meter and you'll find us.* Because tombs had been constructed of wood and adobe, most of them would have collapsed upon themselves centuries ago.

She was stupidly unprepared. She didn't even have a shovel. She wasn't the Tomb Whisperer. She'd *never* been that. The word *fraud* began sneaking through the hallways of her brain, but she flung it back into its cell and locked the door. Still, the word managed to leak out through the keyhole. She'd found so many tombs not because of her archaeological skills, but because of the voices. And she hadn't even done that alone. In each case, she'd marked the general area where the voices were the loudest, then five or six people, depending upon the availability of enthusiastic interns or grad students, would carefully excavate until they reached the tombs.

Claire walked the length of the ridge, then slid down into the edge of the sugarcane field. Carefully skirting the rustling plants, she made her way to the shore, rough with rocks and reeds.

Plovers skittered across the narrow beach, running in and out of the pale yellow foam pushed ahead of each wave. Two brown pelicans swooped low over the water, their shadows swimming beneath them.

Claire shielded her eyes against the sun as she gazed out over the white swells gently rolling toward her. Well, crap. What now? She couldn't find King Chaco's tomb without the voices. She needed help. She needed Denis.

Chapter Four

Sochi
Friday, March 17

Sochi Castillo tried not to worry, but like Mima always said, worry tells you what part of your life needs attention. Sochi chuckled. Since she was always worrying, her entire life obviously needed attention. When everything felt broken, it was hard to know where to start.

Sochi tried to ignore both the waxing moon—still bright as a spotlight—and her racing heartbeat as she crouched near a scrubby bush worrying about the next two minutes. At her side, Rigoberto raised his meaty hand, and the five men behind them stopped. The shaman hovered farther back, not needed for this part of the operation.

Sochi leaned forward, straining to hear. Just over the sandy ridge, the looters talked quietly among themselves, arguing over who would win the World Cup now that the Peruvian team had crashed and burned early in the event. Shovels dug into the sand. One man coughed. The ocean, less than a mile away, salted the warm night air. Sochi's nostrils flared as she detected the closer smells of hot sweat and cigarette smoke. The leaves of a nearby algarrobo tree rustled quietly.

Rigo lightly touched her shoulder and spoke into her ear. "Let me and the men do this. It may get rough. We do not know these looters."

Looters. How had her life come to this? Gods, what a mess. Reminded her of one of Mima's sayings: *If you feel as if life is falling apart, it probably is. Stop and fix it.* Her grandmother would deliver this homily with a shaking finger. Sochi shuddered. If Mima knew what she was up to tonight, it'd kill her, but when Deep Throat had waved the Peruvian flag in Sochi's face and given a moving plea for patriotism, she'd agreed. She was doing this at the request of a governmental minister, not because looting was fun. It wasn't.

"Remember," she whispered, "no violence."

Rigo kept his voice low. "Never, *jefe.*"

Jefe. Boss. That also felt weird, even after all this time. When she nodded, Rigo motioned to the men and they crept forward, pulling bandanas up over their faces. They wore T-shirts, lightweight pants, and sandals, all covered in dust. With the moonlight turning their sticks into ghostly weapons, Rigo and his men dashed over the ridge.

The looters let out startled yells. Rigo commanded that they abandon the dig site, which most of them did immediately. Sochi felt their pounding footsteps through her feet. Keeping low, she crested the ridge to watch, then motioned the shaman forward.

In the circle of light thrown by a Coleman lantern on the ground, a sole looter remained. The middle-aged man's torn khakis and brown shirt were nearly white with sand. He wore a T-shirt tied around his nose and mouth to keep out the dust. The lantern illuminated the devastation his team had wrought on yet another ancient Peruvian tomb.

"No," the man said. "This is our site. We are locals. Go find your own place to dig."

Rigo laughed. "Move on, old man."

One of her men, feisty Tomas, approached the man with a length of pipe, clearly intent on using it. "Gods," she muttered. "I *knew* it." One of these days, Tomas would go too far.

Sochi rose to her full height and strode down the slope into the maze of holes and piles the looters had created. The man saw her approaching in the lamplight.

"*Jesus Cristo,*" he breathed. "La Bruja sin Corazon." The witch without a heart.

Tomas stopped and looked over his shoulder. She glared at him.

"Bruja, why bother us?" the man cried. "This is our only way to earn an income."

When she began her career as La Bruja, Sochi had done her best to *become* the Heartless Witch. She took credit for any dead body found from Lima up to Ecuador. She paid a few motormouths to talk her up, and soon she had a reputation that frightened even her. She and her men had never actually harmed anyone, but thanks to the power of social media, the country believed the opposite.

Her name, Witch Without a Heart, had been meant to inspire fear, but she just thought it was stupid. Much of what Deep Throat came up with was stupid. But here she was, with a powerful reputation that preceded her. Very few women ran looting gangs, since most of the older men believed women at dig sites angered the spirits.

"You will find another way to put food on the table," Rigo told the remaining looter, who thrust out his chin in defiance.

"Leave, or my men will help you leave," Sochi said. "I am afraid they are not at all gentle. And do not return to this site."

Disgusted, the man raised his shovel in defiance, then stomped off, moonlight bleaching his stooped shoulders until he disappeared into the blue-black night.

Sochi sighed with relief. Another band of rival looters vanquished without violence. This had just been a group of local guys, unarmed and willing to back off. One day she and Rigo were going to stumble upon Carlos Higuchi's crew, and that encounter could have a very different ending.

Rigo motioned to the man who'd hung back from everything. Julio Rojas, shaman to looters of every nationality, stepped forward. Personally, she didn't see the need for a shaman, but the men did. Disturbing burial sites could anger the gods. Julio walked in a wide circle, speaking Quechua in a singsong voice, sprinkling crushed-up cigarettes over the ground. When he was done, Sochi handed him a roll of dollars, preferred over the Peruvian currency, and thanked him for his time. With a wave to the others, Julio trudged back up over the sand dune.

As everyone grabbed a discarded shovel, Sochi's jaw tightened to see the pile of now-broken pots the local looters had tossed aside as worthless. Idiots. "Remember," Sochi said. "Preserve everything you find. Collectors will pay us good prices. You crack a pot, I crack your head." Really, it would be Rigo, since she could barely swat a fly without being overcome with guilt.

Rigo wasn't the brightest star in the constellation, but he was a warrior and he understood how to lead men. And he was almost more devoted to the Chimú and Moche cultures than she was. "It is midnight," she continued. "We will dig until five a.m., then pack everything into Rigo's van. He'll sell the artifacts and split the proceeds into shares. As usual, Rigo will take two shares, the rest of you one, and myself none. All of the bounty goes to you and your families."

The men nodded, pleased to be working for the fairest looting boss in all of Peru. They spread out and began to dig.

Sochi retrieved a metal pole abandoned at the edge of the site. While her men dug in pits already opened, she would seek new dig sites. She moved out of the weak circle of lantern light and used only the moonlight to choose a spot. She pushed the sharpened end of the pole into the sandy ground as far as she could. She met resistance, which meant there was no tomb cavity below. She took a few steps and repeated the motion. Her arms would be numb with exhaustion by the end of the night, but she had already achieved her goal. Word would quickly spread that any treasures found in this tomb, ninety miles north of Trujillo, now belonged to the second-most successful looter of Peruvian antiquities—La Bruja sin Corazon. This would remind the most successful looter—Carlos Higuchi—that he wasn't the only fish in this large pond.

As she took a few steps and probed another spot, her long brown hair stuck to the back of her hot neck. Checking over her shoulder to make sure no one watched, Sochi stuck a finger under the edge of the wig and scratched the base of her skull. She hated this damned wig. She also hated the brown contacts, but both were necessary. Not even Rigo knew she wore a disguise. Deep Throat had insisted that he be the only one who knew what she was up to. But wearing contacts while digging in the sand meant her eyes stung most nights, and were red-rimmed by morning. She didn't participate in the digs every night, mostly to give her eyes a rest and grab some sleep.

As Sochi repeatedly jammed the pole into the ground, the breeze moaned through the flat, broad leaves of the abandoned avocado grove next to the tomb, as soft as Claire's sighs during…Damn it. Sochi shook herself. Damn that woman. She hit a rock with the pole, wincing at the shock to her upper arms. Stop thinking about Claire. Just stop it.

She diverted herself with thoughts of her parents. She'd always been grateful to them for giving her a native name instead of a Spanish one, even though Xochiquetzal was Aztec, not Chimú or Moche. During three years of middle school in the States while her mother was posted to the Peruvian embassy, Sochi had grown tired of teachers and students freaking out over the X, so she started using Sochi. It was an okay name, but she loved the Quechua language. Mima spoke it almost more than she spoke Spanish, and Sochi had picked up a surprising amount. Some day she was going to get a dog and name it Suyana, which meant "hope."

An hour later, winded, Sochi leaned her sweaty forehead against the pole. The humid March air was hot against her skin. Claire had taught her to love with her whole heart. She had taught her how to need a person so desperately that sometimes neither words nor thought could fill the need—only touch would do. Then she left, with only a few nasty words as her farewell, teaching Sochi what it felt like to be tossed aside like a broken pot.

Claire had destroyed her life. All Sochi wanted was five minutes with that woman—to tell her exactly what she thought of her, then push her straight into the Pacific Ocean. Well, maybe she'd kiss her and have sex one more time, *then* she'd push her into the ocean. Sochi laughed softly so the others couldn't hear. Could she *be* any more messed up? No, she didn't want sex. She wanted revenge. She wanted justice.

A low whoop from one of the men drew her back to the main dig area. Rigo and Miguel had uncovered a small cache. Sochi watched as her men cleaned off the items—a gold and turquoise ear ornament, a gilded copper drinking cup, four carvings of deer, and two spouted bottles decorated with reddish brown and cream glazes. It wasn't the Lord of Sipan's tomb, or King Chaco's tomb, if that fabled tomb even existed, but still, a nice haul. Her eyes filled as she scanned the soil-encrusted artifacts. Incredibly beautiful. With a heavy sigh, Sochi resumed her work.

For a while, she and Rigo worked together. He told her more of what he knew about Higuchi's main crew boss, Nopa. "He's a killer," Rigo murmured. They all spoke softly to avoid attracting attention.

"Does Higuchi ever work the sites, or is it just Nopa and his men?"

"Nopa does his dirty work, no matter what it is," Rigo said, sounding deeply disgusted. "Nopa is not a man you want to meet out here, in the dark. Some of our men have talked about carrying."

"I don't like guns," Sochi said. "Surely it hasn't come to that." She'd asked Deep Throat about weapons the last time they'd met in his favorite dark alley, but he'd refused.

Hours later, her back ached. Deep Throat wouldn't pay for guns, but she was going to insist he buy them a metal detector. The new ones could detect man-made objects as deep as six meters. She stretched. In a short time, the sky behind the mountains would lighten to a soft, hazy blue. She took Rigo aside. "Denis will buy most of this."

"I will contact him today," Rigo said, his eyes gleaming, his fingers already rolling a San Pedro joint. As part of their post-dig ritual, her men smoked tobacco soaked with the hallucinogenic San Pedro cactus sap. Rigo said they hoped to commune with the dead whose tomb they'd just desecrated, but she knew the ritual was mainly an excuse to get high after a hard night's work.

When she was satisfied he knew how much each item was worth, she left the men to their hallucinations and trudged back to her car, which she'd parked on the gravel road leading to the highway. Pleased but exhausted, Sochi drove as fast as she dared. On the outskirts of Trujillo, she pulled into a deserted gas station and parked in back. She pulled off the coarse wig, scratching her head frantically until her cropped, white blond hair regained its body. She removed the brown contacts. Her hair and ice blue eyes didn't match the deep caramel color of her skin, which Sochi loved. The contrast confused everyone. She squirted drops into her burning eyes, sighing with relief.

Then she grabbed the hanging travel bag from her backseat and stood next to the wall, out of sight of the highway, and changed from her digging clothes into a blue raw silk suit with a pale peach silk blouse. She kicked off her sandals and slipped into moderate heels.

Back on the highway, Sochi checked her watch. Crap. She would be late for the meeting. She finally reached the city, passing the yellow and white cathedral that always reminded her of a wedding cake. Gods, she loved this city. She loved all of Peru. True, the northern part was mostly hills of stone and sand, but the land had captured every shade of beige and brown ever created, and thus shone with its own sort of beauty. After being dragged from embassy to embassy by her parents, when Sochi finished college she moved back to Peru. Finally, she had stability, something she'd never gotten from her parents. She was home. She was here for life. She knew this because not even Claire—when they'd still been speaking—could lure her away. Peru was more than her home. Peru was her *responsibility*.

Sochi pulled into the parking lot behind the building, relieved to find a spot, then dashed for the back door. The organization's name was artistically hand-painted on a sign above the door: *Centro Nacional de Tesoros Peruano*: CNTP. National Center for Peruvian Treasures.

She clattered up the steps, nodded to the receptionist, and hurried down the polished hallway. She loved this old building. "I am so sorry to be late," Sochi said as she nearly ran over her boss, also headed toward the conference room.

Executive Director Aurelio Mamani glared at her. "I was about to start without you." His flared nostrils proclaimed that he disliked delaying meetings for a mere assistant.

Eight people waited in the conference room, sipping coffee and nibbling *alfajores* cookies. Aurelio flashed his politician's smile around the table. "I'm delighted to welcome all of you CNTP regional directors to Trujillo. I'm sure you've met our newest director, Maria Menendez, from the southwestern region." Everyone nodded and smiled at the stunning brunette seated next to Sochi. When the attention was back on Aurelio, Sochi snuck a peek at Maria. Turned out Maria was doing the same to her. When they exchanged shy smiles, a jolt of pleasure zipped through Sochi.

Aurelio's voice was pompous. "I know Lima is a more convenient location for most of you when it comes to our meetings, but I felt it would be good to increase the visibility of northern Peru by meeting here in Trujillo this month."

He nodded at Sochi, so she ran through some of the mundane items on the agenda, then turned the meeting back over to him.

He leaned forward, gazing into each director's eyes for a moment. "Today's topic is looting. It's getting worse. We need to brainstorm new methods for stopping the total destruction and export of our culture and our history. This country has lost more artifacts to looters in the last forty years than in the last four hundred. I hope you have brought your ideas and thoughts to share with the rest of us. Between Carlos Higuchi and La Bruja, we have a war brewing between looters."

Suddenly exhausted, Sochi sat back and listened as Aurelio directed a lively discussion. She took notes without paying much attention, often flexing her right hand, stiff from slamming the pole into the ground for hours on end. Her ankles itched from the sand. Her eyes ached. But still, it had been a productive night's work.

Deep Throat would be pleased. As he often said, the best way to keep Peruvian artifacts from leaving Peru was to steal them before looters could. Sochi struggled with her conscience every day, but a job was a job. And besides, she agreed with him.

CHAPTER FIVE

Claire
Saturday, March 18

Claire wasn't the sort of person to have lots of friends. People were surprised at that, as if blond people naturally bonded with everyone. She used to have that sort of life, but once she hit her thirties, her hair couldn't decide if it wanted to be blond or brown. Brown seemed to be winning, which Claire liked to blame for having fewer friends, even though she knew that made no sense. But then she didn't have to pay attention to her mom and believe that it might be her depressed personality that pushed people away.

Claire had counted Hudson as a friend, but they'd drifted apart. Sochi had been her closest friend, obviously. Maggie and Drew from college would always be in her life, even though they often went months without connecting. But the one good friend she could always count on, especially in Peru, was Denis Valerga.

Saturday afternoon as Nancho dropped Claire off at Denis's house, she bent down to Nancho's open window. "Are you sure you don't mind waiting around?"

"I have many cousins. My cousin Mariposa lives a few miles away, so I will visit her family. Just text when you're ready."

Denis Valerga lived on the eastern edge of Trujillo in a sprawling home set into the dramatic foothills of the Andes. Stark and modern, the all-white home was the perfect backdrop for Denis's collections of pre-Columbian antiquities. Every item mounted on his walls, displayed on simple pedestals, or set into professionally lit niches, had been purchased from looters.

Claire would be hard-pressed to explain to other archaeologists why she and Denis had such a strong bond. Part of it was a love for the cultural treasures buried up and down the Peruvian coast. She loved that he used his great wealth—earned from the sugarcane industry—to keep Peru in Peru.

Part of it was the trust they shared. No matter what the topic, they were always open and honest. No lies. No secrets. They'd agreed to that the day they'd stood in the Trujillo airport watching Denis's daughter Liza board her flight to Jacksonville.

Liza came out to her father when she was twenty-one. He'd already figured it out and admired her courage and determination to be herself. But after two difficult years, he worried that Peru's conservative attitude was crushing her spirit. Claire shared his concern. Liza had insisted on being out and proud, but it was proving dangerous. Even the police constantly harassed her, only stopping short of physical harm because she was a Valerga.

Denis had come to Claire, his face rigid with fear, for advice. She called her cousin Randy in Jacksonville, and two weeks later, Liza went to live with Randy and his boyfriend Mike. Five years later, Liza was now twenty-eight and living happily with Heather, a fourth-grade teacher. Liza called Claire every Christmas. Helping Liza still made her swell with pride.

After Liza had boarded her plane to Jacksonville, Denis had turned to Claire and held both her hands. "The greatest gift I give to my three children is my honesty and my absolute loyalty. I hereby pledge the same to you, with my deepest gratitude."

With that, she became part of Denis's family. With her parents constantly running off to their next crazy adventure, it had been nice having a Peruvian family.

"*Mi hija*, at last you have returned," Denis said as Claire stepped into his welcoming arms, pleased he still called her his daughter. She returned the hug as well as she could, given Denis's impressive bulk. He wore his usual garb—featherlight trousers with a tunic, and simple sandals. He smelled of eucalyptus, and other than a little more gray in his slicked-back hair, he hadn't changed. Denis moved with quiet confidence.

"You look great," Claire said.

"As do you. The extra pounds look good on you."

She laughed. "You weren't supposed to notice." A new Paracas textile hung on the wall behind him, the red and orange tones still brilliant, the fabric showing men fishing in long reed canoes. "Very nice."

Denis shrugged. "My latest."

"Looted."

Now he laughed. "You weren't supposed to notice."

They talked nonstop for an hour. Describing her job took about three seconds, but she enjoyed entertaining him with the story about tracking down the Egyptian necklace Bob had accidentally packed into a crate heading for Brussels.

After he'd told her all about Liza and her brothers, Roberto and Miguel, he leaned closer and took her hand. "I never believed the headlines, the lies they told about you. Yet you left before I could tell you this. And you dropped off the face of the earth, not replying to any texts or calls."

Claire wasn't sure Denis was ready for the truth, but they'd promised honesty to each other. "Well, here's the thing." She met Denis's kind eyes, cocoa brown in a pale face. "The headlines—and the stories that went with them—were, for the most part, true."

He grunted in surprise. "You actually heard voices?"

"One day I...well, it's not important how it started, but just that it did. I began to hear voices speaking Quechua. Those voices led me to the five tombs I discovered."

Denis leaned back, folding both hands over his chest. "If we were in America or some European country, I would be concerned about your mental health, but this is Peru. We inhale the same air as our ancestors inhaled for centuries. Why didn't you tell me?"

"I told no one for weeks. It was just too weird. But after the fifth tomb, and all the attention I was getting as the archaeologist with the golden touch, I had to tell someone. I told Sochi. We had a fight about...about something else...then Sochi..." She clamped her jaw shut.

Denis's eyes widened. "She didn't!"

Claire nodded, surprised to be filling with anger so quickly. "She told the press."

"Mi hija, I am so sorry. But these voices. Tell me what you hear."

"That's the thing! They're gone."

"I am relieved to hear this."

"But it's a good news/bad news sort of thing. The voices are gone, but I'd been planning to use them to help me." How did she bring up Chaco's tomb without sounding even crazier than a woman who heard voices of the dead?

The solution rested in her pocket, so she removed the three eggs and handed them to Denis. His breath quickened as he looked them over. Then she handed him the note, suddenly wanting the eggs back in her hand. Her fingers actually twitched, but she resisted the urge to snatch back the copper egg.

"The deeper etchings are obviously Chimú, but what are these lighter scratches?"

"Don't know. But am I crazy to think that these eggs really could have come from King Chaco's tomb?"

Denis gave her a conspiratorial smile and handed back the eggs and the note. Then he leapt from the sofa with the energy of a much younger man. "Come."

As Claire followed him down the hall, she stopped to examine a Chimú water vessel, noticing that the black glaze was especially shiny for the period.

"Don't look at that too closely," Denis said with a chuckle.

She shot him a look. "Seriously?" Carefully, she lifted it from its wall niche and examined it further, then snorted. "Denis, it's a fake!"

He shrugged. "Liza needed some way to focus her artistic skills in high school, and she continues to help me out now and then from America. It's her hobby." He winked. "But she prefers the term 'reproduction' to 'fake.'"

Wild. Hearing that the premier collector in all of Peru displayed "reproductions" was akin to learning that the Smithsonian's Hope Diamond was really made of plastic.

One of Denis's many rooms was devoted solely to maps. He opened the top drawer of an antique map chest and pulled out a thick file. "Since you left Peru, my sons have also left the nest. So when I have time on my hands, I research my newest hobby." He spread out several handmade maps. "One day I asked myself: If King Chaco's tomb actually existed, where might it be?"

"Denis, you've done all the research."

Two hands the size of catcher's mitts landed gently across the maps. "If you find it, my fee for this information is one gold item."

He would find a way to acquire such an item illegally, so Claire might as well save him the risk. At her brisk nod, he removed his hands. Together, they studied his maps of known tombs.

He had overlaid the photocopied maps with a square grid, then X'd through those pieces of the grid that didn't need searching.

"This is so much work. How did you put this all together?"

"Finding Chaco's tomb has always been a secret obsession. I read all the material written by the Spanish missionaries. I visited each grid to see if it had been developed or not." He separated three maps from the pile. "I've eliminated the area between Chepen and Pacasmayo. And I checked most of the area south of Chan Chan to Chimbote."

"But what about the far northern coast?" She ran her finger all the way up to Punta Sol near the border with Ecuador.

"The material written by the missionaries puts Chaco's city farther south, somewhere along this thirty-mile stretch of coast. His city was much, much smaller than Chan Chan, so it has gone undetected. The missionaries wrote of Chaco's large and impressive tomb, but they never mentioned a location for either the tomb or his city."

"Wouldn't they have been in the same location?" In Chan Chan, when a ruler died, he was entombed with wives, concubines, llamas, and riches, then the tomb was closed.

"Not always. We know that much from the missionaries. A ruler's tomb could be built well outside of a city." Denis rubbed the gray stubble on his chin. "I have narrowed it down to three areas. The first is here, south of Pacasmayo."

Claire studied the map. Most of the grids had been X'd. Only five had small, perfectly formed question marks. Denis had also marked the more than seventeen archaeological sites that stretched north from Trujillo—Galendo, Huaca Prieta, Mocollope, Caballo Muerto, among others. She could avoid those spots, since they'd already been excavated.

"Okay," she said. "What's the second area?"

He switched maps. "The second is on either side of Chicama."

This map had more question marks than Xs, so it hadn't been intensely searched.

He flipped to another map. "Here's the third area, along the five-mile stretch north of Chan Chan, including Chan Chan itself."

Claire shook her head. "Almost all of that area has been excavated to some extent. And didn't I read that La Bruja sin Corazon has been working north of Chan Chan?"

Denis shrugged. "She is all over."

"Sounds like a real bandit."

"Bandit to some, savior to others. She is not nearly as dangerous as Carlos Higuchi."

"Why do you say that? They both sound horrible."

"Higuchi has developed too much influence with our country's ministers. He's been behind many pieces of legislation—both national and regional—that favor his businesses. He's also rumored to be behind a number of unsolved murders."

They took the maps back into the living room and Denis refilled their wine glasses. "I read about him before I came," Claire said. "What's his story? Is he native Japanese, or born here?"

"Japanese-Peruvian," Denis said, "which might explain why he punishes Peru by looting, then smuggling everything out."

"Why punish Peru?"

"Do you know anything about what happened in Peru during WWII?"

She shook her head and settled back against the cushion.

"The Japanese came here in 1899 as laborers, but many of them worked their way into professional life. It was mostly men who immigrated from Japan so they married local women and their children became Peruvians. I think by 1930 almost half ran their own businesses."

"Enterprising people."

"Then WWII came along. Once Japan entered the war, your country put its Japanese citizens in internment camps. Then the Americans began to panic about all the people of Japanese descent in Peru and other South American countries, thinking they might help the Japanese. So America made a deal with Peru: We'll give you all sorts of wonderful military equipment if you'll gather up your Japanese to put in our internment camps."

Claire grimaced. "Wait. Peru sent its people to prison camps in the U.S. in exchange for tanks?"

"The camps were in Nevada, New Mexico, Texas, and a few other states I can't remember. I am not proud of this, but in our defense, the same thing was happening elsewhere in South America. We arrested most of the Japanese-Peruvian families and sent them to U.S. camps."

"Was Higuchi's family involved?"

"Don't know, but if his family was here during WWII, they must have been."

"Well, if mine had been, I'd have a chip the size of Mt. Everest on my shoulder." She wondered if having a chip that large made a person dangerous or just pissed off.

She checked her watch, then nodded toward the wine bottle. "If we reach the bottom of that, I won't be able to sleep tonight." She texted Nancho to pick her up.

As they stood, Denis rested a hand on her shoulder. "I do not know if I truly believe Chaco's tomb exists, or if I am just indulging in a childhood fantasy. I cannot guarantee any of these three maps will help you."

"Denis, you've given me a place to start. Without the voices, I must do this the old-fashioned way, with research and skill and lots of luck."

"You'll also need this." He pulled a brand new metal detector from a nearby closet.

Claire whistled. "A Garrett 2500 Pro. Nice."

"Do you need a dig kit?"

"No, I brought my own." Her kit—pins, cords, tape measure, line level, notebooks, and plastic bags for sherds and other finds—hadn't gotten any use since she'd left Peru.

Denis made photocopies of his maps and a few pages of notes. "I entrust these to you."

"I will tell no one." Claire pulled the eggs from her pocket. "And the knowledge that I possess these three possible artifacts from the tomb of King Chaco?"

Denis placed his hand over his heart. "I will tell no one."

Claire left, excited to have a place to start looking, even if the area to search was daunting.

Chapter Six

Claire
Monday, March 20

The day dawned perfect for a treasure hunt—clear blue skies, temperatures warm enough for Claire's standard clothing choice— two tank tops, cargo shorts, and hiking boots. She hated wearing anything else. If it'd been chilly she'd have gone with cargo pants and a denim shirt over the tank tops. It had been a relief to leave all her DC office clothes hanging in her closet at home.

Last night, Claire's head had swum with Denis's information about the Japanese in Peru, so she'd spent the evening reading more about it. While she avoided sympathy like you'd avoid an erupting volcano, Claire did let herself wallow around in some empathy for the guy. But still, resentment over mistreatment didn't excuse anyone from murder and mayhem.

She stood in the courtyard of her hotel waiting for Nancho, who was taking her treasure hunting. La Casa del Sol—House of the Sun— was a former colonial mansion, two stories high and painted a warm brick red. The pilasters and elaborate pediments around the heavy wooden doors were painted bright white, as were the decorative grills over the first floor windows. She'd been enchanted since the first time she'd seen it. In fact, when she took the job at Chan Chan, she lived here for a month until she found an apartment. The courtyard was outlined by red and white Moorish arches and filled with palm trees and flowering bushes. In the far corner, a cool archway led to a staircase with a swirling iron railing and her room.

That room clearly demonstrated that Señora Nunez, the hotel's owner, cared nothing for decorating principles, instead mixing orange and yellow woven rugs with scrolled iron floor lamps and lacy tablecloths and drapes. The room was a mash-up of colonial Spanish—elegant and refined—and Peruvian bold. Claire loved it.

When Nancho drove up, she pushed hard against the nine-foot high door to shut it; it tended to swell in the heat and scrape against the flagstone.

Their starting point was Pacasmayo, which was about thirty miles north of Trujillo. Pacasmayo was located near the Jequetepeque River, one of more than a dozen rivers flowing through the desert like green, irrigated ribbons, reaching from the mountains down to the coast. Several Chimú cities had been built near the river.

Using the coordinates on the map and the GPS on her phone, Claire had Nancho drive them to the first X in Denis's grid, at the edge of a small town. Other than a dog barking in the distance, the community seemed asleep or gone.

She loaded up her battered leather bag, slung it over her chest, and handed Nancho the metal detector. "We'll trade off, one using the probe pole, the other the detector. Just swing this baby from side to side, like this. When it starts to beep, stop and call me over." They spread out across the dusty ground, covered mostly with rocks, and a few bushes determined to survive without much rain.

The detector hummed happily in Nancho's hands. Claire stopped every ten feet and punched the ground with the probe. The only thing she discovered was that punching the ground with the probe hurt. She hadn't searched for treasure this way for a very long time.

"Mrs. Claire?"

"Yes, Nancho."

"What am I to tell people that we are doing during the day?"

Claire stopped walking. "Is your wife worried?"

He looked at her, eyes wide. "No, of course not, Mrs. Claire. But I just…I need to know if I should admit that we are looking for King Chacochutl's tomb."

She cursed, then bent over for a second. "*Seriously?*"

"Yes, I am serious."

Claire groaned. Sarcasm flew over Nancho's head with the same velocity that poetry zoomed over hers. But how the hell did anyone know what she was doing? "How did you know we were looking for Chaco's tomb?"

"I was with my cousins last night. As I have mentioned, I have many. They asked if I was just going to drive you around, or if I was going to help you search for Chaco's tomb."

Claire covered her angry face by wiping sweat off with a bandana. Who else could possibly know? She had told Denis, but that conversation took place at the same time Nancho was being grilled by his cousins. "I don't know how your cousins found this out, but yes, you and I are searching for Chaco's tomb."

He grinned. "Good. My cousins think I lead a boring life. When we find Chaco's treasure they will sing a different melody."

They resumed hunting, but Claire's brain was caught in a fairly unproductive loop. Who knew she was even here?

She stopped. The person who sent her the eggs knew why she'd come. "Nancho, tell me about your cousins. I only have three myself, so I'd love to hear what it's like to have more."

For the next hour, as Nancho happily chatted about his cousins, Claire listened closely for anyone who might have been in the position to possess the eggs. But that was her problem—*no* one should have had the eggs. The location of Chaco's tomb was a mystery.

Some cousins were farmers; others were goat herders. Mariposa and two others had a stand selling fruits and vegetables in the Trujillo Market. One cousin moved to Lima and cut hair. Another moved to Bolivia and designed websites.

"Oh, but then there is poor Mardonio." Nancho shook his head. "If he survives the year it will be one of God's miracles."

They switched tools and continued on. While the metal detector was heavy, using it to scan the ground was easier than slamming the pole. "Is Mardonio ill?" she asked.

"Mardonio is a *mochilero*."

"Oh, no. Not good, Nancho." *Mochilero* was a person who carried a backpack over the mountains, specifically a backpack filled with cocaine.

"He lives down in Huanta, where he carries cocaine over the Andes once a month. It is very dangerous. Narcotics police hide and watch for *mochileros*. Other traffickers beat and rob them. Sometimes the drug boss hires someone to steal the cocaine, then the boss tells the man he must pay him back the value of what was stolen from him. Two of Mardonio's friends have died. He has been beaten twice. Another friend fell off a cliff. The mountains are dangerous enough by themselves without men with guns walking them."

"I suppose there are lots of traffickers working the area." Peru now exported the most cocaine of any South American country, and at least one third of it traveled by foot.

Nancho slammed the probe into the ground with a grunt. "Only one. Carlos Higuchi." He worried the inside of his cheek. "Mardonio is terrified of him."

They stopped for a short lunch of dried jerky and Coke, Claire's mind chewing on Higuchi. She asked Nancho if he knew about the internment during WWII.

"I didn't finish secondary school. Only made it through third year, so I know very little history." Claire suspected that was true for more people than just Nancho. She hadn't known her own country's fingers had reached so far when it came to the Japanese.

She did the math in her head. If Higuchi was in his early fifties, then a grandfather would have been an adult in 1942, and likely would have been caught up in the dragnet that sent everyone to the U.S. Claire never knew her grandparents—her mom's parents were killed in a car accident, and her dad was raised in the foster system. But then she thought about Mima, Sochi's grandmother. Even though Claire hadn't seen her for three years, she still felt fiercely protective of her. To think of Mima being treated poorly ignited a burning in her chest.

In the afternoon, they stumbled into someone's yard and Claire quickly explained they were lost. The woman looked pointedly at the metal detector in Claire's hands, then waved them away. Later, a few dogs scared the crap out of her when they rushed them from behind, but they were just looking for a handout. They ended up walking beside her for a while, happy to get affectionate pats. Once, when Nancho wasn't looking, Claire whispered to the nearest dog, a small, brown mix, "Do your feet smell like toast?" She bent to sniff, then grimaced. "Okay, that's a *no*."

The dogs eventually wandered away, and Claire suggested to Nancho they call it a day. It was a long walk back to the car. As

Nancho put the equipment away, Claire pulled out Denis's map to mark off what they'd covered. By comparing GPS coordinates, she discovered that they'd only covered one-quarter of the first X on the map. "Shit," she muttered. One quarter of one X? But they had spent all day out here.

"Mrs. Claire?" Nancho slid into the driver's seat. "I must ask. In searching for the tomb, are we doing the illegal?"

"No. I should register with the CNTP, but we don't have a specific dig site yet."

Nancho started the engine. "Maybe illegal depends on what we find," he said.

"Or on what we do with it," Claire added. While what they were doing wasn't "the illegal," she also wasn't practicing archaeology. She was prospecting for gold, nothing more.

And by the look of the map, Claire would be as old as Mima by the time they searched all the Xs left. No wonder Denis had stopped.

As Nancho drove, Claire tried to stay positive. Things would go faster once they had a few days to practice. Maybe this particular X was mismarked. Perhaps they spent too much time talking and not enough time walking.

No matter what she tried, her brain spun back to the truth: There was no freaking way she would ever find King Chaco's tomb this way.

Claire stared out the window at the ocean sparkling brilliantly on the horizon. She might as well fly home. Without those damned voices to lead her, she was as clueless as everyone else.

The solution to her problem popped into her head and began a lively conversation with another part of her brain—the smart part.

No, no, no.

Yes, yes, yes.

I hate this idea.

It's your last option.

Damn it! Damn it!

Claire stopped, since fighting with herself was as weird as it sounded. Heaving a huge sigh, she pulled out her phone.

CHAPTER SEVEN

Claire
Monday, March 20

Claire had met Hudson Petroski in college, late one night in the Brass Monkey as she was trying to drown her sorrows in a margarita. She'd just figured out it wasn't working when this guy plopped down onto the bar stool next to her and tried to pick her up. She finally fiddled with her phone, held it so he could see, and began flicking through the photos of nearly naked women her friend Maggie had put on the phone as a joke.

"Why do you have photos of hot babes on your phone?"

Claire raised an eyebrow.

"Oh, okay. Got it." Then they proceeded to bond over a less-than-appropriate discussion of the other women in the bar, a sexist activity but one that helped her forget her heartbreak over Amanda, who had left her yet again. Amanda would dump Claire, then come running back six months later. Claire'd be so happy for six months, then Amanda would leave again.

Claire's bond with Hudson deepened a few months later when he figured out what was going on. He met a woman in his physics class named Melissa Chen who was depressed because *her* girlfriend, also named Amanda, kept dumping her every six months. It turns out Amanda was just bouncing between Claire and Melissa. Technically, Amanda didn't cheat on her, but still, the betrayal cut deep.

Monday evening, her fourth day in Peru, Claire entered the small bar in the hotel's courtyard. The cozy space was enclosed by the former mansion's two stories and was filled with potted ferns and other lush greenery. The scent of pink and white frangipani ripening in the heat hung over the wicker tables and chairs scattered among the potted trees.

She stared at the mirror behind the bartender and groaned. She looked like shit—hair snarled from the wind, nose sunburned, eyes lined with exhaustion.

"What will it be? Wine? Sangria?"

"Something with lots of vodka or rum and some fruit and an umbrella." Not her usual poison, but she needed a comfort drink.

"Ah, that would be an American Hippie."

Claire nodded as the bartender rattled off the ingredients—coconut rum, watermelon vodka, triple sec, and pink lemonade, topped with a skewer of pineapple and maraschino cherries.

"Perfect."

She collapsed onto a nearby chair with a blissfully comfortable cushion and took a sip. The sweet, cold liquid cooled her down. When she rolled the glass against her sunburned cheeks, she gasped at the chill.

"Do you even own anything but tanks and cargo pants?"

Chuckling, Claire stood. "Hudson. Thanks for coming."

Tan, tousled, and as cocky as ever, Hudson laughed when she, to both their surprise, flung her arms around him in a bear hug. "It's good to see you."

He squeezed her hand as they sat down, then called to the bartender for a Pilsen Callao. "You look good."

Claire rolled her eyes.

"Seriously. You're rocking the extra pounds."

This would be a great moment for a smile. Claire tried forcing her muscles into the right configuration but gave up. She knew she came off as intense, but there wasn't much she could do about that. She couldn't fake being charming, but luckily Hudson knew that. "Screw you," she said.

He threw back his head and laughed, and Claire actually smiled. She'd forgotten how much she enjoyed hanging out with him. Claire had followed him on so many adventures and all had ended well. There'd been his midnight, semi-naked, ping-pong party, when she'd hooked up with the total hottie—Hudson's words—named Janine. This was, of course, during her non-Amanda time. There were the Jell-O shots slurped without the professor's knowledge during their Theory of Archaeology final.

Claire took a sip of her drink. "Are you mad at me?"

"For avoiding me for three years, or for not telling me you were coming?"

"Both."

"Jury's still out. I'll let you know."

"Nice," she said, feeling the opposite. "You always did like to keep people guessing. So, how's the job?"

"Fine, fine, except for the irritating stuff. I think I've gotten more of that than you ever did."

"Stuff like…?"

"Stupid budget cuts. Everyone at the top says there isn't enough for Chan Chan, yet they're all driving bigger cars every year. Even Silvio's gone corrupt. He drove up in a shiny red Lexus SUV the other day.

"And the sea turtles. The goddamned turtles. They're nesting along the coast near Chan Chan, so there are fuckin' tourists wandering through the compounds looking for the beach, paying no attention to where they're walking or what they're walking on. The maintenance crew's getting worked overtime. I hate those sea turtles."

He leaned forward, elbows on the table, his eyes shadowed by the philodendron towering over them. "I hear you've come back to search for Chacochutl's tomb."

"Holy *Christ*. How did *you* know?"

"It's a small town."

"Trujillo has a population of over 800,000. It's a huge city."

Hudson shrugged. "People know who you are. They talk." He downed the last of his beer and motioned for another. "Chaco's a wild goose chase."

"I know. That's why I need your help."

"I can't help you find what doesn't exist."

"You don't know that."

"Look, I meet lots of people in this job. You did too, right? And some of them tell me the most bizarre stuff. I even followed up on some of these wild tips, but never found a thing. I finally wised up after I spent over an hour wasting my time listening to a wacky old lady up in Chepen who said she had proof Chaco's tomb existed. She said she possessed actual treasures from the tomb, rattling on about three precious metal eggs, and how her boyfriend knew the tomb's location. Turns out the woman had dementia and thought she was an Incan princess married to Hernando Cortez."

Claire gripped her glass with both hands to stop herself from reaching for the eggs in her pocket. Why didn't she take him into her confidence? Hudson had been her archaeological twin, her dig site shadow, her most patient listener when she'd fallen for Sochi Castillo faster than a stone could drop down a well.

She told him about the note she'd received, leaving out the three eggs. "So that's why I'm here, to spend a few days looking for King Chaco's tomb."

"You realize how crazy that sounds?" He scowled. "I suppose you're going to use…your skills?"

"They're gone, which is why I need your help." Claire inhaled and let the air out slowly. There was no turning back if she did this. "I need to do San Pedro again."

He gazed into his foam-rimmed mug. "How long did your freaky voices last the first time we did that?"

She swallowed. "They didn't stop when I left Peru. I heard them for months in DC, but only when I passed a cemetery. I couldn't go anywhere near Arlington or my head would threaten to explode from the voices."

"God, how awful."

"It gets worse. One day I went geocaching up in Huntley Meadows Park and started hearing single voices. It was horrible. I walked off the trail until I was standing right over one of the voices. It was some guy calling himself Winston, and he was moaning about being murdered. I did that four more times and marked the sites on my park map."

"What did you do with that information?"

"After thinking about it for a few days, I drove to the nearest police station and insisted on talking to a detective. They led me to a black guy sitting at a desk, where I dropped copies of the Trujillo and Lima headlines about me hearing voices. The guy scanned the headlines. 'Yeah, so?' He wasn't impressed.

"That's me, I said.

"'Good for you,' the guy said.

"Then I handed him the park map. 'I still hear the damned voices, but now I hear them *here*. You have five bodies in this area of the park, probably the work of a serial killer. If you think it was me, check the records. I've been in Peru for the last three years.' Then I left."

"Did they dig up five bodies?"

The memory still made her shudder. "Yes, they did."

"And yet you want to take San Pedro again, even knowing you'll suffer the effects for months."

She nodded. "Crazy, huh?"

With a shrug, Hudson pulled from his pocket a vial of clear capsules, each capsule containing a slice of yellow resin. "I always carry a little with me. Where shall we do this?"

They'd been in Chan Chan when they'd taken the San Pedro before, thinking they'd have better luck if they were close to the Chimú spirits. Chan Chan was also where the voices were loudest and most insistent. "Chan Chan," Claire said.

As he drove them to Chan Chan, Claire remembered their first experience...

..."No, I don't want to," Claire said.

Hudson clutched at her hand. "Please. I keep reading about how shamans use San Pedro to connect with the spiritual world. I need answers, Claire, but I can't do this alone."

"Shouldn't we have someone with us who's not high?"

"The trip won't be that bad. I've done peyote before, so I'm guessing this will be similar, since they both contain mescaline. We'll be fine."

She stared at the capsule Hudson put into her palm. An unexpected fear shivered through her. She heaved a sigh. "Okay."

"Excellent." They were at Chan Chan, tucked into a far corner of the ruins, leaning against a stubby wall.

The afternoon's fog hung so low moisture lightly tickled her skin. "I still don't know why we're doing this."

"It's for the vision. It will happen, and it'll blow you away. Life becomes entirely clear."

He swallowed a capsule and handed her his water bottle.

Claire once again considered the San Pedro in her palm. "It's pathetic to think the answers to life's mysteries can be found in a stupid cactus." She swallowed the pill and they waited for something to happen.

Hudson lay back on his elbows. "So, are you and Sochi still serious? Is she open yet to a threesome?"

"Don't be gross." Claire stretched out her legs. "I think she's the one, Hud. Seriously." Whenever she thought about Sochi, which was about fifty times a day, she wasn't fixated on the woman's generous hips or her melted caramel skin or ice blue eyes. What astounded her every day was the energy coiled inside Sochi. Being next to that woman was like standing next to a small rocket about to launch. Claire wanted to be on board when it did...

"Claire? We're here," Hudson said as he drove into the Chan Chan entrance.

She snapped to attention. Dusk was beginning to settle over the adobe ruins. "Okay, let's do this." They marched to the same spot, a far corner of the Chol An compound, and sat on the sandy ground, leaning against a bench for tourists. Hudson handed her the capsule, and once again, she hesitated. Six months of hearing anguished voices rising from the earth, in exchange for the chance to find Chaco's tomb?

She swallowed it.

At first, nothing happened. They stared at each other.

"Anything?"

Claire shook her head. "How often do you take this stuff?"

He shot her a little kid smile. "Not since the first time." He shrugged. "Just makes me feel cool to carry it around, I guess." She was relieved he wasn't a regular user.

Suddenly, a weariness settled over Claire, so pervasive that she no longer had the strength to hold herself upright. She lay back onto the sandy ground, her skin instantly sensitive. Each individual grain of sand pressed a perfectly round impression into her flesh. Touching the sand with her fingers was like caressing warm beads.

"Wow," Hudson breathed, now stretched out beside her. "Heavy. My body's so heavy."

The dark gray sky overhead became a canvas splashed with swirls of thick cream. Claire breathed as calmly as she could, noticing that all her senses seemed to have receded except for her hearing. She could hear the blood pumping through Hudson's veins. She could hear the flapping wings of a brown pelican skimming the ocean nearby. Her heart expanded to fill her entire body. She didn't need love from anyone. She *was* love, and sympathy, and nostalgia.

"Fuck," Hudson moaned. "I can't move. I'm paralyzed." He sobbed quietly.

Claire reached for his hand. She would heal him with love.

"It's so dark," Hudson whispered. "I'm all alone."

Claire didn't respond because the sky had exploded into colors and heat and love that rained down on her face and trickled gently into her mouth, nose, and ears.

Time seemed to expand, or maybe it stopped altogether. She wasn't sure. She relaxed and let herself drift, as if floating on the waves. Soon the voices would start.

❖

Claire woke up to a dark sky lit with the Milky Way, always more brilliant when viewed from the Southern Hemisphere. Beside her, Hudson snored like an old dog with asthma.

She blinked, her eyes stiff and dry, then raised herself up onto her elbows. She listened for the voices. Nothing. No sound but the surf crashing up onto the beach, then falling back. She pulled her aching body up onto the bench. Still no voices.

God *damn* it.

She needed the voices to find Chaco's tomb, but even with this fresh San Pedro trip, the voices were gone for good. Using Denis's maps would never work, so she'd come to Peru only to fail with amazing speed.

Claire reached into her pocket for the copper egg. She found it calming to hold. Its imperfections appealed to her, the verdigris still stuck in its grooves. But as she rolled the copper egg around in her palm, it began to tingle. She stared down at the egg. What the hell? The tingle worsened to a buzz. Then, as if she had zero control over her own hand, her fingers curled protectively around the egg. Now she clutched live electricity. She tried to force open her hand but couldn't. Christ! Her palm was on fire. She slammed her eyes shut. Images flashed. Fuzzy, then sharp, then fuzzy. She could smell the sea. Smell warm llamas.

A native girl kissed a llama's nose. People hurried down a street between one-story adobe buildings.

When was this? Where was this?

The girl was back home now; she passed through a room into an inner courtyard.

"Come here, Ixchel," said Uncle.

Uncle and Auntie gave her a present. To celebrate. "You are ten cycles."

She was thrilled. She'd never been given a gift before. There just wasn't enough for extra things like gifts. She opened the small bag and pulled out a small copper egg.

"It's from your papa," her uncle said.

Ixchel jumped up. "Papa? You've seen him? Is he here?"

Uncle and Auntie exchanged a glance. "No, your papa isn't here," Auntie said, "and he won't likely come to visit. But he managed to get this egg to Uncle. It's for you."

Sadness coursed through her. Ixchel missed her papa. He left five years ago, but she didn't know when—or if—he was ever coming back. She looked up into the sky, as if it could tell her where her father might be. The night sky was bright. Clusters glowed.

Something had gone wrong five years ago in King Chaco's city. She didn't know what. People had been crying in the streets. Papa had been very upset. The rest of her memories about that time were confused, so she pushed them away. All she knew was that she hadn't seen Papa since that day.

Claire gritted her teeth, trying to force her hand open with the other, digging at her fingers. She tried opening her eyes but couldn't do it. Her breath was harsh and loud in her ears. She tried calling to Hudson for help, but her mouth wouldn't open.

"How can Papa afford this?" She caressed the copper egg.

Uncle said, "Do not worry about that. Your papa wants you to have this egg."

Ixchel glowed. No one she knew had a copper egg.

Auntie said she must carry this egg with her always.

Ixchel was afraid she would lose it. "I will hide it under my sleeping pallet," she said.

"No," Uncle said. "This egg is very, very important to your safety. You must carry it with you from this moment forward until the day you join our ancestors in the sky."

Auntie gripped Ixchel's hand. "Promise you will do this for us."

Ixchel promised.

Claire gasped and bent forward. She unfurled her fingers and let the burning egg drop onto the sand. Then she slowly folded herself over her knees. Everything ached, as if she'd run two marathons back to back. She licked her dry, cracked lips.

Chills began skittering through her, raising goose bumps along her arms. She glared down at the egg as she hugged herself. It hadn't been the usual voices. It had been one specific person, a vision, as if Claire'd been right there with the child Ixchel, seeing everything through her.

This was different from the voices in her head. This was like watching a movie trailer, but only the first few minutes. She wanted more. What was this girl's connection to the egg, to Chaco?

One of her favorite treasure hunts was searching for answers. Unfortunately, this was often the hardest booty to dig up.

Claire woke Hudson, relieved he didn't seem to remember his bad trip. By the time he dropped her off at La Casa del Sol, her brain was racing. She no longer heard voices, but she might have tapped into something even better.

CHAPTER EIGHT

Sochi
Tuesday, March 21

Tuesday morning, Sochi sat in her CNTP office studying the website with rising fury. Not even the bag of pastries she'd picked up at Las Dulces on her way to work could calm her down. The Higuchi Collection, a Japanese antiquities dealer owned by relatives of Carlos Higuchi, had just posted ten new Peruvian artifacts. Since the CNTP no longer allowed legal export of antiquities, the Higuchi cache had come from looters.

A low growl rumbled up her throat as she scanned the photos. A set of ten flutes made from pelican bones. A *quipu*, or knotted string, that the ancients had used to record information because they didn't have a written language. Horns made of deer and llama bone. Pottery dated to 1000 B.C.

Sochi squeezed her short hair until it hurt, using the pain to focus. These items must have come from Caral, one of the oldest civilizations in the Andes Mountains. The inhabitants of this elaborate city, filled with temples, pyramids, and sunken plazas, had existed two millennia before the Moche or Chimú had settled along the coast of what became Peru.

"Fucking bastard," Sochi spat. The Higuchi pipeline, through which Peruvian wealth flowed straight to Japan, was as strong as ever. She had failed to make even a dent in Higuchi's smuggling. She rested her forehead on her arms, exhausted. Peace. That was all she wanted…just five minutes of peace. But it was out of reach. She couldn't relax for a second because of the constant looting. Despite the mindboggling increase in looting since the Lord of Sipan's tomb was discovered in 1987, experts estimated that at least one thousand tombs still remained undiscovered, including the fabled tomb of King Chacochutl.

How could Sochi watch a movie while Peru was being looted? How could she enjoy fresh seafood at El Mar Azul while Peru was being drained of its lifeblood by a vampire like Higuchi? The only one who could tamp down Sochi's anxiety had been Claire. She'd always found a way to pull Sochi out of her head with conversation, dance, sex, or something as simple as a light touch on her shoulder. Sochi shivered at the memory.

Damn it. She forced herself to sit up straighter. If she ever saw Claire again, she would be cold, glacial even. She wouldn't ask Claire why she'd abandoned Sochi to a loneliness so deep it took most of every morning to claw her way out of it.

While the rest of the world worried about the Middle East or Ebola in Africa or terrorism, the excavation work continued in Peru. It rarely made the international news, but each week something new appeared on the "Peru This Week" feature of archaeology.com. The only people monitoring Peruvian archaeological finds were archaeologists digging in Peru. It was like a fraternity; dissent was common between members, but the public face was unified. Everyone knew what everyone else was doing and which university or nonprofit was paying for it. Each team was close-lipped about the precise finds but always willing to hint that it would be a "game changer" when revealed.

She wished the looters had the same sort of network, one she could exploit to bring Higuchi down. With a heavy sigh, she realized how much she missed her sense of humor. She used to laugh. She used to make others laugh.

She laced her fingers together and stared at her nails, painted a light mauve so she'd keep them out of her mouth and stop biting them. The humor thing might be what she resented most about Claire's abandonment. After Claire left, pain moved into Sochi's house and kicked humor out on its ass. Her sense of humor had been homeless ever since. It still hung around, nose pressed sadly against the glass looking for a way back in, but Sochi was ruthless.

She pressed her fingertips against her forehead. No more thoughts of Claire. No more thoughts of Higuchi. Maybe she needed to call up a friend. Sochi sighed. Once she'd created La Bruja, staying connected to friends had been hard, even her oldest friend Lila. Not only was Sochi twice as busy now, but it was easier to slip into La Bruja if she didn't have her friends' voices in her head. It had been months since she'd talked with any of them. The isolation felt like penance.

❖

An hour later, Sochi sat in her boss's office, wondering what new scheme Aurelio had come up with now. Beside her sat Manuel Sosa, another of Aurelio's assistants. Sochi had more seniority, but Aurelio—although he'd never dare say it—felt more comfortable with a man by his side to help pick up the pieces in case she, a mere girl, failed. Manuel, tall and bony with deeply set eyes and a patchy beard-in-training, drove her crazy. The guy was so busy kissing Aurelio's butt he probably had a permanent kink in his spine.

"I want us to think big," Aurelio said. His pewter gray hair, swept straight back, was gelled so intensely that his comb left tracks that never moved, even on a windy day. He was the ultimate politician, interested less in what he could do for the CNTP than in what the CNTP could do for him.

"Big," Manuel parroted.

"Think grand, think dramatic. What did that American president say about Iraq—shock and awe? That's what we want. That's how we're going to beat these looters. We'll be heroes."

Sochi sighed. It would be her job to implement Aurelio's crazy-assed ideas.

"Here's what I'm thinking. We need drones. That's the wave of the future as far as looting control. Manuel, because engines are involved, you'll be in charge of that."

Sochi snorted. Manuel wouldn't recognize an engine if someone opened his car hood and pointed. But Manuel was a guy, so he obviously knew more about engines than she did.

"The drones must be quiet and outfitted with cameras, the kind that see at night. Screw the budget. Just go out today and buy them."

"Yes, sir. I'll get right on that." Manuel shot her a triumphant look, smug because he clearly had been given the prime assignment. He was going to play with cool airplanes. The drones, however, could be useful in photographing sites and then creating 3-D maps. They could also help with encroachment, watching to make sure developers and squatters respected boundaries. Most sites—there were over 100,000—weren't protected, so developers would just start bulldozing, assuming no one was paying attention. They would disturb the site then say it was now clearly archaeologically worthless. That was like ripping out random pages of a book then pronouncing the story full of holes.

"Sochi, I've been hearing rumors of a tracking device unlike any other," Aurelio said. "It is a liquid that can be painted on. When it dries it is invisible and cannot be detected by scans."

"With all due respect, sir, a liquid can't transmit a radio signal. What you're describing is science fiction."

Aurelio waved impatiently. "I trust you will find out. Ask the Americans, since they have their greedy fat fingers in everything. But we will use this device to conduct a sting operation."

"A what?"

"We will use some of our artifacts as bait, but they will be marked with this new technology. Then we will announce to the country that we've found an amazing treasure. Let's say we've found Chacochutl's tomb to really get the looters excited. Neither Higuchi nor La Bruja will be able to resist. One of them will steal the marked artifacts, and you will follow, thus discovering their smuggling route. You will call for police and the looters will be caught. We will cut the country's antiquities losses in half with this plan."

Sochi kept her face impassive. Her boss's plan was less "shock and awe" and more "stupid and idiotic."

"Sir, there are so many ways this could go wrong. I'm not sure we can tempt the looters with just a handful of artifacts. And how will they steal them? Perhaps we should take some time to refine this idea."

"No time to delay. The details I leave up to you. Remember, my friends, shock and awe."

She should feel satisfied because Aurelio actually gave her the more difficult assignment, but she just felt tired.

❖

As Sochi locked her car, she looked around the Chan Chan parking lot, saddened at the lack of other cars, taxis, or tourist buses. The whole world wanted to visit Machu Picchu, but did any of those people even know that Peru was home to hundreds of archaeological treasures *beyond* the restored mountain city? Few knew about the amazing wonders displayed at the museum in Sipan, or the discoveries at Keulap.

When Sochi knocked on Hudson's open door, he scowled like a man confronting his worst enemy. Pleased, Sochi smiled. "Got a minute?"

"For you, no. Go away. Unless, of course, you have my backflap in your bag." Dressed in khaki shorts, a Tommy Bahama shirt, and sandals, Hudson Petroski didn't look like any of the other Chan Chan subdirectors.

Sochi sauntered into Hudson's office, a dusty place where every flat surface was covered with stacks of papers or boxes of broken pottery. She moved a pile of books off a chair and pulled it up to Hudson's desk. "Any historical site in Peru would be thrilled to have a personal visit from the assistant to CNTP's executive director."

"From *one* of the assistants to the executive director. When do I get my backflap back?"

"Say that ten times," she said with a wry smile. "But don't hold your breath. The backflap isn't yours. It belongs to Peru." She scanned the office, marveling at how different it felt without Claire in it. Gone were the potted plants, the clean shelves, the tasteful tapestry on the walls. Now the office looked like a cross between the set for a low-budget samurai movie and a surf shop. Hudson would always be the last surfer dude on the beach, still irresponsible long after the other "dudes" had started families, paid mortgages, and stashed their unused surfboards in the corner of the garage.

"I found it," he snapped. "It belongs here in the Chan Chan museum."

Hudson's backflap was stunning. The enormous gold blade flared out in the shape of a half-moon. The handle along the top was made in the image of a snarling spider man grasping a severed head. The CNTP's other backflap was less gruesome, but larger and therefore more valuable.

"We're taking good care of it."

"You should know I've petitioned your boss twice for its return, and I think I'm wearing him down."

Sochi held tight to her neutral expression. Aurelio was the kind of man to hand over an artifact permanently if it could buy him even five minutes of American goodwill. Asshole. "I have plans for your backflap. What do you know about Carlos Higuchi?" Somehow, sparring with Hudson was helping her recover from the shock of seeing Claire.

Hudson's eyebrows arched in surprise. He was her height but carried a lot more muscle. With his broad shoulders and thick neck, he must have been a wrestler in school. She knew the female CNTP employees' descriptions of Hudson ranged from "adorable" and "charming" all the way to "hot," but Sochi found him none of the above. He was as obstinate as a child, unable to let go of the backflap as if she'd really stolen it from him. It was an amazingly valuable find and could never be protected well enough at Chan Chan. She also detected a deep undercurrent of insecurity in Hudson that made her nervous. She suspected that he constantly compared himself to Claire, which couldn't help since Claire had been known as one of the most creative and resourceful archaeologists to have worked in Peru for decades.

Hudson shrugged. "Carlos Higuchi. Wealthy businessman who has his finger in all sorts of industries in this country. He's sansei, third generation Japanese in Peru. He reestablished contacts with relatives in Japan during the nineties, and some of them now run a gallery specializing in pre-Columbian artifacts from Peru."

"Who's his source? How's he getting stuff out of the country?"

Hudson shrugged. "I have no idea. My job is to excavate Chan Chan. It's *your* job to catch smugglers, not mine."

"I just thought you might have heard something."

"I don't know anything about Higuchi's operation. How could I? *I'm* not a smuggler."

Sudden panic made her ears ring. Did he know? Impossible. The voices of a group of German tourists drifted through the open windows, along with the scent of salt water and humidity. Despite traffic noise from the Pan American, she could hear the ocean caressing Peru, one wave after another.

She picked up a sherd, pretending to admire the black glaze while waiting for her heart to beat its way back to normal. "Okay, fair enough. But how about a new tracking material based on nanotechnology? Something that was likely developed in America, something that can emit an electronic signal?"

A half-smile flickered across Hudson's chiseled face. "You think because I'm an American I know everything that's going on? I wish." He leaned his chair back on two legs, his faded T-shirt stretching across his chest. "Guess you drove all the way out here for nothing."

Sochi smiled mysteriously.

His chair dropped back to the floor with a hollow thud. "Wait a damn minute." He smacked his forehead with the heel of his hand. "You said you have plans for my backflap. Then you ask about Higuchi, then about some mysterious way to track an artifact."

Sochi waited. If he was worried about the backflap's safety, he'd be motivated to help.

He roared to his feet. "You're going to use my backflap as bait to catch Higuchi."

She smiled. "You're quicker than I thought."

"You can't do that. Higuchi's too good. You give him the backflap and we'll never see it again."

"Not if I have access to that new technology."

"What am I supposed to do about that?"

Sochi stood, shoulders squared against his anger. "You have connections at the largest museum system in the world. I need that tracking technology. If you find it for me, and I can catch Higuchi smuggling the backflap out of Peru, you may display the backflap here at Chan Chan."

"I don't believe you." His green-gray eyes went dark with fury.

Sochi made a face. "We may disagree about the backflap, but I have never lied to you."

"Why not use the one in your vault?"

"Because it's larger and contains more gold. It has the rattle along the handle with the metal beads inside. Your flap lacks the rattles." Chambers along the edges of backflaps usually held pellets that rattled when the leader walked in order to summon supernatural forces. "The larger one is more valuable. I can't risk—"

"You can't risk losing yours, but you can risk losing mine."

She shrugged.

Hudson's gaze dropped to his desk as he worked to control himself.

"I don't have much time," Sochi said. "Find me that tracking material, or you'll never see your backflap again." She left before he had the chance to start whining.

❖

That evening, Sochi jumped when her looting cell rang. Rigo.

He was gasping for breath. "The Swedish dig...outside of Cartavio..."

"Rigo, calm down. What happened?" Sochi leapt to her feet. Rigo never lost his cool.

"Their security guards wouldn't take our bribes."

"What happened?"

"Tomas and the others didn't want to back down. There were only three of them, and seven of us."

"Tomas, that *asshole*. He's going to be the death of me."

"I managed to get everyone out of there before guns were drawn. The guards were armed to the teeth, *jefe*. That means they are guarding something big."

Sochi began to pace, tugging at her hair. "And if our bribes are being refused, then the guards are being well-paid, which means the Swedes might have found something of value."

"We need to get in there, *jefe*, even if it means taking out the guards."

"No. We've been over and over this. No violence."

"*Jefe*, think. This could be the big score we've been looking for. We have to see what they've found."

She growled deep in her throat. "You're talking about crossing the line we said we'd never cross."

"We don't have to kill them. Maybe drug them. Or just tie them up. Now that we know they're armed we'll approach the site differently."

"I hate this."

"I won't do it without your approval," Rigo said. "But there is only one answer you can give me."

Sochi folded her upper body over her kitchen island. She felt like a deflated balloon. "Okay, but do only what's necessary to subdue them so you can check out the dig."

"Thank you, *jefe*, but I am worried. We've had no big finds in weeks. The men grow restless. Everyone has families to feed."

"I know." She chewed the inside of her cheek. With Higuchi so successful, more of Peru was leaving than she and Rigo were retaining. If her men became too desperate for money, they would dig on their own or join Higuchi.

"We need a big score," Rigo said. "We need to get the men excited again."

She pulled out a folded paper from her pocket. "I went through our records this morning. In addition to the Swedes, there are two German teams working farther north. There are five American teams scattered along the coast south of Lima. The digs are supposed to report any significant finds, but we know they don't. You and the men could start with these digs. Take them over if they aren't guarded."

She slowly read down the list while Rigo took notes.

"You need to be careful. Get in and out quickly. See if they're focusing on one spot. Maybe get one of our guys on each team. I suspect these digs might be smuggling artifacts out, so we're within our rights to take what we find."

"Good. We will start tomorrow night."

"But make sure you don't run into Higuchi's men. That could lead to a bloodbath."

"I have no desire to run into Nopa. He is the devil himself." He hesitated.

"What?"

"One more thing I must ask, but I fear I will sound like a crazy man."

"We are partners, Rigo. Ask."

"What about Chacochutl's tomb? That's the sort of big score that could really make a difference."

She smiled at his embarrassed cough. "It would be nice, I know, but archaeologists believe it's a myth."

"But it might be true."

"Rigo, consider how unlikely it is that the tomb exists. If it did, someone should have found it by now. And add to that the totally unrealistic myth that one family has been caring for the tomb for centuries. Members of that family would have had to remain in place even after the Incas captured all the Chimú as slaves. They would have had to survive the Spaniards, their swords and their diseases. No, it's just not possible." Despite this, she, too, felt the pull of the undiscovered treasure.

"I believe in the myth, *jefe*. The tomb exists. It has likely collapsed because you are right—at some point someone in that family probably messed up and stopped caring for the tomb. But that doesn't mean we can't find it."

"Our men need cash. I can't justify sending them on a fantasy hunt."

"But, *jefe*, there is someone in the area who is actively seeking Chaco's tomb. She's been here a few days and has already gone out looking. I could follow her, see in which areas she digs."

Sochi froze. "She who?"

"The woman they called the Tomb Whisperer."

She tried to swallow, but her mouth was as dry as the desert surrounding Trujillo. "Claire Adams?"

"Yes, that's her. One of my men saw her. Five years ago, she shut down a dig he and his family had been working, so he had good reason to remember her face."

Sochi, suddenly dizzy, touched a finger to her desk for balance. She felt as if she'd been sucked up into a dust storm then spat out. No, it was as if someone had held her up by the ankles and shaken her. No, as if her lungs had turned to concrete and could no longer flex.

"*Jefe*? You okay?"

Sochi blinked rapidly and managed to gasp in more oxygen. The woman who had opened her like a shy flower, then left her to shrivel up like a plant without water, was here, in Trujillo. She pressed her lips together. "You would like permission to follow her."

"Yes. If she finds the tomb, this will be the big score we have been seeking. Even if the other digs have discovered something big, it cannot compare to King Chaco's tomb."

"You won't hurt her?"

"*Jefe!*"

She could easily imagine the affronted look on his chiseled face. "Sorry."

"I must follow her. We cannot afford to let her find it and then turn everything over to the CNTP."

"No, we can't." Sochi's jaw tightened. If Claire found the tomb, La Bruja sin Corazon and her men would steal its contents. It was the only way to keep them safe.

"She is at La Casa del Sol?"

"Room 206. She should be there now. I followed her before driving to the dig and heard her tell the proprietor she was in for the night."

Sochi struggled to repress the trembling coursing through her hands. "Thank you, Rigo. I am glad you weren't hurt tonight. Stay safe."

"Always, *jefe*."

Claire, back in Peru. Shit. Here was Sochi's opportunity to confront her.

She paced her office, roughing up her hair. She sat down hard on her chair and closed her eyes, remembering the first time she'd seen Claire Adams....

...Huanchaco Beach. Here friends had taught Sochi to surf. Here she'd convinced an old fisherman to help her make her own *caballito de totora*, the narrow, woven reed boat used by the area's fishermen for over 3,000 years. She had loved her *caballito*, surfing on it until the boat finally succumbed to sun, salt water, and years of pounding surf.

Today, the beach was surprisingly busy for November, but the days had been warm, which always attracted surfers. Long-haired, tanned, dressed in shorts, sandals, and Tommy Bahama shirts no matter the weather, they lent the town its Bohemian atmosphere. Today, both the beginner's area and the advanced breakers out beyond the pier were filled with boards and caballitos.

Through the congestion of people and colorful umbrellas, a woman strode as if late for work. Her tank suit, bright orange, revealed an athlete's body, lean and taut, the opposite of Sochi's own curves. The woman's blond-brown hair billowed back in the breeze. What captured Sochi's attention, however, was the serenity on the woman's face. She oozed so much confidence Sochi found herself rising to her feet. Here was a woman who knew where she was going. Sochi hungered for such a keen sense of direction. She had a new job at the CNTP and loved her work, but something was missing.

Sochi struggled through the soft sand as she walked parallel to the woman. When the woman angled up from the water, Sochi could see she was heading for the *caballito* rental run by Pedro, a small, wizened man who no longer fished. Only one *caballito* remained. Sochi walked faster.

Just as the slender woman on long, sure legs reached Pedro, Sochi called out, "Hey, Pedro. Thanks for saving a boat for me."

Close up, the woman's face was more sharp angles than curves, but when she raised her sunglasses, her heavily-lashed eyes were kind.

"Oh," Sochi said. "I'm sorry. Did you want to rent this *caballito*?"

The woman's smile, barely perceptible, was languid, as if she'd just rolled over in bed to face her. Sochi's skin tingled. "Not if you've already reserved it," the woman said.

Sochi's knees weakened. An American with solid Spanish skills. The woman's low voice was as sultry as that American actress from the 1950s—Lauren Bacall. In Sochi's crowd, no self-respecting lesbian remained ignorant of Bacall and her voice.

"Have you ever surfed on a *caballito*?" Sochi asked.

The woman shook her head, smiling ruefully. "I thought it would be an adventure."

"How about this? I will let you rent this last boat if you let me give you a lesson. I've been surfing them since I was ten."

The woman's gaze dropped to Sochi's ankles then slowly drifted back up to her face. "Deal," the woman said, thrusting out her hand. "Claire Adams, Subdirector of Excavation at Chan Chan."

Sochi shook her hand. "Xochiquetzal Castillo, recent CNTP employee and surfing expert. Call me Sochi."

Pleased to find they worked in the same field, they chatted happily as they headed out into the gentle surf of the beginner's area, the eastern part of the cove between the long pier and the curve of the beach. Not once did Claire complain about the cool water. For twenty minutes, Claire struggled to master a wave, but fell before succeeding. Each time she fell, her clear laugh, rich with happiness, brought another smile to Sochi's face. Once, Claire laughed so hard she took in water. Sochi looped an arm around her waist and held Claire up until she stopped coughing.

"God, you're strong," Claire said.

Sochi set her back down into the water. "I think I need to be on the *caballito* with you." She showed Claire where to sit, a few feet back from the curved front of the boat, then they paddled out together. With the first good wave, Sochi said, "Now," and they both rose to their feet. Sochi placed her hands firmly on Claire's hips, guiding her, and in seconds they were riding the crest of the wave.

Claire's earthy shout of joy pumped Sochi so full of energy she thought she might explode. When the wave exhausted itself, Sochi reluctantly released Claire's hips.

They repeated their success four more times. Then, laughing, they waded from the water and collapsed on the wet sand, dragging the boat with them. When Sochi gazed at Claire, she realized her heart felt strange, its rhythm off. Oh, gods, no.

They talked for another hour, about jobs and life and family, until Sochi was sure heaven had come to earth and taken the shape and voice of Claire Adams.

Finally, Claire sighed. "I'm afraid I have an appointment this afternoon, so I must leave."

They returned the boat to Pedro, then strolled the winding concrete trail lined with palm trees to the parking lot. By the time they reached Claire's dark blue Fiat, which she'd borrowed from a friend, Sochi's heart pounded. She knew what she wanted but was terrified to take it, even though there was no one else in the lot. Never had she been so bold.

Claire paused before unlocking her door. "Do I owe you anything for the lesson?"

Sochi gently pressed Claire up against the car, then slid her hands up Claire's back. They were nearly the same height. "You owe me nothing," she said. "But I think you should know that I—right here, in this parking lot, on this perfect day—am about to kiss you. So if you need to run away or scream for help, you have about four seconds…three seconds…"

Desire flared in Claire's eyes. Sochi moved in closer, stopping just shy of her lips.

"Two," they whispered together, then, "one."

Salty from the sea, Claire's lips slid over Sochi's with such fire that her knees buckled. Claire caught her as the kiss deepened. Such a public display wasn't always safe in this area, but there was no way Sochi could stop now. When they finally broke for air, Claire nuzzled her way to Sochi's ear. "Thanks for pretending to have reserved that last boat."

Sochi chuckled. "Dinner on Friday? La Paloma's?"

"I'll be there. Eight p.m." After another languid smile and one more kiss, Claire climbed into her car and left.

Sochi headed back toward the beach but only took a few steps before she sank to her knees, trembling. Her stomach roiled, as if her insides had been totally rearranged. You can't fall in love in just a few hours. How ridiculous. But this was exactly what had just happened…

Back in the present, Sochi cursed softly. Her life—three years of heaven—had turned into a living hell when Claire had left. Neither of them had tried to contact the other, but given the note Claire had slid under her door, Sochi never wanted to speak to her again.

But Claire was here, in Peru again. It was time to face the bitch.

Sochi marched into the bathroom and stared at herself in the yellow-framed mirror. Her eyes were bloodshot, her hair stuck up as if she'd been electrocuted. Her skin looked almost gray, and the fine lines at the corners of her eyes made her look tired instead of friendly. This wasn't the face Claire had fallen in love with all those years ago.

It was the face of a woman obsessed with a problem she could never solve and the face of La Bruja sin Corazon spending too many nights digging in the dry desert.

Sochi set the building's alarm and locked the door behind her. La Casa del Sol. Three blocks away. Claire was there now. Fury rose in Sochi like a swollen river flooding its banks. She could finally tell Claire Adams exactly what she thought of her.

She covered the three blocks in less than five minutes. Heart pounding, she pushed open the hotel's massive outer door and headed for the staircase in the courtyard. Claire loved this old mansion and had put all her visiting relatives here since there hadn't been room for them at Sochi's small house.

Sochi took the stairs two at a time, then marched down the hall until she reached 206. Her breath sounded like a snorting bull in her ears. She raised a fist toward the door.

She stopped. Her anger drained so quickly she glanced down at the floor to see if it had puddled around her ankles. She tried again to pound on the door, but instead her arm dropped to her side, weak and unresponsive.

She stood there, eyes closed. She began trembling again, not from anger but because Claire was on the other side of this door. Tall, strong, but soft in all the right places. The woman who melted in Sochi's arms whenever she nibbled on her earlobe.

Damn it. Sochi pressed the heels of her hands against her wet eyes. What a fucking idiot she was.

She turned and retraced her steps, trying not to run.

CHAPTER NINE

Claire
Wednesday, March 22

Six days in Peru and Claire finally had one bit of information: The copper egg was somehow connected to the life of a Chimú girl named Ixchel, who was somehow connected to King Chaco. Was it a stretch to think there might be a link between Ixchel and the tomb?

Unsure what to do next, Claire knew the best way to clear her head of one problem was to focus on another. So she looked up the geocaching sites in the area, hoping to find something new. There wasn't, since Trujillo wasn't a hotbed of fanatical geocachers. But she downloaded a handful of cache locations that she'd already found just to get her mind off of Ixchel.

Nancho was disappointed they weren't prospecting today, but he was very willing to take Claire on her adventure. The first two caches were in Trujillo parks and easy to find. For the third she chose one that was up in the foothills. Nancho drove her south of Trujillo and followed a snaking, dusty road up to a grassy flat spot that doubled as a parking lot. By the time they reached the lot, they'd left all traffic behind, including a dark gray SUV that had been behind them since Trujillo.

When Nancho dragged a chair, cooler, small boom box, and a six-pack of beer from his trunk, Claire laughed. "I see you'll be just fine as I go exploring."

The Andes were etched with walking trails, some new, some older than Chan Chan. Using her GPS, Claire headed for the cache. The trail snaked through patches of trees, then out onto a meadow filled with chittering birds, then back in the cool shade of the forest.

Caches can be placed by anyone, but they must follow the guidelines set out at geocaching.com. The container must be marked with the geocaching logo and be stashed not too far off the trail. She reached the coordinates, which could only bring her within five to ten meters of the cache, and began scanning the forest. The fake rock was easy to see. Inside was an easy coded message, which quickly yielded the next set of coordinates. She remembered searching for this cache with Sochi. Geocaching on the weekends had given them a break from their crazy jobs.

At the next set of coordinates, Claire found what she sought immediately, bringing the treasure hunt to a close. The larger fake rock blended in so poorly she laughed. The first time she and Sochi had tracked this cache, they'd walked around and around this stupid rock, growing increasingly frustrated that they couldn't find the cache.

She lifted the fake rock, light as cardboard, to find the small metal box. Inside each box, or cache, would be a logbook and a trinket. Tradition was if you took the trinket, you left one in its place for the next person to find, but you never left anything of value.

When she removed the logbook, intending to record today's date, she gasped. In the bottom of the box was a shell. It wasn't just any shell; it was *their* shell.

Claire had found the shell when she and Sochi had traveled up the coast to Ecuador one long weekend. The moon snail shell was a perfect Fibonacci spiral. Its two colors, warm peach and soft white, curled tighter around each other as the spiral deepened. Sochi said they were like the peach and the white, growing closer together every day.

When Claire had given Sochi the shell, she'd stroked the smooth surface. "I'm going to keep this in my pocket forever." Sochi had recently lost the pottery sherd she'd carried with her since she was a kid, and was delighted to have a new talisman.

Now Claire stared at the shell, surprised at the pain. What had she thought? That Sochi would carry the shell for the rest of her life? *That* was messed up. Claire picked up the shell and ran her thumb over the smooth surface. She traced the small, cool swirl with her finger. Sochi could have just thrown the shell back into the ocean, but leaving it here was a message. Trinkets left in caches had little or no value.

Claire fought back her emotions as she recorded her name in the logbook. Then she pocketed the shell and dropped into the cache box a little pig keychain that worked as a flashlight when you squeezed it. No message intended, just a cheap trinket, as the sport called for.

Claire shouldn't have been tired, but she was. She hiked back down the trail to a clearing, then sank down onto the ground and leaned back against a warm and fairly comfortable rock.

She was pretty good at controlling her actions; too bad she wasn't as successful controlling her thoughts. No matter how hard she fought it, she kept circling back to Sochi. What was she up to? Did she still work at the CNTP? Did she have a girlfriend? Still surf? Regret pierced Claire's armor—if Sochi hadn't betrayed her, they'd still be together and Claire wouldn't be feeling like a freaking ship with a broken rudder. And why had Sochi responded so brutally to Claire's letter of apology?

Claire pulled out the three eggs from her pocket, letting all three nestle in her palm. Gold, silver, copper. She dropped the gold egg into her lap and watched it roll to a stop between her thighs. Highly polished, the egg was stunning. The silver egg dropped next, rolling until it nestled against the gold. Together they were royalty and his mate.

The copper egg was polished, but had a roughness about it, a sense that it'd been created not to be beautiful, but to be useful. What use could Ixchel, or anyone, for that matter, have had for a copper egg?

Claire had held the copper egg a dozen times since taking the San Pedro, but nothing had happened. Now, however, by the time she realized the egg was once again burning in her hand, it was too late to drop it. Her fingers curled around it as before. Damn it. She didn't want to have a vision so far from people. What if something happened? The meadow around her faded into a heavy, dark fog.

"Who are you?" Ixchel asked the girl who hovered near the llama pens. The girl was dressed in old clothes but was clean. She didn't belong here. Ixchel was so, so curious.

"My name is Cualli," the girl answered. *She had long black hair, delicate features, skin the color of hot sand.*

Claire struggled to stay present in the vision, but it swirled around her like an elusive scent, teasing and promising then slipping away, then circling back to envelop her. It wasn't finished with her because she couldn't drop the egg.

Cualli was on an adventure...seeing where the copper eggs lived. She confessed she was the daughter of a wealthy city administrator. "But life inside the city walls is boring. I want to meet people outside the city."

"How old are you?" Ixchel asked.

"Thirteen summers." This was the same as Ixchel.

When Cualli smiled, Ixchel felt a pull deep within her body. Cualli's smile was brighter than the sun. Ixchel had never had a friend before. Only llamas.

"Show me your life," Cualli said, hand outstretched.

Ixchel took her hand. "If I show you, you will run back inside the city walls and never return."

Cualli squeezed her hand. "No one ever knows what I will do. Even me. Best to remember that."

Ixchel showed her how llama necks smelled. She showed her Uncle's forge, where sheets of copper and silver utensils hung from the rafters. She showed her lambs in their pen, bleating in alarm. Ixchel watched Cualli learn, watched her laugh at what she didn't know. Her fingers itched to show Cualli the copper egg. It was her best secret.

Cualli had so many questions. Questions about Uncle and Auntie. Ixchel said nothing about Papa. Ixchel instead asked questions about Cualli's family.

"My family is proud," Cualli said. "I am learning to spin and weave and cook and make chicha. I will be a good wife one day."

Ixchel felt sick. Why did the thought of Cualli belonging to someone else make her feel this way?

Cualli glowed like moonlight on the water. She sparkled like a wet seal. She smelled like the crops and the flowers and the earth. Ixchel felt that tug again from somewhere inside her.

Ixchel began to pray every day that Cualli would like her as much as she liked Cualli.

Claire opened her eyes. The meadow once again spread out before her, the tall wildflowers bending gracefully in the fresh mountain breeze. She rubbed her forehead, grateful there weren't headaches like with the voices. She replayed the vision, looking for clues about where Ixchel might have been, but the entire vision had taken place inside a compound of adobe walls. It wasn't Chan Chan, because Chaco had never ruled there, but since most of the Chimú cities were built using the same materials, they probably all looked similar. Ixchel could have lived in any number of Chimú cities that had hugged the coast but no longer existed.

Even though Claire couldn't narrow things down, she jumped to her feet, actually excited for the first time in days. If she could keep having these Ixchel visions, and hopefully see things when Ixchel was outside the city walls, she might be able to figure out the location of Chaco's city. If she found the city, she could find the tomb.

Nancho drove back down the mountain, and as they left the dirt road behind and pulled onto a paved road, a gray SUV with tinted windows, just like the one Claire had seen earlier, reappeared behind them. She took note of the license plate and ignored it the rest of the way home. But when Nancho pulled over to let her out at La Casa del Sol, the same SUV drove past.

CHAPTER TEN

Claire
Thursday, March 23

The overcast sky actually let loose with a desert storm as Claire stood under the archway near La Casa del Sol's massive open doors. She loved the summer rains in Trujillo. They were so rare that people always looked a little startled, as if the sky were actually falling.

Claire had finally convinced Hudson to take her to the elderly woman who'd spoken of the three eggs. He insisted it was a waste of time, but caved when she bribed him with the promise of beer.

Nancho picked her up, then she directed him to Hudson's apartment on the north edge of Trujillo, noticing that the same gray SUV from the other day once again fell in behind them. An old orange Volvo was behind the SUV. Claire forced herself to stop focusing on the cars behind them. Paranoia was irritating in other people, but absolutely infuriating in herself.

Hudson strolled out, unconcerned by the rain, and hopped in beside her in the backseat. They talked nonstop for half of the 110-kilometer drive, Hudson amusing her with stories of people she'd known at Chan Chan, or classmates he'd kept in touch with whom she'd let slip away like water through her fingers. But then they fell silent and stared out the windows.

When her phone chimed, Claire read the text. It was from Mac.

"That tracking device you asked me about?" Claire said. "My boss pulled in a few favors from some higher-ups at the Smithsonian, and here's your answer." She handed the phone to Hudson. *Sorry. Turns out the tracking device, called NanoTrax, was a bust. Didn't work. US government pulled funding.*

Hudson handed back the phone with a shrug. "Okay, thanks for checking." He pulled out his own phone and sent a text.

After a short pause, he suddenly added, "You know I followed you to Peru, right? I never told you, but I'd been offered a job in England digging in those fucking bogs, but you were in Peru. So I followed you here and hung around until you hired me. But then you left and I found myself in a foreign country without you. I finally found some…like-minded people, but I was lost for so long."

"I'm sorry. I became really wrapped up in my own pain."

He turned away, ending the topic just as abruptly as he'd begun it.

As they thrummed along the highway from Trujillo to Chepen, Claire remembered how, five minutes after Sochi had first met Hudson and he'd drifted away to refill his beer glass, Sochi'd said, "You'll outgrow him one day."

Claire had been a little insulted. It made her relationship with Hudson sound childish, as if he were a bad habit, like wetting the bed. Sochi had predicted that she and Claire, on the other hand, would last because they were always surprising each other. Yet their ending had been much more painful than the drifting apart that Hudson and Claire had done. Claire had wondered a few times, over the years, if she might have been wrong about Sochi revealing her secret, but what the hell did she do with *that* thought? If Claire were wrong, it'd meant she'd thrown away the only relationship that had ever mattered. Ever. No, she wasn't going there. Besides, she'd apologized in the letter. She'd agreed to stay in Peru, but vindictive Sochi had rejected that olive branch.

Hudson shifted in his seat. "Nancho, can't this steed gallop any faster?"

Claire snorted. "You sound like some snooty British lord."

"Two generations back on my father's side. Call me Sir Hudson."

"Sir Asshole is more like it."

"My family has some of those too." They bantered for a while, which felt good and familiar, until Hudson grew serious. "Are you going to see Sochi while you're here?"

She jerked at the question. "I don't know. It's over." They reached the outskirts of Chepen, a small city of 40,000.

"Yeah, but she was the love of your life. At least that's what you said ten times a day."

Claire swallowed. "I might speak to her, for closure."

"Closure? I hate psychobabble."

"Mrs. Claire, we are here to the old people's asylum." The rain had stopped, but the blanket of clouds hung overhead. The city of Chepen was curled around three small foothills that disappeared into the fog. The city smelled clean.

Hudson led the way into the surprisingly cheerful nursing home, its walls painted cerulean blue, orange, and a warm yellow. With a charming smile and his wit, Hudson learned that Señora Facala was still a resident.

An attendant led them into a large room filled with active seniors playing checkers and chess, knitting, or watching TV. A few simply stared into space. The woman they'd come to see sat in a molded plastic chair, her body a collapsed *S*, her gaze locked onto a spot on the floor ahead of her.

"Señora Facala, you have visitors."

The woman's lined face brightened as she straightened a bit and reached out both hands, gnarled into swollen knots by arthritis. "How lovely you are. Please sit with me."

Claire nodded and they pulled up chairs to sit close. The woman wore a heavy lavender perfume. She glared at Hudson.

As they talked, it seemed that the woman's memory was intact, but shuffled badly, like library books shelved by someone who didn't know the alphabet. It took Claire ten minutes of gentle questions to bring Señora Facala around to the topic they'd come to discuss. Every time Hudson tried to participate in the conversation, however, the woman shut down and looked away.

"Who told you about the tomb?" Claire asked.

"My boyfriend." Her watery gray eyes actually twinkled.

"What was your boyfriend's name?"

"I called him Mr. Handsome. So devoted. So kind."

"What was his real name?" she asked.

Señora Facala cocked her head, then shot another look at Hudson. He was clearly making her nervous.

"How old were you?"

She refused to answer, folding her arms and scowling at Hudson.

Claire turned to him. "Could you ask someone at the front desk if they know her age, and where she lived before coming here? That information might be in her medical records."

"Good idea."

As soon as Hudson left the room, the woman grabbed her hand. "I can't talk in front of him. He's an evil man."

"Hudson?"

"He came to visit me one day. I told him about the eggs. Then he left. Then the next time I looked for the eggs, they were gone."

Claire's eyes widened. "You actually had the eggs in your possession?"

She nodded. "My boyfriend would be upset to know I lost them. He said they were more precious than I could imagine. But they're gone. A man took them."

"Did he look like my friend Hudson?"

She took time to sift through her memories. "No, but I forget that sometimes. I am afraid every man is here to steal the eggs. This man came into my room. He said, 'Excuse me, Auntie,' then searched through my drawer and took the eggs."

"What did the man look like?

"He was broad, like a bear. He was indio. Square, native face. Cheekbones like anvils."

Finally! A clue to the person who might have sent her the eggs. Claire pumped her for more information, but she couldn't remember much, so Claire switched back to the boyfriend. "Did he ever take you to the tomb?"

She shook her head. "I wanted to see it, but he said only family could visit the tomb. He was very proud of his family. Said they'd cared for this tomb for over seven hundred years, and that he was the only one in the world who knew where it was."

"Did he tell you where it was?"

"No, but NP did say it was soon time to tell his son the location, even though he believed his son was incompetent. He said the tomb was located in a place where no one would think to look for it."

"What does NP stand for? Were those his initials?"

Señora Facala's attention shifted to the television in the corner, but she nodded. "He said that one day—through his son or his grandson should he have one—King Chaco would rise from the dead and see through new eyes, breathe through a new mouth." She spoke slowly, as if hypnotized by her thoughts.

"King Chaco rise from the dead? That's unlikely."

Señora Facala squeezed Claire's hand. Her pale, cloudy eyes looked into hers. "It could certainly happen with enough sacrifice. Life demands it of all of us. You must not be afraid."

Hudson returned. "They don't have a previous address, and they wouldn't tell me her age."

Señora Facala had begun to ramble on about needing to see her favorite show, so Claire thanked her, gently returned her hug, then followed Hudson.

"Nancho," Hudson said as they approached the car. "Back to civilization please!"

Nancho blinked but stayed silent.

"Nice," Claire said under her breath as they slid into the car. "Nancho is *from* Chepen."

"Sorry, man," Hudson called. "It's a rocking town."

A tiny thrill ran up her spine at what she'd learned. NP knew the location of the tomb, had removed the eggs, and given them to Señora Facala. Since she spoke of him in the past tense, he must have died. He was the only one who knew the location. That would explain why the person who sent the eggs needed Claire. And the man who'd stolen the eggs from the señora hadn't been Hudson, but an indigenous man. Claire was gathering information but still couldn't see how any of it linked together.

As Hudson rambled on about not liking nursing homes because they smelled like old people, Claire clutched the copper egg in her pocket again. Once again, nothing happened. No vision.

"Hudson?"

He stopped, surprised at the interruption.

"Do you know any shamans?"

He frowned. "Yeah. I know one."

"I need to talk with him."

"Why?"

Claire pursed her lips, still hesitant to share the eggs. "It's complicated."

He barked a harsh laugh. "It always is with you." He thumbed through his phone contacts. "Julio Rojas."

She keyed in his name and number. A shaman wasn't scientific, but then neither was holding a little copper egg and seeing through the eyes of a Chimú girl who died centuries ago.

Halfway home, despite her best attempts to ignore the traffic, Claire began paying attention to the cars behind them. That damned SUV was right on their bumper. When the road curved, Claire saw the orange Volvo, and behind that a small blue pickup truck. The caravan followed them all the way back to Hudson's, then to La Casa del Sol.

Was it paranoia, or was she really being followed, not just by one person, but by three? How long had they been tailing her?

Instead of panicking, Claire got pissed. One tail she could understand—maybe it was the guy who'd sent her the eggs. But three felt like overkill.

Claire and Nancho had ceased searching for the tomb days earlier, but she decided they would start up again. They would give an impressive performance of two people determined to find King Chaco's tomb with a map and a metal detector. Claire would take a perverse sort of pleasure in messing with these people, at least until she figured out who they were.

CHAPTER ELEVEN

Claire
Friday, March 24

As soon as Claire's parents retired, they went a little crazy. Hiking in the Himalayas. Visiting Machu Picchu. Touring China for four weeks. Signing up for a three-month volunteer stint as teachers in Point Lay, Alaska, where meat became available only when the Inuit killed a whale, chopped it up into chunks, and gave barrels of it away to everyone in the village. Her dad still shuddered whenever she mentioned Alaska.

Her own life, however, had been considerably less exciting. Thanks to the Indiana Jones movies, everyone thought that archaeologists led dramatic lives. Not so. The drama was in the stories that unfolded as they dug and measured and examined and theorized. Not many people understood that. Claire might have carried a battered leather bag like Indiana's, but the similarities went no further.

Yet here she was, sitting in her hotel room eating another pastry from Las Dulces, trying to wrap her head around the suspicion that she was being followed. Yesterday those three vehicles had followed Nancho's car all the way from Chepen to Hudson's apartment then back to La Casa del Sol, where Nancho dropped her off.

If she were being followed, and not just paranoid, her little caravan of drivers were no doubt interested in King Chaco's tomb, since the entire country seemed to know she was here searching for it. But she wasn't skilled enough in the art of being followed to know what to do next.

She called her mom and got the message: *River rafting in Mexico. No cell service. Please leave a message.* She considered calling Maggie, her oldest friend besides Hudson, but she'd worry herself into an ulcer over this. Claire couldn't think of anyone else to call.

She sighed. Nothing like the warm, fuzzy feeling that comes over you when you realize you don't have any friends close enough to consult about being followed in a foreign country. She tried Denis, but there was no answer. As she thought, she toyed with the stone on the leather cord around her neck. She'd taken it off the day she left Peru and put it on the moment she arrived. Not sure why. Sochi's Mima had given it to Claire after she'd known her for a while. "It's amazonite," Mima said in halting English, "from the Amazon River."

Claire had nodded. "This gem supposedly adorned the shields of the Amazons." She shot a look at Sochi, proud that Mima thought she was tough.

But then Mima had rattled off a string of Quechua that made Sochi smile. "Mima says the stone is to calm your soul." Claire had made a face. Her soul needed calming? More Quechua, more smiles from Sochi. "She also says the stone will awaken compassion in you by allowing you to see both sides of a problem." Mima thought she lacked compassion?

Still, it felt right to wear the cool, light green stone around her neck. Perhaps her soul did need a little calming.

Claire skimmed through one of Denis's books on the Chimú. Human sacrifice—of both girls and young women—was a routine part of the ceremony when a ruler died. The ruler was buried with all the food and riches he would need on his journey, along with the bodies of llamas to carry his possessions and the bodies of women to act as his attendants.

Her heart lurched. Was Ixchel to be one of these sacrifices? No, there was no reason to think that. Still, Claire couldn't bear the thought of one day gripping the egg only to witness Ixchel's death.

She stood, frustrated, and began pacing her small room. She'd spoken with Señora Facala. She knew that NP must have known the location of the tomb since he possessed the eggs. Her brain spun in ever-tightening circles, for now she was right back where she started.

If NP knew the location, why did he need her? He had to be dead. If so, who had stolen the eggs from Señora Facala?

Claire stopped, staring out her picture window into the courtyard below. Could the person who'd stolen them be the one who'd sent them to her? Was he or she one of the people following her? Or a hired thug? Private investigator? It was like constructing a jigsaw puzzle without the image on the box.

She let her mind wander. Would the CNTP have more complete records she could use? Claire imagined herself in her most provocative dress (she actually owned only one dress, so it would have to do), her legs still looking great despite the few extra pounds. She'd sashay into the CNTP office and give Sochi nothing but a haughty glance as she Marilyn-Monroed her way down the central hallway to the research library.

Claire scrolled through her contact list and stopped just before she dialed Sochi.

"Whoa!" She put down the phone. No, no, no.

Well, wait. Maybe she should just call her and get it over with.

She couldn't. Finally, Claire dialed her boss. "Hey, are you still in business even though I'm gone?"

"Just barely," Mac said. "The bankruptcy lawyers are circling like buzzards."

"How's Roger?"

"Much better. He misses you."

"When I get home, may I have him?"

"To borrow or to keep?"

"To keep. I like how his feet smell."

"You're a bizarre woman, Claire."

She chuckled. "Roger's a lucky dog to be so loved. But he's not why I'm calling. I have a question for you," Claire said. "If you were in Peru and suspected that your car was being followed by two, possibly three people, what would you do?"

She could imagine his face screwing up in surprise. "Hmm. Which foreign country? Iraq? Iran? Indiana?"

"Peru."

"Peru, Indiana?"

"No, *the* Peru."

"And here I thought you'd gone off to Mazatlan or something."

Claire chuckled. "Nope. Trujillo, Peru. What would you do? Call the police?"

There was a long pause. "Claire, does this have anything to do with all the rumors going around when you came to work for me, stuff about you being in Peru and hearing voices of the dead?"

She clenched her jaw. They'd never talked about that, so Claire assumed he hadn't known.

"Possibly. I suppose you think I'm a freak for hearing voices."

"Nah. My grandmother saw ghosts. Used to scare the crap out of me. I'd be sitting in the living room with her, and she'd start talking to someone—not me—even though we were the only two in the room. Said she was talking to the nice woman in the long dress and big hat with a feather in it."

"Wow."

"So what if you heard voices? The world's full of crap we can't understand. Do you know why these people are following you?" She could hear his chair creak as he leaned back, assuming his thinking position.

"They know I'm looking for something and they probably want it."

"So you're not in danger until you find this something."

"That's my guess."

"I wouldn't call the cops. I'd get out of the car, walk through an area full of people so you'll be safe, then take quick peeks over your shoulder to see if they follow you on foot."

"And if they do?"

Mac's breathing deepened as he considered her question. "I'd either stop looking for this something and get my ass out of Peru, or I'd lead them on such a wild goose chase that they would give up and leave me alone."

Her plan clicked into place at his words. "Mac, you're brilliant."

"If that's true, then why did I hire Bob?"

"Gotta go. Thanks!"

She drained the last of her tea as she planned her route. Downtown Trujillo wasn't huge—a grid of seven streets crossed by eight streets—so it was very walkable. The whole thing was bordered by Avenida España, which traced the site of the original wall that had surrounded Trujillo. The area enclosed by the Avenida was shaped, ironically enough, like an egg. If she walked to the Plaza de Armas, the approximate middle of the egg, then she could visit a few churches to put Mac's plan in motion.

One block brought her to the Plaza, where she strolled past its handful of towering palm trees and the Freedom Monument, which celebrated the city's proclaimed independence from Spain in 1820. Then before she crossed the street to the yellow and white Cathedral, she used the excuse of looking for oncoming traffic to glance over her shoulder. A Japanese man in a suit stood off to her left, supposedly reading a newspaper in the middle of the sidewalk. Otherwise, people were in groups of two or three, or waiting for the traffic light with her.

Claire strolled past the Cathedral, then turned left and walked up Pizarro and over to Bolivar to the El Carmen Monastery. This massive white building took up the entire block, its horizontal trim painted a deep red. By now, some of the foot traffic had dropped away, but there were still a fair number of people on the street. At one point, she shifted her bag from across her chest to just dangling from her shoulder. She let it fall a few minutes later and saw a woman behind her quickly turn away, a *beautiful* woman, tall with bountiful black hair and sunglasses. She wore slacks and a pale yellow blouse.

As Claire passed by the church, the only other person who caught her eye was a native man dressed much as she was—cargo pants and a black tank top that revealed muscles much more impressive than hers. He had cheekbones sharp as anvils, just like Señora Facala had described. Claire's heart beat a little faster. Might this be the person who'd sent her the eggs?

She'd planned to do an about-face and retrace her steps, but for some reason she didn't want to walk right past these people. So she walked down to Ayacucho and turned right, heading back toward the Church of San Agustin, which was only a block from where she'd started. Hyper-intent on the people behind her, she forgot that the CNTP building—two stories of pink stucco—was on Ayachucho until she walked right by it. Claire held her breath as she picked up the pace. What if Sochi came out the front door right now? What would Claire say? She'd stop and say, "Your betrayal told me more about our relationship than a ring ever could." She'd thought of that bit of stinging dialogue this morning in bed, and resolved to use it should she find herself face-to-face with Sochi.

A block later, Claire's breathing returned to normal. She pretended to bump into a guy and drop her bag again. The Japanese man, the gorgeous woman, and the man with the cheekbones were all still behind her. How much more evidence did she need?

The Church of San Agustin was a lovely cream building with twin towers, its horizontal features also painted brick red, which seemed to be a theme in Trujillo. Claire stepped inside the quiet church and moved down the aisle. There was no service in progress, but fifteen or twenty people were scattered around, sitting or kneeling in prayer. When she slid into an empty pew, her three shadows did the same. Either they were terrible at following people, or they just didn't care if she knew they were there.

She texted Denis: *Please come to San Agustin. Need help.*

Twenty minutes later, the pew shifted as Denis sat down beside her. "What is it, *mi hija*? Spiritual crisis?"

"See the man over my left shoulder? Japanese in the expensive suit."

Denis took a look. "No Japanese guy in a suit."

Claire verified that the guy was gone. "Then over my right shoulder. Indigenous guy in black tank."

"No indio back there."

Damn it! He was gone too. She blew out a huge breath. "How about the black-haired woman behind me in the yellow blouse?"

Denis turned and looked. "Ah, yes. She's lovely."

"She's been following me all morning." Footsteps of the worshippers echoed in the soaring church.

"Too shy to ask you for a date?"

She smacked Denis on the knee. "Three people have been following me." She explained about the cars yesterday and now this morning. "Who are these people?"

Denis worried his upper lip. "I do not know the woman."

"Could she be La Bruja?"

"No, she isn't."

"Wait a minute. You don't know her, but you know she's *not* La Bruja. Logic tells me you, therefore, know La Bruja."

He waved her comment aside. "Fallacious logic. But because the two men left, I suspect they know me, or know who I am, and didn't want to be seen following you."

As they discussed the possibilities, Denis texted someone once, but otherwise he gave Claire his complete attention. They suspected that one of the people might be working for Carlos Higuchi—likely the Japanese guy, and one of them working for La Bruja—her bet was on the native man. They had no idea about the woman. "But the native guy could be the one who stole the eggs from Señora Facala and sent them to me," Claire said.

"Possible. Who else knows you have the eggs?"

"You." She hesitated, then told him about the Ixchel visions. "I'm going to see a shaman to ask about the visions, but otherwise no one knows I'm having them."

He frowned. "This is a mess. Both La Bruja and Higuchi would love to get their hands on the treasure buried in the tomb with Chacochutl. The man who sent you the eggs could be associated with one of them, or acting entirely on his own."

Claire shifted on the hard pew, ready to get back into the sunshine. "I'd like to put both of those looters out of business." She lowered her voice as an elderly couple sat down a few rows ahead of them. "Why won't you tell me the identity of La Bruja?"

"I didn't say I know it. But between the two, she is the lesser of two evils. She makes sure everything her men find stays in Peru. She sells to me, to other collectors, and to small, private museums that don't require authentication."

"Do you think I'm in any danger?"

"From La Bruja and her men? No. They won't harm you. But remember that Higuchi has his fingers in all sorts of things—drugs, and legitimate businesses as well—and that he does not hesitate to use violence to advance his goals. His influence is hidden, like the roots of an old tree. You can't see them, but underground lies a network of complex connections that could harm the tree if severed. So it worries me that one of his men might be following you."

It worried Claire, too.

They stood and hugged. "I think I'll stay for a few minutes," he said softly. "I hear confession is good for the soul." A tour bus must have just unloaded outside because the volume of voices increased. "If I were you, I'd exit through the side door over there. You'll avoid the tourists."

"Good idea." Claire worked her way toward the right side of the church and entered the narrow hallway, which was made even narrower by two rows of stacked chairs. She squinted at the bright light streaming through the open door, which made the hallway dark as a tomb. A woman, probably trying to adjust to just stepping into the dark hallway, was silhouetted by the sun as she walked toward her. Claire turned sideways to make room, even prepared to smile politely as she passed.

Claire froze directly across from the woman. Ice blue eyes. Shock of short white-blond hair. Caramel skin.

The woman stood just as paralyzed. Sochi Castillo.

Fuck a *duck*. Sochi Castillo stood right in front of her. Claire's mouth opened, but nothing came out. Her own shock must have been reflected in Sochi's face—wide eyes and open mouth. Claire scanned her and she scanned Claire. Sochi had lost weight. Where was the glowing skin, the generous hips?

Concentrate! When Claire trained new movers at work, she pounded home the idea of thinking through every step, of planning ahead to see trouble spots before they happened. She'd planned for her first encounter with Sochi. Now was Claire's chance to tell her how much she'd hurt her. To proclaim, "Your betrayal told me more about our relationship than a ring ever could." The words jammed up like moviegoers trying to flee a burning theater. Her heart raced. Then, without saying a word, Claire turned and ran out the building.

She made it twenty feet down the block before she collapsed against the church. Her hands shook. Her knees shook. Her teeth rattled.

Idiot! Instead of saying what needed to be said, she ran away. Instead of confronting Sochi about the letter, she ran away. Claire straightened and kept walking in case Sochi followed her. She didn't want to talk to her because the shaking wasn't from fear.

Claire shook with anger.

CHAPTER TWELVE

Sochi
Friday, March 24

Sochi staggered into the church, but Denis was nowhere to be seen. Of course not. The fucking asshole. He'd set her up. *Meet me in the east side entrance*, he'd texted. She reached for the nearest pew and lowered herself before her legs collapsed. She gasped for air, drawing a scowl from a nearby worshipper.

Sochi held her head in shaking hands. Gods, what an idiot. Claire had been there, right in *front* of her, but Sochi hadn't been able to make her mouth or her brain work. All she could do was scan Claire's body and think how lush it'd become. And think about how much she hated her. And tremble. All she could do was stand there and tremble.

Sochi grasped her hands together, forcing them to stop shaking. She was so angry she wanted to run up to the altar and scream. Angry with Denis, angry with Claire for leaving her, for sliding that hateful letter under her door, and angry with herself for not pulling off the scornful reunion she'd planned for three years.

After thirty minutes, she was able to stand and leave the church. As she drove back to work, her brain spun with all the things she should have said. She'd been dreading running into Claire, but now she wanted it to happen again so she could have the chance to do it right.

By the time she pulled into the parking lot, she'd pushed thoughts of Claire Adams away. She would focus on what she could control, so she marched into Aurelio's office and gave him the bad news: NanoTrax was DBA, dead before arrival.

❖

That evening the CNTP office was so quiet that Sochi's breath sounded too loud in her own ears. She sat at her desk, inhaling the silence, letting it flow throughout her limbs. Gods, she was tired. She dropped her shoulders, pressing them toward the floor as her physical therapist had trained her. *You store all your tension across your shoulders, Sochi, and this tension will block your body's healthy flow of energy.*

When had her life become so damn complicated? Her twenties had been exciting, fun even. But her thirties were proving to be nothing but heartache and hard work.

Sochi closed her eyes with a heavy sigh. She was pathetic. She had a challenging and fulfilling job (two, if you counted the looting), and yet she'd never been lonelier in her life. She needed to get off her butt and find a social life, but she lacked the energy.

A soft chime rang in the hallway, meaning someone had entered the building. High heels tapping rhythmically on the hardwood floor told her the visitor was female. Was it Claire? Was she coming to finish what they'd never really started in the church? No, Claire would never wear heels. Sochi pinched her cheeks to look more alert and opened a file on her desk.

"Hello, Sochi. I'm sorry to interrupt."

It was Maria Menendez, the new regional director from Lima. Appointed to her position by the country's president, Menendez came from one of the oldest and wealthiest families in Peru, a family highly invested in sugar and silver. Sochi smiled and waved her in. She scanned Maria's well-curved body as the woman sat down. She was dressed casually in leggings and a tunic that clung to her hips.

"No problem," Sochi said. "What brings you back up to Trujillo?"

Maria swept her long black waves off one shoulder with a graceful flip of her hand, then, back straight, she leaned forward just enough that her top stretched enticingly.

Sochi's body responded. Huh. This was interesting. She hadn't felt even the slightest twitch of sexual interest in anyone for three years. Could the long, frigid winter be over?

"I'm taking a few weeks off. I needed the break from work." Maria's clear voice and bright smile pierced Sochi's gloom. "So I'm here to visit Chan Chan. I've never been. I also have plans to go surfing tomorrow with friends. I've seen videos of people on those *caballitos de totora*, but I've never tried it myself."

Sochi felt a flutter in her chest. "I haven't been on a *caballito* for ages, but in high school one was permanently attached to my feet." The feel of a *caballito* was entirely different than a board.

Maria sat back, looking pleased. "I thought you might be a surfer, since you're in such good shape." Her thickly-lashed gaze dropped to Sochi's chest then back up to her face. "My friends just backed out. I could go by myself, but it would be more fun to go with someone who already knows what she's doing."

Sochi opened her mouth to decline, then surprised herself. "I'd love to, although I'm so rusty I may not be of much help."

Maria dismissed her with another graceful gesture. "We'll have fun. I thought I would tour Chan Chan in the morning, then surf in the afternoon."

"Sounds good. Why the sudden interest in Chan Chan?"

"I know quite a bit about the Moche, of course, since their sites are so prevalent in my region. But—and this is a bit embarrassing to admit—until I recently read an old article in America's *Smithsonian*, I knew almost nothing about Chan Chan or the Chimú. The article described the Chimú's charming belief that their people hatched from three eggs."

"Gold, silver, and copper."

"Yes. The article made me curious about the Chimú and how much their culture and agricultural practices overlap with the Moche."

"Chan Chan is a good place to begin." Sochi leaned back in her chair, relaxed now. How long had it been since she'd spent time with a beautiful woman? This was exactly what she needed to take her mind off Claire. "You, of course, are a gold egg."

Maria tipped her head, confused.

"The gold egg hatched the ruling class. Didn't the president's appointment letter mention you are a direct descendant of one of the first Spanish to settle in Peru?"

Maria blushed. "Yes, I suppose that would have made sense three hundred and fifty years ago, but today?" She shrugged. "My family grows sugarcane. We are not rulers. But what of you? From which egg would *you* have hatched? Surely you have an Incan princess in your lineage somewhere. Perhaps we are both gold eggs."

Sochi laughed. "Hardly. Most of my blood is native, but there are no records tracing my ancestry. Goat herders didn't spend too much time working on family genealogy."

"Ah, a copper egg then."

Sochi spread her hands. "In the flesh."

"It's very nice flesh."

Now Sochi felt her own blush spreading up her neck. She diverted the conversation back to the Chimú and printed a few articles for Maria. While Maria skimmed through them, Sochi wondered what it would be like to run her fingers through that thick hair. Where might the surfing date lead? Her thoughts skipped from surfing straight to sex, since both gave her a rush impossible to describe. Would it happen with Maria, or would she be one of those women to ruin it? For Sochi, sex itself was the communication—sighs, moans, gasps were all she needed. No words required. Nothing brought her out of the mood faster than a woman constantly talking.

"Thanks for these," Maria said, snapping Sochi back to reality.

As they talked, Sochi began to actually look forward to their surfing date the next afternoon.

Maria then rose. "I should let you get on with your evening. I'll pick you up at your house." Sochi gave her the address. "I drive an older model orange Volvo," Maria said, "so you can't miss me."

"I look forward to it."

Perfect. It didn't even matter if Maria was straight. Sochi just needed to spend time looking at her. It would replace the image in her mind of Claire standing in the church, green eyes huge, mouth open in shock.

❖

Sochi couldn't go home and collapse in front of the TV because looters worked at night. She joined her men at their dig, remembering just in time to stop and don her wig and contacts. Exhaustion was making her careless.

After an hour of digging, Sochi tucked the edges of the bandana into the neck of her T-shirt, but it didn't help much. She was gritty with sand, inside and outside her clothes, inside her nose and mouth. Sand packed itself under her fingernails, filled her socks, and parched her exposed skin. She didn't doubt there was probably sand working its way up toward her ovaries.

Gods, how she hated sand. This land had once been lush with plants and wildlife—monkeys, jaguars, pumas, iguanas, parrots. The Chimú had built an effective network of canals and sluices. But first the Incas came, enslaved the Chimú, and destroyed the irrigation systems so no one could grow food in the area. Then the Spanish came and destroyed the environment with the need for charcoal and other products. All that was left now was desert, and stupid sand.

At the new moon, the night was as dark as the deepest well. Stars arched above her but shed no light. They'd turned off the lanterns at Rigo's insistence to avoid detection, but she worried that in the dark someone would accidentally get a shovel in the face.

She worked at Rigo's side, her brown wig nearly searing her skull as she worked. She slitted her eyes to repel sand. The other diggers had spread out in teams, focusing on those areas the Swedes had yet to excavate. She could just barely see their shadowy shapes. As they dug, Sochi told Rigo about NanoTrax, and that it didn't work.

"Good. Such a thing would make selling our finds much harder."

He wasn't wrong, but still, she would have loved to use such an amazing device to catch Higuchi.

As she tossed the sand aside, her uncooperative brain swung back to Claire. Damn that woman, haunting Sochi in her own backyard. And seeking Chaco's tomb. A ridiculous task. What on earth had driven Claire to think she could ever find it?

"I'm going to check on the guards again." She spoke loudly enough that Tomas could hear. His fluid movements turned rigid as he dug. She glared at him, but he didn't look up. He knew she didn't trust him.

The three guards lay next to an excavated pit, arms and feet tied. Sochi wiped fresh blood off the beefiest Swede's forehead. Gods, these were a pale people. Tomas had kicked the man in the head while Rigo was cuffing him. Tomas danced toward a cliff of violence, and if he fell, he'd take the rest of them with him.

Rigo was guzzling water when she returned, letting it run down his chin and into his T-shirt. "The Swedes may have been telling you the truth when they said they have discovered little of value."

Sochi lifted her bandanna and drank deeply. "Perhaps, but I suspect many of these international digs have learned the CNTP won't challenge them when it comes to their reports. Ever since that French team walked away with so many valuable artifacts, other teams do the same thing. Yesterday, the Swedish guy seemed awfully satisfied for the leader of such a failed dig. His tone didn't match his words."

Based on her hunch alone, Rigo had chosen to return to the Swedish dig for tonight's looting. He picked up his shovel and resumed work. "Perhaps this time a foreigner was telling the truth. We have been digging for four hours without—"

"Quiet!" Tomas cried. Digging ceased as he tapped the ground with the edge of his shovel. There. A hollow tap. Tomas and the man nearest him dropped to their knees and dug with their hands. In seconds, they lifted up an eighteen-inch gold mask.

Sochi clutched her chest, too overcome to speak. They gathered around as a flashlight played over the mask. Inlaid with what might be turquoise, although the mask was too soiled to know for sure, the tooth-lined mouth snarled at them. The mask shook in Tomas's trembling hands.

"*Jesus Cristo,*" one of the men murmured.

"Good job," Rigo said to Tomas. Then he looked at Sochi. "The Swedes said there was nothing here, which proves that everybody lies, *jefe.*"

Nothing fueled looters like finding gold. Within the hour, they'd filled two cloth sacks with more gold, hammered silver, ceramic figurines, and a handful of well-preserved weavings. While the others tossed aside the human bones they uncovered, Sochi stashed hers in neat piles. Since they didn't have the shaman here, it seemed a good idea. Rigo had told tales of looters spooked by the spirits of those they'd disturbed. If she kept the bones together, perhaps their spirits would be less likely to harass. She ignored Claire's voice in her head lecturing about destroying the integrity of the site by not following proper procedures.

The mood at the dig became electrifyingly giddy. Only taking breaks to smoke or pee, or in Sochi's case give the guards water, they increased their haul to three bags.

Ready to quit, with raw blisters stinging like hot needles, Sochi stopped digging. "Rigo, you said everybody lies."

"Yes?"

"What if Hudson's information about NanoTrax was a lie? What if the test was meant to fail so the Americans wouldn't have access to it? What if NanoTrax really does work, but they lied about it?"

Rigo nodded thoughtfully. "Then we would want to know that, *jefe*."

Sochi laughed, excited again. She pulled out her phone and texted Hudson: *As thanks for looking into NanoTrax for me, would you like to visit your backflap in the CNTP vault? Come to my office next week at your convenience.*

She wiped off the sand crusted along her lips. The Swedes lied. Hudson—or his source—might have lied. She was going to push and bribe and blackmail until she had the means to carry out Aurelio's crazy scheme to catch Higuchi.

❖

Just when Sochi thought she couldn't dig another shovelful, the text came from Deep Throat. *Same place, thirty minutes.* Sochi waved good-bye to Rigo and strode to her car. Thirty minutes later, she parked in the short, dark alley near the university that Deep Throat preferred. It struck her as stupid and clichéd—the secret name, the dark alley—but he was the paranoid one, not her. Deep Throat was so terrified of Higuchi that he refused to take chances. She knew she should be terrified too, but she had nothing left to give the asshole, not even fear.

Deep Throat huddled in the shadows next to a row of trash bins. The guy was a minister in the regional La Libertad government, but he was positive Higuchi would have him killed if he knew the truth—that Deep Throat was working against him.

"I need an update," Deep Throat said.

She knew his identity, but after three government employees from the next region were murdered, Deep Throat went "undercover."

"Things are changing," Sochi said. "We can't keep doing this. The CNTP will soon be using drones, so it'll be too easy for me to get caught. But the drones are good news for you—they'll help bring Higuchi down."

He shook his head. "No, the drones will bring Higuchi's men down, but won't affect him at all. He'll still be in control of nearly everything."

"Sir, I'm sorry. I know you had hopes that La Bruja's presence would push Higuchi into making a mistake and getting caught, but he's too smart for that." Sochi licked her lips, relieved to be finally voicing the words she'd been waiting to say for days. "I want out. It's just too hard to work for you and the other ministers as La Bruja *and* work at the CNTP. Looting wrecks me."

Deep Throat stepped forward, revealing his long, tired face. "But Sochi, you can't quit. La Bruja is driving Higuchi to take more risks. No one in the government can confront him directly, so giving him competition from La Bruja is the only way."

Why did she have such a problem saying no to authority? Deep Throat had given her this secret assignment and identity nearly two years ago, and she'd been flattered. But now she was exhausted. And the idea of looting with Claire in the country made her sick to her stomach.

"No, sir, I'm sorry. You're going to have to find someone else to act as La Bruja. Rigo is a flexible man. He'll be able to switch his allegiance to another woman. He doesn't even know who I really am anyway."

The man moved closer. She could feel him attempting to intimidate her, but they were the same height. "Sochi, I am sorry about this, but the stakes are too high. I cannot allow you to quit."

"I'm done."

"I am told you have a beloved grandmother whom you call Mima. She is healthy for her age. You wish her to remain so?"

Sochi grabbed Deep Throat by his suit lapels and shook him. "Don't you dare threaten my family."

"Sochi," the man gasped. "This is bigger than you or me or your Mima. We must exorcise Peru of Higuchi's influence. The CNTP has no power. The regional government has no power. As a regional minister, all I can do is advise the president. But he has let things go too far with Higuchi. You cannot quit now."

"What if I'm caught?" She released him and he fell back a step.

"I will, of course, reveal that you are working for me."

"If Higuchi is so harmful to our country, why don't you just kill him?" She was shocked to hear those words come out her mouth.

"We're too afraid to try. If we fail, we're dead."

"You keep your fucking hands off my grandmother."

Without replying, Deep Throat scurried down the alley.

Sochi climbed into her car, drove home, and ended the night the way all her nights ended...exhausted and alone. The only difference was that today she'd frozen in front of Claire Adams, and tomorrow she was going surfing with a beautiful woman.

Anything could happen.

CHAPTER THIRTEEN

Claire
Saturday, March 25

The key to hunting for treasure was always being on the lookout for clues. And the key to seeing clues was a simple one: Observation. Claire learned this early in life, probably during her family's annual Easter egg hunts. Her little brother, Nick, would run out into the backyard, wide-eyed and crazed, dashing everywhere. Despite his energy, he'd find few eggs. On the other hand, Claire would stand on the deck and observe. She knew the eggs would never be hidden higher than her brother could reach. She knew nature wouldn't be harmed in the hiding of the eggs. With those constraints, the hiding places soon became obvious. When she was ten, she found every single candy egg. Her brother was despondent, so she shared. The next year they worked out a system. Claire would stand on the deck and shout directions to Nick: "In the crook of the oak tree. Behind the bird bath. Under the sprinkler." They'd split the take, one-third for her, two-thirds for Nick, since he did the running, and they were both happy.

Claire applied the same observational skills in bars during her twenties. Friends would ask her advice on whether they should approach a particular woman and offer to buy her a drink or ask her to dance. Claire would have already observed how the woman responded to others around her, so she had a good idea of her friends' chances. If Claire recommended a friend approach a particular woman and she was successful, the friend had to buy Claire a drink. Too many nights Claire's success resulted in a killer hangover the next morning, so she switched her fee to a used book.

So here she was in Peru, facing the same need to observe. She'd already determined that Denis's maps covered too much territory, so were useless. She was hoping to pick up clues through careful observation during the Ixchel visions, but these things were so random that she despaired of ever learning anything. She needed more clues.

Bored, Claire sat in her hotel room in the overstuffed chair, laptop on her thighs. She skimmed the science news and found an article about how Dr. Neil deGrasse Tyson had spotted an error in James Cameron's movie, *Titanic*, which she'd seen once and refused to watch again because she hated to cry over movies. During the scene where Leonardo DiCaprio and Kate Winslet were in the water, staring up at the night sky, Tyson recognized that the sky was wrong for 1912. Talk about brilliant. Tyson "nipped at my heels," as Cameron said, for about ten years until Cameron agreed to change it if Tyson would send him the proper star field.

Of *course*. Excited, Claire sat back and braided her hair quickly to get it out of her face. The night sky might give her another clue. Using her computer, she quickly established the longitude and latitude for 50 km north of Trujillo, and 50 km south of the city. Given the writings of the Spanish missionaries and Denis's maps, King Chaco's city had to be located somewhere between the two points. Find the ancient city's location, and she'd have a better chance of finding the tomb.

She plugged the coordinates into SkyCentury. This amazing website, designed by two German university students, took a GPS location—latitude and longitude—and nearly any day in time, and came up with the star field that would have appeared in the sky that night. The most-entered date was December 25 in the year 0, of course.

The night skies change over time because of the earth's wobble. The earth isn't a perfect sphere, but wider at the equator, so gravitational pulls from the sun and the moon cause the earth to wobble like a spinning top. Basically, the earth's axis carves a circle in the space above the planet, but it takes 26,000 years to complete one circle. People in the Northern Hemisphere currently used Polaris as the North Star, but in 13,000 years, the North Star would be Vega.

Claire chose the year 1200 for her search, since this year fell about halfway between the 900 to 1450 time period in which the Chimú dominated the coastal region of northern Peru.

While the program chugged away, Claire read more about the Japanese in Peru. During Peru's rocky economy in the 1980s, Japan's was taking off and needed labor. So a reversal of what happened in 1889 began—instead of Japanese coming to Peru for work, the Peruvians who could prove they were of Japanese descent could emigrate to Japan for work. The Japanese called them dekasegi, or migratory workers. As more and more Japanese-Peruvians emigrated to better jobs, the non-Japanese wanted in on it. A person adopted by someone of Japanese descent would legally be Japanese and could move to Japan. In 1992, one Japanese-Peruvian woman adopted sixty people, all of whom dashed off to Japan for jobs. People paid up to three thousand U.S. dollars to be "adopted." The Peruvian government didn't care because the dekasegi sent back over $120 million to their families in Peru.

Reading about these Japanese leaving Peru reminded Claire of her own exit...

...Claire finished the last of her coffee, then checked her phone. Nancho would be here soon to drive her to work, so she grabbed her leather satchel, feeling almost positive.

True, yesterday she and Sochi had fought over where to live, basically rejecting each other's proposals of marriage. And Sochi had left "their" hill without a word. But by the time Claire had walked back to her office, she realized how stupid she'd been, and stubborn. She began composing a letter of apology, offering to stay in Peru with Sochi. She kept getting called away to deal with problems, but then she'd return to her desk and scratch out a few more lines. Hudson was often using her computer, so she had to shoo him away a few times. She recopied the final draft, put it in an envelope, then after a consultation with the subdirector of restoration over a crumbling wall, she grabbed the envelope and had Nancho drive her straight to Sochi's house.

She'd knocked and knocked without an answer. Since they'd fought, it seemed inappropriate to use her spare key, so she slid the envelope under the front door. Claire wasn't going to give up on Sochi, but she also wasn't going to give up on her career. She could find a job in Lima or at Machu Picchu. She and Sochi would kiss and make up, and then slide those rings onto each other's fingers in a small but beautiful ceremony.

But here it was the next morning and there'd been no response to Claire's letter. She and Sochi had to find a way to work things out. She'd never loved anyone as much as she loved Sochi. Could it be true? Were they really over?

When her phone chimed, Claire quickly tapped the screen. A photo from Sochi. Claire enlarged the photo and gasped. Sochi held a match to the envelope, which had caught on fire. Claire's throat closed up and she dropped her phone.

So. Now she knew. Apology not accepted.

When Claire forced herself to straighten up, grab her bag, and open her apartment door, a paper fluttered in her face. Someone had taped up a newspaper article with the word FREAK scrawled across it in red Sharpie.

She pulled it off the door. *Tomb Whisperer Hears Voices* screamed the headline. Claire groaned as she read: *Reliable sources confirm that Dr. Claire Adams, Subdirector of Excavation at Chan Chan, used more than her archaeological skills to uncover tomb after tomb these past few months. Adams claims to be able to hear voices of the dead spirits inhabiting the tombs as they call to her.*

Claire stopped reading. Holy shit. What a nightmare. She hurried down the stairs and flung open the front door. A dozen men and women surged toward her.

"Dr. Adams, can you confirm that you hear—"

"Ms. Adams, how often do you use San Pedro? Are you addicted?"

"If you can hear voices, why haven't you found King Chaco's—"

Nancho fought through them and took her arm, pushing the reporters aside as she hurried to the car. On autopilot, she slid inside and Nancho closed the door behind her. The reporters pressed in close, shouting questions through the glass.

Nancho pulled away from the curb. "Mrs. Claire, are you okay?" Her hands shook as she reached for her phone. "I'm fine. Thank you for helping me."

Claire's favorite archaeology blogs all buzzed with the same story—her. A few dismissed the report as bogus, but most jumped on the bandwagon, calling her a fraud or a freak or a pathetic excuse for a professional. Anger seemed to pulse from each entry she read, anger that one of their own would be so ignorant as to suggest that the dead spoke to her. *I Hear Dead People* read one of the headlines.

She hiccupped. This news was all over the Web. What about here in Peru? She slid forward because Nancho always had three or four of the day's papers on the front seat. Before she could grab one, he swept them off onto the floor, out of her reach. But she'd seen the headlines.

Too stunned to think through how this happened, all she wanted to do was call Sochi and cry into the phone. The need to hold her was so sharp Claire imagined she'd been stabbed in the gut. Who had told her story to the press? No one could have been eavesdropping, for they'd been on a barren hill. There would have been no place for anyone to hide. As the truth dawned slowly, Claire wrapped her arms around herself and rocked quietly. Apparently, setting Claire's apology letter on fire hadn't been enough for Sochi.

"Mrs. Claire, I take you to door." Nancho meant that literally. He honked at the reporters crowded around the entrance to the admin offices at Chan Chan, then drove onto the broad sidewalk and right up to the door.

Claire jumped out, dashed inside, ran down the hall to her office, and slammed the door. An avalanche had just barreled through her life, destroying everything in its path. She could barely breathe. Her anger was so frightening, so raw, that for now all she could do was turn her back on it.

Claire shuddered and wiped the tears off her face. There was no going back from this sort of betrayal. There was no going forward. There was just the end of her relationship with Sochi.

She'd never been this angry, almost paralyzed by the churning fury. She hadn't yet found a new job, so there was no reason to leave Peru, but she couldn't stay here, not with the press, the ridicule, and the knowledge of what Sochi had done. She went home, packed, then that afternoon Nancho drove her to the airport. When he announced their arrival, his voice was husky. Claire paid him generously, checked her bags, then left Peru...

When her computer dinged, Claire shook her head to clear away the unwelcome trip down memory lane, then opened up side-by-side windows in SkyCentury to view the results. Eight hundred years ago, the night sky 50 km north of Trujillo looked, not surprisingly, very similar to the 50 km south of Trujillo. She leaned forward to study them. Even though she'd lived in the Southern Hemisphere for four years, she'd forgotten how different the sky looked.

Claire picked out Sirius, Canopus, and Alpha Centauri, the three brightest stars. The Carina Nebula spread itself across the sky, as did Omega Centauri, a bright cluster with topaz, orange, and red stars.

Claire stared at the screens until her eyes burned, and then she saw it. The vertical line of the three brightest clusters in the Carina Nebula tipped just slightly to the left at 50 km *north*, and just slightly right at 50 km *south*. It was almost too slight to notice, but it was there. Now if, during a vision with the copper egg, Claire could see the night sky through Ixchel's eyes, she might be able to narrow down the location using the three clusters in the Carina Nebula.

She rubbed her burning eyes. Treasure hunts were exhausting when you had to reach toward the ridiculous for clues.

CHAPTER FOURTEEN

Claire
Tuesday, March 28

Claire's plan was to irritate the three people following her as much as possible. She had nothing else to do since she couldn't control when the copper egg gave her an Ixchel vision, and that was now her only source for clues in this crazy treasure hunt.

So for three days, Claire and Nancho went fake treasure hunting. Each morning, by the time they passed Chan Chan and Claire had gazed at the mountain horizon to the east that she loved, they'd acquired all three vehicles. Nancho would ask if she wanted him to "be loosening those sons of guns," but she declined.

"They'll just find us again." The three had given up any attempt at concealment. Whenever Claire and Nancho would return to the car, their three shadows would be parked along the road—the Japanese in the SUV, the woman in the orange Volvo, and the indigenous man in the pickup truck.

At least being followed injected a little excitement into Nancho's day, since their prospecting was yielding few finds. Claire knew they were just going through the motions, but poor Nancho didn't. She thought about telling him the truth, but decided the truth was better kept to herself. She even considered sneaking out on her own and "planting" a few pots for Nancho to find, but that would have just been cruel.

So on the third day when the metal detector began clicking loudly in Nancho's hands, they were both surprised.

Nancho beamed. "I has found it!"

"Not so fast, cowboy."

The area they'd been pacing was an uninhabited stretch of desert southeast of Pacasmayo. They were far enough inland she couldn't hear or see or smell the ocean. This was an unlikely site, given the Chimú's dependence on the sea for food.

More sweeps of the detector determined that the majority of the clicking was concentrated in a five-by-five-meter area. In the nearest corner, they gently shoveled off the thin layer of grass and topsoil, then got to work. Within minutes, they began to encounter pottery sherds. Her heart beat a little faster, even though she knew it wasn't what they sought. Still, anything that had been in the ground for centuries was, in her book, treasure.

Then Nancho bent over to scoop something up. He wiped it off and handed it to her. "Gold bead," he said.

"Nice, but don't get your hopes up. This could just be your average burial site." His grin shouted maybe *not*.

"The bead is tumbaga, a gold-copper alloy used by the Moche and Chimú. Let's try a soil sample before we get too excited." Claire retrieved her dig kit from her leather bag. Nancho pushed the hollow soil probe in, twisted it, then brought up a sample. She dropped a spoonful into a test tube.

"What are we doing?" Nancho asked.

"I'm adding hydrochloric and ascorbic acids to the sample." She capped the tube and shook it. "We're looking for high-phosphate soil, which indicates human habitation. Bone, urine, and other organic matter contain phosphate." The liquid in the test tube turned deep blue. She grinned at Nancho.

"Blue is good?"

"Blue is great."

Her training took over. She marked off one square meter with cord, then they switched to trowels and brushes. "Okay, anything you find, no matter how small, put into this bucket. I'll bag it up later. We are cutting so many corners here it's pathetic."

By the end of the day, they'd dug down barely a quarter of a meter, but had found Chimú pottery sherds, many more beads, and a broken Tumi knife. Claire sat back, filthy and tired.

"Mrs. Claire, this is slowly going."

"It is, Nancho. Definitely slowly going." For a second, she was tempted to use her shovel to dig recklessly, but then an artifact would be useless without the context in which it was found. That was what infuriated her most about looters like La Bruja—their disregard for the story each tomb told.

"Will it be safe tonight?" Nancho asked.

"This is an isolated spot. It should be fine."

It wouldn't be. Her trio would be falling all over themselves tonight in this location. She recorded the coordinates in her notebook, and began the long walk back to the car.

On the drive back to Trujillo, the car was stifling hot so Claire barely moved as sweat ran down her back. Nancho cranked up the AC. Her fingernails were cracked and flaky and her teeth crunchy after a day of working in sand. Every muscle in her body protested as she stretched her arms and shoulders. In three years of deskwork, she'd forgotten the physical realities of her field. But it felt good. Very few of her muscles were challenged by emailing customers or training employees how to safely pack a seventh century Chinese vase.

❖

That evening, Claire and Denis had dinner downtown at his favorite seafood restaurant. She hadn't spoken to him since she'd nearly run right into Sochi in the church.

She opened the conversation. "I don't appreciate being set up at the church the other day."

Denis had the good sense to blush. "I am sorry, but the tension was driving me crazy. I knew you weren't going to call Sochi, and she certainly wasn't going to call you. I had to get the two of you together in one room. Consider it an intervention."

"Yeah, well, it didn't go well."

"You fought? Exchanged harsh words? I am saddened to hear that."

She laughed. "We exchanged nothing. After a few seconds, I freaked and ran."

Denis scratched his earlobe. "It is better to get that first meeting out of the way so you can move to the next step."

"What's that?"

"I don't know. That would be up to the two of you."

Claire thanked the waiter for the glass of wine he placed in front of her. "There is no next step. We were done three years ago. We're still done."

Denis steered them to safer ground, and the rest of the meal was a delight. She'd forgotten how nice it was to have someone to talk with. Her affection for this man came rushing back—he was a great father and good friend. He told the truth. Yes, he purchased artifacts from looters, but he did so to keep the treasures here, in Peru. And he truly loved the cultures he collected, especially the Moche and the Chimú.

While waiting for desert, she slipped her hand into her pocket and touched—for the hundredth time—the copper egg. Nothing ever—

As Ixchel watched Cualli walk closer, warmth flooded her face. Desire froze her tongue. She never knew when Cualli would come visit, but she loved seeing her. Cualli was like walking sunshine.

Cualli took her hand. "I have escaped my family again. Come with me."

They spent the evening strolling through stalls and watching a woman weaving a basket. Finally, when the sun had sunk into the ocean, Cualli tugged at Ixchel's hand again, pulling them toward a sunken field. It was dark, but Ixchel was willing to follow Cualli anywhere, any time.

They climbed down a short ladder into one of the shallower fields. Most fields had to be dug the depth of two men to reach water, but not this one.

Ixchel stumbled, but Cualli caught her. "Come."

There was a bare spot in the field so they lay down on the warm soil. Ixchel arched her back, looking up at the world of stars.

Yes! Claire's brain screamed at Ixchel. Stay there. Don't move!

Cualli leaned over Ixchel. "I think of you all of my days."

Ixchel's heart pounded. She slid her arms around warm, soft Cualli.

Move! Claire yelled at Cualli. Move your head! The Carina Nebula is behind your head!

Ixchel felt the welcome weight of Cualli's body against her own. Soft lips slid over her mouth. Cualli touched her, confident, strong, as their bodies pressed into the fertile ground. Ixchel clutched soil, arched, and shattered into bits of light and floated among the stars, a need she'd never understood finally met.

"Claire?"

She shook her head. God *damn* it. "Yeah, I'm okay. Sorry."

"Did you have a vision?"

She nodded. In this vision, Cualli's libido had literally come between her and the clue she needed. Claire was happy for the two women for connecting, but crap, so frustrated.

Her hotel was only four blocks away, but Denis insisted on driving her. Just as he pulled to a stop in front of the massive doors, her phone chimed and she stared at the photo. "What the hell is this?" She showed it to Denis. A woman sat slumped over in the sand, tied to a stake, the water lapping at her knees.

Denis cursed. "Is this real?"

Another ping. This time it was an email with GPS coordinates and this note: *Look at the cache I've hidden. Be the FTF. And do it soon. This photo is hours old. Tide coming in.*

"Seriously?" Claire growled. "Some asshole has cached a human being?"

"FTF?"

"First to find." Her pulse increased. By now the tide could have drowned the woman. "It might be a prank, but I need to check it out."

"It could also be a trap."

"I'll call a taxi."

"No time," Denis snapped. "Direct me."

In twenty minutes, Claire's GPS brought them to the parking lot at Huanchaco Beach, empty except for an old orange Volvo, one of the cars that had been tailing her. Dusk had yielded to darkness. With Denis struggling through the sand beside her, shining his phone as a flashlight, she followed her GPS.

They reached the coordinates, but it was too dark to see much. She scanned the waves for a head. "Hello? Is anyone here?"

A muffled cry came from farther down the beach. "Denis, over there!" Claire yelled.

A head was just barely visible in the darkness. Claire flung off her bag and dug her jackknife from her pocket. They waded into the surf and stopped beside the woman, struggling to keep their footing in the active water. The water lapped at her neck, and her eyes were wide above the strip of duct tape over her mouth. Denis gently began removing it while Claire knelt behind her and began sawing through the wet rope. The surf knocked her over once, but she clung to the rope and scrambled back onto her feet.

"There," Denis crooned. "You'll be all right. You're safe now."

The woman began to cry softly as he comforted her. Finally, Claire's knife sliced through the rope. They lifted her to her feet, but she was so unsteady she leaned heavily against Denis.

"Who did this?" Claire asked. The woman bit her lip but wouldn't look at her.

"Let's get her back to my car," Denis said. "We're going to freeze standing here."

Claire shivered in the chill breeze skimming over the surf. "What's your name?" she asked. "Who tied you up?"

The woman grew stronger as they walked, but didn't say a word.

"Who are you?" Claire lost her patience as quickly as parents lost kids in the grocery store—in the blink of an eye. "Really? We save your life. We drag you from the surf minutes before you drown, and you can't tell us your name? You can't tell us who did this to you? And while you're at it, why don't you tell me why you're following me? Are you going to steal—"

"Claire," Denis said. "She's likely in shock."

At that, the woman shook them both off and stomped across the lot to the Volvo. She fished keys from her pocket and climbed in.

"I don't care if you're in shock or not," Claire yelled. "A little gratitude wouldn't kill you."

And she was gone in a dramatic squeal-out, red taillights disappearing down the street.

"What is *wrong* with people?" Claire snapped. She was stunned not only at the woman's rudeness, but at her own failure to charm a beautiful woman. As Mima always said, "If you don't use it, you lose it." She'd been scolding Sochi about speaking Quechua, but it also applied to Claire losing her touch with women.

Denis dug out two towels from his trunk and they dried themselves as best they could.

"What was the point of putting that woman's life in danger and sending me after her?"

Denis shook his head. "I don't know, but I don't like it." Once in the car, Denis turned to her. "Please do not take this the wrong way, *mi hija*, but I want you to leave Peru. Now."

She set her jaw. No freaking way. Shame drove her away last time. She wasn't going to let fear or intimidation do it this time.

CHAPTER FIFTEEN

Sochi
Wednesday, March 29

Last Friday, Sochi had invited Hudson to visit his backflap. She'd expected him to show up first thing Monday morning, but then she realized he probably didn't want to appear too eager. When he finally showed up in her office on Wednesday, Sochi bit back a triumphant grin. She knew he'd be unable to resist. She led him down the narrow stairs, advising him not to trust the rickety handrail. At the bottom, she held up her hand and commanded, "Turn your back."

Hudson did so, turning toward the stairs leading back up to the CNTP offices while Sochi tapped in the access code.

With a satisfying click, the vault unlocked. "Okay," she said, swinging open the heavy door. She flipped on the bank of switches, but even with all the lights on, the CNTP vault could have been the set for an adventure movie, a room with deep shadows and towering shelves filled with mystery, the somberness broken by the sly twinkle of gold and gems. It smelled of dust despite the constant air filtration.

Sochi watched Hudson's face as he stepped into the packed room. He was trying not to look impressed but was failing. "Nice," was all he said.

"Your backflap is over here." A wide metal cabinet with shallow drawers was nestled between two shelf units groaning under the weight of Moche pottery. She unlocked a middle drawer and slid it open. The backflap, about twenty inches long, rested on a firm cushion of foam.

Hudson stood at her elbow, eyes gleaming. "I'd forgotten how amazing this was." He reached for it, then hesitated. "May I?"

Sochi nodded.

He cradled it like a baby, running his fingers over the dull gold.

"I've never really understood the concept of the backflap," Sochi said. "The thing dangles over the warrior's butt. But why? He's afraid someone's going to stick a spear up there?"

Hudson chuckled. "Or something else." He nodded toward the nearest Moche water vessel, topped with the figurines of two men having sex.

Sochi waited while Hudson took his fill of the backflap, the most significant find of his career. He finally placed it back into the drawer.

"I think NanoTrax works," she said.

"My source told me it didn't."

"Everybody lies, Hudson. Maybe the developers decided to keep the product to themselves. Fool the Americans into thinking it didn't work, then be free to use it at will without suspicion."

Hudson shook his head. "Nah. Sounds too farfetched."

"Push harder. Find another source. Get me a sample."

"I told you. The stuff doesn't work."

"No. It must. Get me some and the backflap is yours."

"I don't know how—"

"Figure it out."

Hudson flung up both hands. "Christ. You and Claire are just alike. You only focus on what's important to you. You give absolutely no thought to anyone else and what he might want or need."

"We're not alike," Sochi snapped. "She's so ambitious she's unwilling to sacrifice her career for anything or anyone."

"What about you? You're just as obsessed with Peruvian artifacts. It's scary to think how far you might go on behalf of a few dusty pots."

"What the hell is that supposed to mean?"

"It means you two deserve whatever pain you've inflicted on each other."

This was dangerous territory. "Get me NanoTrax and I'll see that more of the budget is allocated specifically to Chan Chan excavation."

"I can't be bought."

"Sure you can. You and I will come to an agreement—we just haven't yet found what will motivate you."

Hudson pressed his lips together, then scraped a hand through his surfer hair. He scanned the dim room. "I hate that you're going to use my backflap as bait for Higuchi."

"We'll announce some stupendous find, like Chaco's tomb, then plant the backflap there."

"You'll need more than just the backflap to convince the looters the site is real."

"We haven't gotten that far in the plan yet."

Hudson worried his lower lip. "Let me choose the other items to dangle in front of Higuchi."

Sochi's eyebrows shot up. "Why?"

"Because I've never been part of an archaeological sting operation before. It'll look good on the résumé."

Sochi glared at him. "I'd have final approval," she said.

"Of course. I get NanoTrax for you, help choose the bait, then when you've caught Higuchi with his fingers in the cookie jar and recovered the backflap, you'll return it to Chan Chan."

Sochi licked her lips. "Deal." They shook on it, actually smiling at each other.

"You know she's back, right?" Hudson said.

Sochi nodded, not trusting her voice.

"Are you going to see her?"

The image of Claire in the church, only inches away, filled her vision. "No reason to. It's been over for years."

Hudson grimaced. "Even if the two of you never see each other again, it'll never be over."

"What's that supposed to mean?"

"Just an observation."

Sochi swung the door closed behind them and engaged the alarm as Hudson mounted the stairs. "Keep your stupid observations to yourself."

❖

After Hudson left, Sochi picked up her phone and keyed in the number. "Denis? It's Sochi Castillo."

"Delighted."

"Yeah, I'm not. I didn't appreciate being set up at the church the other day."

"I was just trying to help."

"I don't need your help." She cleared her throat. "The CNTP, however, does. We're planning an operation that requires someone of your...skill and experience. Please come to my office right now."

"Ahh. Well, I'm no longer a consultant, so—"

"I'm sorry to be unclear. I'm not inviting you. I'm not even asking. I'm telling you to come."

"And if I don't?"

"Denis, you and I have been on opposite sides for a number of years, but we've always managed to get along."

"Thanks to Claire."

"Yes, well, she's no longer part of the equation. The CNTP has never looked very hard at the sources for your vast collection of pre-Columbian artifacts. It would be a shame to be forced to take that step now."

More silence. "I do not respond well to threats, my dear, but I will be there."

Sochi hung up and exhaled loudly. She felt like someone moving pieces on a chessboard without a deep understanding of the game. She needed Hudson to come through with the NanoTrax. She needed funding. She needed Denis to help set the trap.

An hour later, Denis appeared to be lightly perspiring, even though the wide-open window in Sochi's office pulled in a soft breeze. Denis Valerga purchased looted goods, making him a criminal in the halls of the CNTP.

After he settled his bulk into a chair, she rolled tight up against her desk and rested her arms on the polished wood. "The CNTP needs your help."

Denis's mouth curled in a wry smile. "I am your eager servant."

"What we speak of today must remain in this room, to be shared with no one." He nodded. "Do you know Carlos Higuchi?"

"Not personally, but I believe him to be a despicable character. Much of the treasures leaving this country end up in his collection."

She explained their plan to set a trap for Higuchi using Chaco's tomb, the backflap, and a few other artifacts as bait. "But we need your help luring him in. We were hoping you, as a prominent collector, might have some ideas."

Denis tented his fingertips under his generous chin. "Higuchi will never believe your tale of Chaco's tomb. For him to believe, the site must be heavily guarded. Yet a tomb so protected cannot be looted."

"We were hoping you could flash around a few items and claim they were from the king's tomb."

"You realize that Claire has returned and that she searches for the very tomb you will claim to have found."

Sochi's heart skipped a beat. Claire would have to be told so she didn't inadvertently ruin their operation. "Someone will let her know."

"Higuchi will smell a trap if the CNTP claims to have found Chaco's tomb. But if he believed that a looter had found the tomb and meant to keep its location secret, he would be more tempted." He looked her in the eye. "If Higuchi thought La Bruja had uncovered the backflap and other treasures, he would go to great lengths to steal from her."

Sochi's brain began to ache with the complexity of it all. "Okay, good idea. We'll set things up so Higuchi steals not from some fake tomb, but from La Bruja." She swallowed. "How would we do that?"

"I know how to contact her man. You put the artifacts in a van. I'll let it be known I am about to purchase items from La Bruja. Higuchi's men will steal from the van, or steal the van itself, and you'll follow." He coughed politely. "You understand, of course, that I am not in the habit of purchasing artifacts from looters."

Sochi bit back a smile. "Of course." Years ago, Claire had convinced Sochi that Denis, despite his criminal purchases, really was one of the good guys.

Denis nodded but said nothing. It took Sochi a second to realize he was waiting.

"And in exchange for your help, you are asking...?"

"A simple thing. Freedom from threats such as you leveled against me on the phone. While you may not think so, you and I are on the same side as La Bruja. The two of you have more in common than you think."

Sochi felt as if an elephant had just plopped itself down onto her chest. She kept her face impassive and polite. There was no way Denis could know La Bruja's identity. "As long as I am with the CNTP, you need not worry."

"Excellent." He rose to his feet, extended his hand, and their meeting was over.

❖

Mima never answered her door on the first knock since it took her a while to weave her way through her cats and sewing projects. Sochi could hear her grandmother's heels clicking on the floor.

"Sochi, sweetheart, come in!" Mima dressed as if she might be called on to visit the president or preside over a planning meeting for a charity gala. Today her suit was a soft silk, peach, with a flowered blouse.

"Mima, you look beautiful." Her grandmother barely came up to Sochi's shoulder, but had managed to terrify all her grandchildren at one time or another with her stern gaze.

Her grandmother waved off the compliment. "You have come for lunch?"

Sochi smiled, caught. "Well, I needed to talk with you and I was in the neighborhood."

"Ha. Your Mima knows you. Sit down. I will cook us some eggs."

Sochi sat. "Mima, have you had any visits from strangers?"

Mima cracked the eggs smartly. "Strangers? No."

"Have there been any people hanging around the apartment building that you don't recognize?"

As the eggs cooked, Mima turned to her, eyes bright. "What is this about? Are you in trouble?"

"Me? No. It's just..." Sochi chewed her lip. Was Mima really in danger? Was Sochi just making too much of Deep Throat's threat? "In my job I sometimes run into people who are less than honest, less than respectful." Mima nodded. "Well, sometimes that person can turn out to be someone you thought was a good guy."

Mima bustled around the kitchen. "This is true in all walks of life, not just the CNTP."

"Right. Well, one of the supposed 'good guys' thinks he can control me by threatening my family."

Mima made a disgusted noise. "I'm not afraid."

"Is your cell phone charged?"

Mima winced. Sochi sighed, pulling out the new cell phone. "Look, this is a really easy one to use."

"I hate them." She set down two plates of fried eggs and corn salsa.

"I know, but your family wants to know you're safe. We worry about you."

"I'm eighty, not one hundred."

"See this big red button? I've programmed the phone to text me when you push the button. The text says *Help*. It doesn't have to be a huge problem—maybe you can't reach the sugar on the top shelf—but you need to push the button." She handed her the phone. "Will you do that for me?"

"This isn't necessary."

"Mima, I can't do my job if I must worry about you."

With a resigned nod, Mima put the phone on the table. "I do this for you. Now will you do me a favor?"

"Anything."

"Go on a date. Get out. Meet someone. You are too young to be so sad."

Sochi focused on her food. "I went on a sort-of-date last weekend."

"And?"

"We had a great time. Maria and I surfed at Huanchaco."

"She is a nice girl?"

"Yes, and very rich, Mima. She's a Menendez."

"Huh. Big deal. I wish you would call that nice girl Claire. I miss her."

"Mima, no. I told you what she did to me. I'm not calling her, even though she's back in Peru." Sochi bit her lip.

Mima's eyes widened. "She is back? This is very interesting."

Sochi put the dirty dishes in the sink. "Forget Claire. Please keep this phone with you at all times."

Back in her car, Sochi scrolled through her phone's contact list. Claire was still on it. Maybe Mima was right. Maybe they should just get together and come to some sort of closure.

No. She had too much pride for that.

❖

Would this day ever end? She'd been ready to head home when she'd gotten the alarmed call from Rigo. There'd been a fight.

Just before she reached the turnoff to the sandy road that led to the dig site, Sochi braked and pulled over. "Gods," she muttered as she reached for the black bag with her wig and contact case in the backseat. The last thing she needed was to march into a dig as herself.

One of the men waited for her, signaling with a flashlight so she'd know where to turn off the highway. She picked him up and drove down the rutted road.

She looked him over. "You aren't hurt?"

"No, I'm fine. Playing football makes me quick on my feet."

When she stopped the car, her headlights caught the men clustered near Rigo's van, some holding T-shirts against bleeding wounds. Others sprawled on the ground, arms thrown over their eyes as if in despair. She shut off the engine, furious. She'd warned Rigo about this.

She leapt from the car, then forced herself to calm down. "Is anyone hurt badly?"

Rigo stepped forward. "Cuts and bruises only."

Bare-chested Tomas held his T-shirt against his head, rivulets of blood trickling down his bicep like slender snakes. She moved his hand away, wincing at the deep gash running from his temple back into his hairline. "You need stitches," she said. He shrugged. She pressed her fists against her hips. "Okay, spill it. What happened?"

No one met her steady gaze, not even Rigo. She crossed her arms, waiting.

Rigo's sigh could have toppled a small child. "The men at this dig did not yield as others have."

"Who started the fight?"

No one replied, but enough eyes flickered in Tomas's direction that she had her answer.

Tomas straightened. "My son needs new shoes for school, and my wife has lost her job. I need money. We could see they'd found some good stuff."

Sochi's jaw tightened. "Where is it?"

One of the men coughed. "A few of them left with the loot while we were fighting."

Sochi briefly massaged her forehead, hoping to break up the approaching headache. "One of you take Tomas to a doctor to be sewn up. Otherwise, what few brains he has left are likely to leak out. The rest of you, go home. I know you are desperate for money, but we must be smarter in the future. Now that there has been violence, the cops will be less likely to look the other way."

The men gathered up their shovels and water bottles, murmured their apologies, then drifted toward the van. Rigo remained a minute. "*Jefe*, I am sorry. I know—"

"You assured me you had these men under control."

"I did, until Tomas started punching. His frustration level is crazy high."

They stood in silence. Finally, Sochi broke the tension. "I'll get some cash for you to distribute among the men. Desperate men are dangerous."

"I will speak to Tomas."

Sochi carefully turned her car around and headed back toward the highway, concern gnawing at her gut. What the hell was she doing? She had sacrificed everything, including Claire, for this country, and for what? The artifacts didn't care. The dead certainly didn't. Now that there'd been violence, the word would reach the police or the CNTP and both would double their efforts to find La Bruja.

But she couldn't stop. Not only did she fear for Mima's safety, but she still had days when the ten-year-old still inside her couldn't let go...

...At ten, Sochi couldn't bear to sit inside. One cool, pleasant Saturday she was hungry to go somewhere, to do something. In two weeks, they were leaving Peru yet again, this time for America. Sochi had just watched *Raiders of the Lost Ark* for the first time, and yearned to race ahead of giant boulders trying to kill her.

Papa finally agreed. He grabbed two shovels from beside the house. "Follow me," he said.

Delighted to finally be on an adventure, Sochi slogged through the brush beyond the yard. They lived at the very edge of Lima, so she was unclear where their property ended and the desert began.

"Where are we going, Papa?"

"There is a mound just over that hill that I've always wondered about."

Sochi leapt with excitement. Buried treasure!

The mound was about fifteen feet long and four feet wide. It just looked like a pile of drifting sand caught by a bank of weeds.

"Let's start by taking off the crown of soil," Papa said, and they bent to their work, backs strong with enthusiasm. After thirty minutes, Sochi's small fingers burned where they rubbed against the shovel handle, but by then they'd knocked down most of the mound.

"Okay," Papa said, "now we dig slower as we go into the ground. Kind of move your shovel around before digging in too deep. Feel for resistance."

Almost immediately, her shovel clinked against something. She dropped to her knees and pawed at the sand with both hands. "Papa, look!" It was a pottery sherd, glazed orange. Papa showed her how to sweep sand away with a hand brush until she'd uncovered the remains of a pot that had collapsed into itself.

Something took hold of her as she worked quietly beside her father to uncover a row of similar pots. It was almost a feeling of reverence. She was helping to discover her own history.

"Sochi, look," Papa breathed.

She stopped, seeing that he pointed to the mouth of the pot she was excavating. "It's not broken," she whispered. They released the water vessel from its sandy prison.

Papa whistled. "This is a beauty." It was in the shape of a fierce animal, perhaps a dog, with fangs bared. A handle curved from the back of the dog's neck down to its tail. Faded red and orange glaze still covering the pot.

Shaking with excitement, Sochi began working the area next to the line of pots. But when she brushed the sand from something long and white, she rocked back on her heels, heart pounding. "A bone."

She watched as Papa took over, gently brushing the sand aside until enough of the skeleton was revealed to determine it was human. Bits of fabric were still draped across the leg bones.

"Do you think this person made these pots?"

"It's possible. But more importantly, he is an ancestor, Sochi, a person who lived right here, where we live now."

Sochi stayed still, struggling to understand. She touched the femur and shivered.

Papa began mounding the sand back over the skeleton. "This person was loved by someone. He or she was buried with consideration."

"The looters I heard you and Mama talking about—this is what they do? They dig up people like this?"

"They are digging up the valuables. Sadly, they care nothing for the bodies themselves, but just toss the bones aside."

"And they sell the pots and stuff?"

Papa nodded. "Usually to foreign museums or private collectors." He licked his thumb and rubbed sand off the face of the pot, revealing a bright orange glaze. "It's hard to relate to people from so long ago," he said. "Even now, staring at this skeleton, he or she doesn't seem like a real person. But look what this person, or someone like him, created. It's art. It's proof the person who lived had skilled hands, a sense of beauty. What we leave behind matters. Most humans don't last one hundred years, but this pot? It's probably early Moche, so this pot has survived for over one thousand years. The artist is long dead, but this pottery continues. Entire cultures and races have died, but they continue to exist because of their art."

Sochi's eyes stung at the thought of making something that could last that long. It seemed incredible, and impossible, and achingly important. Papa picked up a small sherd of one of the crushed pots. "Keep this in your pocket as a way to remember that."

Sochi stroked the smooth surface. "And the whole pot we found?"

"Would you like to donate it to the CNTP? They will care for it forever."

"Yes."

Sochi and her father shoveled until the skeleton was once against buried under two feet of sand, unaware that the seeds for her degree in museum studies and her job at the CNTP had just been planted.

CHAPTER SIXTEEN

Claire
Thursday, March 30

The next morning, Claire knew what she and Nancho would find when they returned to the dig site they'd started yesterday. They parked and began the walk to the site. Claire was about to warn Nancho not to be upset when he stopped, cursing with despair.

Their flat dig site had been turned into five towering piles of sand next to five holes. Nancho reached the nearest hole first. Four pots and a few dozen sherds lined the edge of the hole. They found the same at the other holes. Someone had dug furiously, tossed aside bones, and left the artifacts as if to say, "See, this was all we found."

Nancho turned to her, wild-eyed. "Me no tell. No tell!" His English skills, not good to begin with, disappeared with his anguish.

She touched his arm. "I know. It's okay, I believe you. It was one of the people following us. They must have tracked us on foot."

Claire surveyed the damage. It was impossible, of course, to know which of her three tails had reached the site first and dug it up. Perhaps they'd encountered each other, so she briefly entertained herself with the image of three groups of angry people digging up a site she knew had very little in it. This site wasn't large enough to be Chaco's tomb.

"Let's go home."

Nancho slumped with despair over the steering wheel. The poor guy was so sure they'd found it.

❖

Claire was starting to worry about always ending up at Las Dulces. There were places where she could buy a nutritious breakfast of beans and rice, or pork and rice, or goat and rice. Yet here she was, once again, stuffing her face with sugar. It was entirely possible that she might be an emotional eater.

She wanted to call Sochi. Every time she closed her eyes, she saw Sochi in the church, every millisecond of their encounter burned into Claire's memory. As a result, sleeping was becoming a challenge. Clearly, Mom was right. Claire needed closure. She needed to work through her negative feelings, her deep sense of betrayal, and move on.

Claire stared at her phone. Now. She would do it now.

"The *orejitas* are my favorite as well. They are worth it even though I always get powdered sugar on my suit."

Shading her eyes, Claire peered up at the man standing beside her. Not until he sat down could she see he wore a suit likely more expensive than her DC condo. His graying hair was short and bristly. His Japanese features revealed no emotion, but his voice, when speaking perfect Spanish, seemed friendly enough. Behind him four men, also in suits, stood in a protective row. One of them was the Japanese guy who'd been following Claire in the SUV. She smiled up at him. "Hey, long time no see. We'll be heading out in about an hour. Shall I text you when I leave?"

The young guy's eyes narrowed, but he said nothing.

"Oh, and I'm sorry about all the work you had to do last night," she added. "I'm guessing you didn't dig up anything interesting."

The older man now seated across from her laughed politely. Carlos Higuchi. Claire refused to be intimidated. She extended her hand and shook his as firmly as she could. "Carlos, good to meet you. I could order another *orejitas* if you'd like."

The smile was strained, as if he were too important to spar with her. "I hear you are an avid geocacher. I hid my first cache yesterday. Were you FTF?"

"Yes, I was. The woman you staked to the beach is fine, in case you're wondering." She spoke over his shoulder to the young guy.

"You might want to apologize to her while you're tailing me this afternoon. Your boss here almost killed her."

"Oh, my, so dramatic," Higuchi crooned.

"Yeah, that's me. So what was the point? Why endanger the life of a woman I don't even know?"

"To show you how serious I am."

Claire sipped her water. "Serious about what?"

"About King Chacochutl's treasure."

"Don't you know that's just a myth?" People around them were staring now, recognizing the country's biggest drug boss and the man who was terrorizing the regional government as he browbeat it into submission. If she'd been in the U.S., she'd have felt safe since people would react if anyone had tried to drag her away from a crowded restaurant and stuff her into a car. But she could see the fear on everyone's faces. Some were even abandoning their food and leaving. If Higuchi and his men wanted to drag her away in broad daylight, they could.

Higuchi shrugged. "We know you are searching for the tomb and that you hear the voices of the dead."

Claire was tempted to bring him up to date on that, but couldn't figure out fast enough if that would help her or harm her. She mimicked his shrug. "Just a tourist, here on vacation."

He shot forward and smacked the table with his open palm. "Cut the bullshit. You need to find it, and soon."

Rattled, Claire slid her hand into the pocket without the eggs and sought out the moon shell she'd retrieved from the geocache. Rubbing her thumb over its smoothness reminded her of happier times, when being with Sochi had seemed to boost her self-esteem. You weren't supposed to key how you felt about yourself to another person and she didn't think she did that, but Claire had felt stronger and braver knowing Sochi was in her life. She played with the shell, struggling for calm.

"Yes, Carlos—" She liked how he flinched at her disrespect. "I am seeking the tomb, but if it had been easy to find, you would have already done so, correct? So back off. I'll find it when I find it."

"Look harder. Stop touring churches."

"Why are you in such a big hurry? The treasure, if it exists, has been there for centuries. It's not going anywhere."

"I think the cache you found demonstrates that I can do anything to anyone. You would be wise not to challenge me."

She didn't disagree but seemed unable to stop her mouth. "Did you send me the eggs?"

His wry smile told her she'd just given away more than she should have. "Ahh, the eggs. No, but I am aware they are in your possession."

Claire frowned. "If the eggs came from Chaco's tomb, then whoever sent the eggs already knows the location. Ask him—or her— where the tomb is. I have no idea."

Higuchi broke off a small piece of her *orejitas*, as if they were buddies, which made her jaw tighten. "Do you know the story surrounding King Chaco's tomb, the story about the family?" He popped the sweet bread into his mouth.

She vaguely remembered but wanted to hear his version, so she shook her head.

"The story says that when King Chaco was entombed, a great miracle occurred. One family, blessed with this miracle, was so grateful that they committed to caring for the tomb into eternity. For centuries the family passed the task on to the next generation."

"That's impossible. The Incas conquered the Chimú and marched them all to Cuzco. Then the Spaniards came and killed off thousands. No way could one family remain at the same location during all that upheaval."

When Higuchi reached for her plate again, Claire hissed with such menace that he withdrew his hand. "But this family somehow managed," he continued. "You know the persistence of the indios in this country. Each generation passed to the eldest child the location to the tomb's secret entrance, and all the things that must be done to keep everything ready for King Chaco's return."

"What sorts of things?"

"Replacing rotting posts, resoaking the torches, oiling the sacrificial altar." He grimaced. "The usual stuff."

Realization dawned. "That chain of caretaking has broken down. The current generation had the eggs but no idea of the tomb's location."

Higuchi watched a woman walk by, too involved in her cell phone to realize who she passed. "This is all I know. My family comes from Japan, of course, so we are not the caretakers. I just repeat what I've been told."

"Why should I work so hard to find it? You're just going to swoop in at the last minute and steal the treasure."

There was that shrug again, oozing with innocence and malice at the same time.

"And then you're going to ship the treasure to Japan, leaving nothing here for the Peruvians."

"Now why would I do that?" He leaned back, face glowing with pleasure.

She took her best shot. "Because you resent the hell out of Peru for what it did to someone in your family during WWII."

He nodded, impressed. "Yes, this is true. My grandfather was taken prisoner by the Peruvian police for doing absolutely nothing, then, in collusion with the Americans, imprisoned in the Texas of your country."

His voice had taken on a sharp edge that reminded Claire just how dangerous this guy could be. The longer this conversation dragged on, the greater the chance she pissed him off and ended up stuffed in the trunk of a car. Claire gathered her belongings together. "While I'm horrified at what my country—and yours—did to all Japanese, regardless of where they lived, your desire to harm Peru seems a little extreme." She stood. "I'd recommend therapy, Carlos. Really, you need it. Time to let the past go. Retribution is so twelfth century, don't you think?"

With that, she whirled and walked back into the restaurant, praying he didn't follow. Then she locked herself in the small bathroom and threw up.

❖

That night after Nancho dropped Claire off, she took stock. She'd had three visions. From these visions she knew that Ixchel lived in Chaco's city, had an absent father, and loving parents in Uncle and Auntie. She loved life, loved llamas, and now clearly loved Cualli, a girl from the nicer side of the railroad tracks, so to speak. Claire hadn't, however, picked up any clues to help her determine either the location of the city or of the tomb. No wonder Higuchi was getting impatient; she was too. Unfortunately, the team she'd assembled to search for the tomb was small: the copper egg and Ixchel.

And the egg was freaking uncooperative. She held that thing dozens of times every day, and nothing happened. There was no rhyme or reason to when the visions came. There was no pattern as to location or time or her emotional condition. She hadn't yet tracked them using her menstrual cycle, but that would be next.

What was the worst that could happen if she didn't find the tomb? Nothing, really. Despite Carlos Higuchi's threats, harming her wouldn't help him find the tomb. She marveled at the man's impatient greed. He believed all he had to do was snap his fingers and he'd get what he wanted. But if Claire wanted to quit, she could be on the first flight home before Higuchi could stop her.

Everything would continue here as if she'd never come. Peru would, like water, close over the ripple she'd made and there would be no evidence she'd even been here. Yes, Higuchi had gotten to her, but he was an idiot, albeit a scary one, if he thought that threats could hurry a treasure hunt.

Higuchi had distracted her from her earlier purpose when she'd been sitting at Las Dulces. She would call Sochi because she couldn't stop thinking about her. Every corner in this city was haunted by who they were before she betrayed Claire.

She scrolled through her contacts until she found Sochi's number. Then, taking a huge breath, she pressed CALL. With her other hand, she nervously reached for the copper egg.

Ixchel looked into Cualli's brown eyes. "Cualli, my heart, do not be sad."

"I am to marry Tochi, but I don't want to."

"It is what women of your class must do."

Waves crashed at their side as the fine mist caressed their skin. Ixchel tasted salt on Cualli's lips. Birds wheeled above.

"But, Ixchel, I love you. I love Tochi only as a friend."

Ixchel felt the love singing between them like a string played by the wind. "We will continue to love. Tochi will understand."

Cualli hugged her tightly. "You are right. We can all be happy together."

Ixchel swelled with happiness. She kissed Cualli—warm and deep and smooth.

Seals barked offshore. Ixchel looked to the north. Nothing but beach and sand stretched in that direction.

Two eggs nestled in Ixchel's pocket. "I have a gift for you. Tochi is royal, which means he is a golden egg. When you marry, you shall be the wife of royalty, or a silver egg."

She slid the silver egg into Cualli's perfect palm.

"Ohhh. So beautiful."

"Uncle made it. He taught me to etch. I etched my copper egg, too."

Shyly, she showed Cualli the copper egg. "Uncle says this will save my life one day."

They exchanged more warm kisses. Cualli's insistent hands slid lower and moved deeper.

Ixchel closed her eyes. Silver egg and copper egg...Cualli and Ixchel.

When Claire came out of the vision, the phone was still in her hand. She put it to her ear. Nothing but silence. The END CALL button still glowed. Had Claire called Sochi? Had she answered? She would have heard nothing but heavy breathing, with Claire's caller ID attached to it.

CHAPTER SEVENTEEN

Sochi
Thursday, March 30

Despite the disastrous fight her men had gotten into the previous night, Sochi let Rigo talk her into going out again tonight. She'd told Deep Throat she was done, yet here she was, still La Bruja.

But as Sochi followed her men toward their target in the dark, her phone vibrated, with Claire's face on the screen. Sochi froze. Should she answer? Would it be cowardly *not* to answer? Finally, she took the call, nervous as hell. "Hello," she said as coldly as she could. But then—nothing. Claire didn't say a word. She just breathed into the phone. Was that supposed to be funny? It was just as cruel as the envelope Claire had slipped under her door the day they'd ended it. At least then Sochi had the satisfaction of setting it on fire. Couldn't do that with a phone call.

She shut off her phone and forced herself to concentrate. The plan tonight was the same as usual—encourage the local looter to go elsewhere so La Bruja and her men could take over the site. Much as Sochi hated being an actual looter, she did take pride in the long list of artifacts La Bruja had recovered and saved from being smuggled out of the country.

As usual, Sochi hung back as her men rushed the looters. But this time the shouts were followed by complete silence. She dashed over the ridge to find a gun pointed at Tomas's head. A native man, as blocky and warrior-like as Rigo, held the gun. No one moved.

Sochi stuffed down her fear and strolled into the scene. While the man held his gun on Tomas, he was glaring at Rigo. The armed man flicked his gaze her way, then sneered and turned back to Rigo. "Of course. You are La Bruja's man."

"And you are?" She walked up to the man, shooting a look at Tomas that said *Don't be an idiot. Stay put.*

"I am Nopa. This is Higuchi's dig. Fuck off."

She jammed her fists into her pockets. "Well, we like this spot. We thought we'd stay awhile."

"Higuchi is furious with you. You interfere. You are not welcome. Go away."

That Higuchi was furious meant Deep Throat's plan to harass Higuchi might be working after all.

Her throat tightened. "We think Higuchi should be more generous and share some of the spoils. Looters should stick together, don't you think? You find more treasures than we do, so let us have this dig. Go use your amazing luck to find another."

Nopa's grin gave her the shivers. The guy was wacko. "We aren't leaving." He stepped forward until he was much closer to Tomas now. "While Señor Higuchi might be upset if I killed you, he won't mind if I pop off your boy here."

His finger curled around the trigger. Fast as a panther, Rigo put himself between Tomas and Nopa. Now the gun was pointed at Rigo's chest. *No!* Not until Rigo stood in front of the gun did she realize how attached she'd become to her second-in-command.

"That won't stop me!" Nopa cried. He stepped closer, jamming the barrel of the gun against Rigo's heart.

The two men stared at each other. "This is not the way," Rigo said quietly.

Sochi licked her lips. "Do you two know each other?"

"Yes," Rigo said, but didn't elaborate.

Tension electrified the air. Sochi scanned both groups, alarmed to see that many of Nopa's men were armed. None of hers had more than sticks or clubs.

"What have you found here?" she asked.

Nopa's gaze stayed locked with Rigo's. "Nothing."

"Then give us the site. Why should you waste your valuable time here?" She wanted to pull Rigo away but knew he wouldn't budge.

"If you know Rigo, you should understand that he is not leaving. This stubbornness has nothing to do with the site and everything to do with the gun you're pointing at him. He will not leave. I don't know your relationship, but do you really want to kill him?"

Nopa looked at her, then leaned forward and whispered something to Rigo. Then he jammed his gun into his waistband and motioned to his men. Silently, they gathered their equipment. "I will let you have the site, but only because Rigo doesn't understand the danger. Next time, I will kill him, and now he knows it."

A few minutes later, when they were gone, the men gathered around Tomas and Rigo, congratulating them on their bravery. Then as they started digging, Sochi moved up next to Rigo. "How do you know Nopa?"

Rigo scowled and bent over his shovel. "I'd rather not discuss it."

She waited, but he refused to say more, so she eventually stepped away.

An hour later, tired and distracted, Sochi sat down in the dark. Insects chattered quietly, and the highway noise was light. After living in the United States as a child, when Sochi returned to live in Peru she'd fallen in love with the silence. Most of the time the only sound heard outside of the cities was nature herself.

Stars and nebulae danced overhead. People in the Northern Hemisphere thought they had a great night sky, with the Big Dipper and the Northern Lights, but it was nothing compared to the sky in the Southern Hemisphere. A Dutch astronomer had once said the Southern Hemisphere held all the "good stuff." It had the two best globular clusters, the largest and brightest naked eye galaxies, and some of the largest nebulae. Sochi lay back and cradled her head in her hands.

What did she want out of life? She wanted to succeed at her job, even if Aurelio could be a jerk. She wanted Mima to be safe. She wanted to find love again. Claire's heavy-breathing phone call convinced Sochi she needed to set up a real date with Maria Menendez in order to distract herself from Claire.

Something changed. Her ears picked up a new sound, soft but mechanical, rhythmic, like a motor. She used her hand to block out the brightest nebula, then scanned the sky. There. To the north. A shadow that was blacker than the sky. She sat up. Gods. A drone was headed right for them.

Sochi leapt to her feet, dashed to the nearest lantern, and kicked it over, shouting for the others to be doused. "Drone," she yelled. "Don't look up. Don't look into anything that might reflect your face up to the camera." Heart racing, she ran for her car as the men scattered.

"Kick up dust with your tires so they can't see the plates," Rigo shouted.

The drone hovered for five minutes as everyone hid in the shadows, then it moved on. If Manuel was getting a live feed from the drone, he'd send the police.

Sochi stood. "Time to leave." The men scattered for their vehicles. Tonight's treasure hunt was over. Before she left, she touched Rigo on the shoulder. "I wish you hadn't put yourself in danger."

"He wasn't going to shoot me, but he would have shot Tomas."

"What about me? Would he have shot me? Higuchi's starting to blame us for taking more out of the ground than he is."

Rigo hesitated. "I don't know if Nopa would have shot you. Let's not find out, okay?"

"Deal." She thought about how sad she'd be to lose Rigo. "Rigo, be careful."

"You too, *jefe*. We make a good team."

"That we do. Good night, Rigo." They did make a good team, but that partnership must end soon. Despite Deep Throat's insistence that she continue, the second Sochi heard the drone she knew that La Bruja had retired.

❖

Sochi opted for a long soak in the tub instead of a shower, sighing wearily as she sank up to her neck in frothy water smelling of lavender, then continued puzzling over her future. She wanted to preserve every item she could from Peru's rich past. Having a settled life with a woman who loved her would be nice, but that hadn't worked out. Her friend Lila had tried to tell Sochi that Claire wasn't the only woman for her, and she'd laughed and agreed. But deep in her core, she knew the truth and hated herself because of it.

And what about La Bruja sin Corazon? What did *she* want? Sochi ran a handful of bubbles up her wet thigh. If she was caught and Deep Throat did not acknowledge her, she could be sentenced to a minimum of ten years in prison. She doubted the Peruvian legal system would consider it acceptable to break the law in order to save Peru's history. Her brain began to throb as she tried puzzling out her endgame as La Bruja, so she gave up. That part of her life was over anyway.

After toweling off and donning faded sweats and a T-shirt, Sochi slouched in her most comfortable chair, a wide-bodied beast with an ottoman as big as the chair, her tablet on her lap. She Googled "Maria Menendez, Lima, Peru," but found nothing other than her connection to the CNTP and her family's sugar business.

Their time at Huanchaco Beach had been the most fun Sochi'd had in years...three years, to be exact. They'd rented two boats, since Sochi wasn't about to share the *caballito* with another woman. Like *that* had worked out so well the first time.

Maria was a quick learner, and soon they'd moved from the beginner waves to the more advanced. Sochi's hair became stiff with sand and seawater, and her muscles ached, but she had felt weightless, a hot air balloon cut free from its moorings.

But Maria hadn't given her any sign that she was gay. She'd flirted more with Sochi in the CNTP offices than on the beach, almost as if now that she had Sochi alone, or at least alone with hundreds of others on the beach, she was afraid to be herself. Or maybe she was straight, and had just been flirting for the hell of it.

Sochi tried different combinations with Maria's name: lesbian, gay, rainbow. Nothing. She even dredged the scummy gossip blogs, trying derogatory terms for lesbian like *marimacha* or *cachapera*. Nothing.

She blew out a breath and tugged at her wet hair. Each tug left a tuft standing entirely upright. She thought about calling Lila, but couldn't, even though her friend had kept her sane whenever Sochi had wanted to break apart after Claire left. But La Bruja had managed to kill even her friendship with Lila.

Maybe the next step would be to ask Maria out for dinner. No pressure. But Sochi would make it clear it was a date.

❖

Friday morning as she dressed, Sochi jumped at an incoming text. It was from Hudson: *Got it. Meet me in 30 minutes near McDonald's.* She hurried downtown.

Half an hour later, Sochi slid into the passenger seat of Hudson's battered Range Rover. The SUV smelled of French fries and catsup.

"McDonald's?" she snapped. "You'd make a classy spy."

"Funny." He tucked his unwashed sandy hair behind an ear, then opened the gym bag on his lap and pulled out a small aluminum box. Inside the box a coil of a clear substance rested in molded Styrofoam, looking like the ghost of a tiny snake. There were only about eight inches of material. A small black receiver with a screen was nestled into the depression next to the coil.

"It's real," Sochi breathed.

"Your hunch was right. The developers gave the Americans a faulty version of NanoTrax to get them out of the picture."

"How did you get it, and so quickly?"

"That information isn't part of the deal." He gently removed the small coil. "Put this in the sun to warm it up—do *not* use a microwave or an oven. You'll ruin it. You'll need at least two inches for a viable signal. Cut it with a knife. Place the NanoTrax on the backflap. Along the seam of the handle would be best." She leaned forward as he explained how to use a warm finger to smooth out the NanoTrax, and then let it set for forty-eight hours.

"Then you'll need to charge it. I'm fuzzy on this part—perhaps jumper cables to a car battery? Or strip the wires from a lamp, plug it in, and touch the wires to the NanoTrax?"

He pulled out the receiver. "Turn this on and set it to the frequency on this card. The screen will show the movement of the backflap superimposed over a map of northern Peru. I'm not sure what will happen if the signal goes off the map, like into Ecuador or something. A new map may appear. I can't actually demonstrate the tracking part without applying the NanoTrax, but you can practice once the material's on the backflap."

Sochi took the box. While she didn't have much faith in Aurelio's plan, this stuff was fascinating. Perhaps they actually *could* shut Higuchi down.

"How much do I owe you?"

"Nothing."

"Nothing? How is that possible?"

Hudson shrugged. "Called in a favor from a friend. That's all you need to know. Now it's your turn. You promised I could pick some items from the vault to use as bait."

"What difference does it make? The items will be wrapped up. He'll take them and be gone."

"Not Higuchi. He'll open every item to make sure it's worth the risk." He handed her a list. "These three items should catch Higuchi's attention."

Sochi winced. The gold and amber pectoral. The small Chimú war shield. The set of Moche nose ornaments, crafted of gold and silver. Suspicion bloomed in her chest, but she ignored it. With the NanoTrax attached to the items, none of them could be spirited out of the country.

Exhausted, Sochi headed back to the office. But just as she parked, she received another text. Groaning, she checked it. Adrenaline filled her veins. It was Mima's *Help* text.

She raced over to Mima's apartment building, barely letting her car stop before leaping out and taking the stairs two at a time. Mima's door was ajar. Sochi flew through the apartment. "Mima! Mima!" A kitchen chair was overturned. A painted, wooden cross had fallen off the wall and split in two.

"Mima!" The cell phone was on the floor, crushed by an angry heel.

This had to be Deep Throat. What the hell was she going to do? Call the police and tell them a respected member of the regional government had just kidnapped her grandmother?

As Sochi stood there trembling, panic clutched at her chest. Where was Mima?

CHAPTER EIGHTEEN

Claire
Friday, March 31

Claire had been in Peru for nearly two weeks, and she was exactly zero percent closer to meeting her goal. She'd been threatened by the country's top drug dealer and had possibly phone-stalked her ex-girlfriend. Hardly a successful trip. It was way past time to go home. This whole trip had been a stupid, stupid idea.

Claire sat on the narrow balcony off her hotel room, where there was just enough room for one chair and a small table, which she'd filled with a bottle of wine, a glass, and a chaotic plateful of cheese and crackers and fruit. She regretted giving Nancho the day off, but he needed to take one of his kids to the doctor.

Also, Claire was tired of leading her trio of clowns on their daily wild goose chase. And she didn't know what upset her more—her scary conversation with Higuchi at Las Dulces, where he'd threatened her, or that she might have dialed Sochi and then breathed in her ear during the Ixchel vision. Both terrified her. Mima had always said if your life was broken, stop and fix it. The only way to fix this was to leave.

Claire stared at the copper egg in her hand and realized she'd almost come to hate it. It would give her short, vivid flashes of Ixchel's life, then it would clam up and give her nothing for days. Hudson's shaman friend didn't have time to see her for a few more days, so all her questions festered in her head.

She lifted up the egg. "Why are you so freaking uncooperative? I need more information. I don't know one goddamned thing about Chaco's tomb. And I blame you!"

There was nothing like yelling at an inanimate object to make you feel like a crazy person. Just as Claire sighed and gave up, the egg came to life.

Ixchel huddled outside her house, crouched below the main window, trembling. A man was inside with Uncle and Auntie. He had a painfully harsh voice, like sand grinding against skin. The voice brought back memories of Papa's fear, and of Papa hiding her in a basket and running. This man was part of her past, but she didn't know why.

"I am King Chaco's chief administrator. I demand to see this Ixchel, daughter of Atl."

Uncle said, "Ixchel is our child, not the daughter of anyone else."

"She is promised to the king as one of his attendants once he dies. She escaped years ago, but luckily our blessed ruler did not then join his ancestors in the sky. However, I have tracked Ixchel to this house because our king is now gravely ill."

Auntie was crying. "You have wasted your time. There is no Ixchel here."

"When my beloved ruler's time comes again, Ixchel will be sacrificed, no matter if she is five or fifteen or twenty-five and with child. She is on my list. Chaco demands she accompany him on his journey when that journey happens."

"Why are you doing this?" Auntie asked. "Why would you despise such a sweet child?"

"It is not her I despise. No, it is her father, Atl. He considers himself far too clever with his hands, with his mind. He thinks he will outsmart me. He hid Ixchel from me once, but I will find her. The best way to destroy Atl is to make sure his daughter meets the fate for which she was intended."

Uncle and Auntie moaned. Ixchel slipped down the alleyway and into the nearest llama stall. She moved toward one of the llamas that knew her, so he barely stirred as she pressed against him. She inhaled his warm fur and wrapped her arms around his sturdy neck. Fear clutched at her. What did this all mean?

It took Claire longer to come out of this vision. It seemed the more traumatized Ixchel was, the deeper Claire's connection to the vision. But of course, even though it was dark, Ixchel had never looked skyward. She'd been too busy eavesdropping on the conversation. But if Ixchel never looked up, Claire would never have a clear view of the stars that might help her pin down a location.

Her phone chirped once, but she ignored it, trying to remember the years of her childhood when the only way people could reach you was by landline. That meant if a person were in a foreign country, in a hotel, the chances of the whole world finding you was slim. You could actually take a break from the normal misery called "life." Now, in addition to hating the egg, Claire hated her phone.

It chirped again, insistent. This time she looked. It was another photo, this one so dark she had to squint at the screen. She ran it through her photo editor and lightened it.

The photo was of an elderly woman tied to a red, wooden chair sitting precariously on a mountainside, on the verge of tumbling down the steep slope. Claire studied the photo.

Mima! Holy shit. She was bound and gagged, and leaning back as far as she could to prevent the chair from falling forward. A second text came with GPS coordinates.

Claire called Sochi immediately.

"Mima's gone!" Sochi cried.

"I know. I just received this photo and these coordinates." She forwarded them both. "Meet me there."

Claire didn't have time to call Nancho or a cab, so Señora Nunez, the owner of the hotel, gave her the keys to a high-mileage Honda Civic. The coordinates led Claire southeast of town and up a narrow road into the foothills. There was nothing at the coordinates but a short widening of the road. She stopped and got out.

Two minutes later, Sochi screamed up in her battered Hyundai. She leapt from her car, and even through Claire's fog of fear for Mima she noted Sochi wore a smoking hot skirt with a tight blouse. Her worn boots meant she was ready to hike clear across the Andes to rescue her grandmother. "Is she here?"

"No, but Higuchi considers himself an imaginative geocacher."

"Higuchi took her?"

"I'll explain later. Look for clues or something that will give us the next coordinates." They waded through tall grass, looked up into the nearby trees, but nothing. They returned to the cars. That's when Claire saw it off in the grass. "Look. Fake rock."

Sochi flew to the rock and lifted it to find a piece of paper. "Another GPS location."

Claire entered the coordinates into her phone. "Okay." She pointed up the pathway. "We go up."

They climbed over rocky patches, through meadows filled with white-yellow grasses and scolding birds. They climbed through stretches of forest and areas that were nothing but rocks. Finally, in the shade of a stand of trees, Claire stopped. "We're here." Because GPS can only get you within five to ten meters of a precise location, they had to do the rest of the work on their own. They began searching through the brush, not knowing if they sought another clue, or Mima herself.

"Mima!" Sochi called. They both held their breath and waited. "Mima!"

A sound came from their left.

Sochi whirled in that direction, flew through the trees and out onto the edge of a steep slope, with Claire right behind her. Halfway down the slope, which was covered in unstable rocks, sat Mima in the red wooden chair.

Slowly, they picked their way down the hill. It felt like an hour, but probably only took fifteen minutes. In that time the front legs of the chair had sunk deeper into the rocks, and Mima was seconds from a nose dive. When Claire and Sochi finally reached her, they each grabbed a side of the chair and began ascending. Back on solid ground, they lowered the chair. Sochi undid the gag while Claire worked on the ropes around Mima's hands and feet.

When the gag was off, such a stream of cursing came from the small woman that Claire was actually grateful she didn't speak Quechua. Every fourth or fifth word was Spanish, however, so she managed to pick up much of her fury. "A child! They pick me up like a child! No, like a child's dolly! How disrespectful they were."

Claire massaged Mima's wrists. "Japanese-Peruvians?"

"Yes," she snapped. "They should have more respect for their elders. Look at my suit. It is ruined." Grass and dirt stained the pale silk, and the jacket sleeves had ripped. "When I get my hands on those young men I am going to cut off their balls!" She flipped the chair upside down, rested the seat on her head, and began stomping back down the trail.

Claire heaved a huge sigh, but was too shaky to follow. "Thank God."

Sochi's usually caramel skin was pale as ash. "No, thank *you*."

"Girls! Come!"

They started down the trail, Claire in front. In just a few minutes, Sochi touched her shoulder. "It wasn't me."

"What?"

"It wasn't me."

"We're going to do this now?"

"Why not?"

"Okay, fine. But it *was* you. You wanted revenge because I wouldn't stay in Peru." Claire struggled to tame her quavering voice. "You told the press so my humiliation would be as public as possible."

"That is *beyond* stupid."

"It had to be you. We were *alone*."

"It was not me. I *loved* you."

"But you weren't willing to leave Peru."

"And you weren't willing to stay."

Claire stopped walking, stunned. "But my letter..."

"Yeah, so moving. A blank sheet of paper with "Good Riddance" printed in the middle. Clearly you didn't regret abandoning me. You didn't miss me."

Claire gasped. "Of course I missed you. It was like having an organ removed without anesthesia. But I...my letter..." Her stomach began churning.

"I did *not* do it. Do you hear me? I did not do it."

Claire wanted to fall into those blue pools and forgive, but she was so confused she could barely speak.

"Girls! Come!"

Claire stumbled down the path, then whirled on Sochi. "You burned my letter."

"Your letter burned me."

Claire couldn't describe how it felt to actually talk with Sochi. It confused her, much like a churning river made things too cloudy to see anything.

They reached the parking area, where Mima was angrily cramming her chair into the back of Sochi's car. Claire was having trouble wrapping her mind around the truth—Sochi had received a different letter, not the one Claire had written.

She stood there, unable to move. "I don't know what to do with this information, but Sochi, you received the wrong letter. I apologized. I offered to remain in Peru."

Sochi drew back as if Claire had slapped her. "What?"

They weren't criers, either of them. They just stood, stiff as trees, arms at their sides, tears tracking down their dusty faces.

Mima was suddenly there, small and dark and concerned. She placed one hand on Sochi's chest, the other on Claire's. "Oh, my loves. I know the heart seems the most vulnerable part of our bodies, the most easily broken, but the heart really is the strongest part of each of us. The heart *always* recovers. It's built that way." She stopped and tapped their foreheads. "It's the mind that stores the hurt and anger and betrayal. When the mind lets go, the heart heals. It's that simple. Now I want to go home and clean up."

Claire watched her stride back to the Hyundai. "That woman is brilliant."

Sochi nodded, then said, straight-faced, "She gets it from me."

As Claire's cheek twitched into a reluctant smile, her knees gave out and she leaned against her car for support. *She gets it from me.* Hudson loved Claire's office because it was so clean. When people complimented Claire on that, he'd grin and say, "She gets it from me."

That day, when Claire had been composing the most important apology she'd ever written, she'd been running in and out of her office. Hudson was in and out as well since she had a better printer. She'd left the letter on her desk. He could have read it. Learned about the voices.

Sochi and Mima drove away without looking back. The scene unfolded in Claire's head, clear as a movie. Hudson had recognized the opportunity to get rid of Claire in order to get her job. All he had to do was replace her letter with *Good Riddance* and seal the envelope, thereby sealing the fate of Claire's relationship with Sochi.

CHAPTER NINETEEN

Claire
Friday, March 31

The first thing Claire did once Sochi and Mima drove away was call Hudson. No answer. She left a terse message: *Call me.* She texted the same message. Years ago, Sochi had told her that Hudson had envied her job as subdirector. Hudson was fond of telling Claire, "You have such mad skills that everyone wants to be you, even me."

Sochi might have been right. Hudson could have sabotaged Claire's relationship with Sochi to get her job. She hadn't known Hudson was capable of that. Her heart died a little, but then she forced herself to wait until he could explain. Innocent until proven guilty.

Since she had Señora Nunez's car, Claire drove herself to the shaman. Now that she wasn't hearing voices all the time, she felt more capable of both navigating and driving. The independence felt good.

She double-checked the address on the southern outskirts of Trujillo. Yup, this was it.

The short, compact man who opened the door looked nothing like a shaman. Dressed in loose trousers, sandals, and a faded blue T-shirt, Julio Rojas could have been a campesino just home from work in the avocado groves. His cropped hair was shot with gray.

"You are Julio?"

"I am."

"The shaman?" came out before she could stop herself.

"You were expecting a feather headdress perhaps, and a bone rattle?"

She grimaced, totally busted. "I'm guessing you don't dance around the house chanting."

"Not unless someone pays me to do it." His wide, infectious grin revealed yellowed teeth. "Right now I'm having a beer and listening to Bob Marley. Care to join me?"

"I'd be delighted."

The small front room was sparsely furnished with a table and two chairs, all with peeling yellow paint, a faded orange recliner, and a massive flat screen TV.

Julio laughed when he caught her quick glance at the TV. "My diverse spirituality extends to soccer and Jose de la Vega's cooking show."

"And reggae." Claire sat in one of the wooden chairs as Julio settled in across from her. "I appreciate you taking the time to see me." The house smelled of cinnamon.

"I give spiritual guidance to all, even godless Americans." He winked, deepening the crow's feet defining his eyes.

"I've studied many of Peru's ancient cultures, and I worked at Chan Chan for a number of years, but I don't really know what a shaman does."

Julio cocked his head, his lined face kind. "Ah, yes. You are the Tomb Whisperer."

She flushed. In the background, Marley sang rhythmically about getting together and being all right. "I no longer hear voices."

"I am glad for you, since it must have been exhausting. Clearly, the San Pedro no longer affects you."

"How did you know?"

"Shamans speak to the spirits of our ancestors using San Pedro."

"You do that often?"

"No. Drugs really mess you up. Most blessings I perform without altering my mind. Before men dig at a site, I make a payment of coca leaves or tobacco, asking the spirits of the tomb about to be disturbed that they protect the men against landslides, and that they produce much treasure."

"You know all the looters and where they work?"

"I believe that information falls under shaman-client privilege."

"But what about La Bruja? I thought women made a tomb's spirits angry."

"Not La Bruja. Her motivation is different from men who only wish to pillage." He folded his hands on the table. "But enough about my night job. I only use the San Pedro during Holy Week, which is kind of like your American Super Bowl. It's a big deal. I might perform ten to fifteen ceremonies that week, traveling from dig to dig." He chuckled. "I'm basically high all week."

"You do this at looting sites."

Julio gave a noncommittal shrug. "Families bring pots of food and jugs of sweet corn liquor. I use San Pedro to request that the spirits draw ancient pottery to the surface so people can more easily dig it up. As you know, Peru's ancient past is never far from the surface."

Claire reached into her pocket. "That's why I'm here." She held out her hand, revealing the three eggs.

"Chimú," Julio said.

She explained about the box and mysterious note claiming the eggs came from King Chaco's tomb. Then, trusting that a shaman would know she wasn't crazy, Claire told him about the visions.

He leaned forward. "Fascinating. Is it as if you are watching a play?"

"No, it's as if I'm actually Ixchel, seeing the play through her eyes. I don't know the language but the meaning goes straight to my core. I'm not translating."

"Do you experience all the senses?"

"I felt mist from the surf, and once, when Ixchel touched Cualli's hair, I could feel it was thick and clean. But why am I having these visions?"

Julio picked up the copper egg and closed his fist. They both stared at his hand for a minute, then he returned the egg. "I experience nothing. For some reason, the egg has chosen you."

"But am I seeing reality or am I just dreaming? What if I'm making it all up?"

"The ancient world beneath our feet is separated from us only by a few shovelfuls of sand. The spirit world all around us is separated from us by only a thin curtain. Souls still walk among us, not conscious, but as ghostly proof they existed."

"I don't understand."

"When the sea turtle crosses hard-packed sand, what does she leave behind?"

"Not much, I guess. Maybe a swiggle from her tail, or a claw mark."

"Precisely. The sign is small, yet you still know a sea turtle has passed this way. As we live our lives our souls leave behind signs of our existence. You are somehow able to breach this curtain between present and past. You are seeing—or rather, experiencing—the 'swiggle' or 'claw mark' that Ixchel left behind."

Claire pursed her lips. "It seems too fantastical."

"You are trying to analyze this rationally, but most of life's mysteries cannot be rationalized. The gods are giving you a great gift. Do not fear it."

"But I still don't understand. Why me? Why Ixchel?"

"I do not know for sure. Perhaps you are being given some sort of message. Something in Ixchel's life might prove valuable in your own."

She fingered the copper egg. "Ixchel's father made the egg. Her aunt and uncle insisted she carry it with her at all times. Uncle said it would save her life one day." Then, with an electrifying tingle, her hand closed over the egg.

Ixchel shook. Wind whipped her hair into her face. "I am doomed. The administrator will keep coming for me."

Cualli held Ixchel, her breath warm on her neck. "No, I will keep you safe."

"You live within the city walls. I am outside them, so he can find me."

Cualli's deep brown eyes calmed her. "No, when the time comes, you and I will leave together. The Chimú live all along the coast. We will go to another city and be safe, together."

"But what of Tochi?"

"We understand each other."

Ixchel held her. "I will go anywhere with you."

They settled back against the rocks as surf licked at their toes. Ixchel was determined to find a way to be together. If only the administrator would leave her alone. At least, if things went very wrong, she had her father's copper egg. But how could a copper egg possibly protect her?

Claire opened her eyes. The light in the house was fading with dusk, but Julio didn't switch on a lamp. Softened by the shadows, his brow was furrowed in concern. She understood now why the locals put their faith in this man.

"You have had a vision?" he asked.

She nodded. "Not much happened. That's the problem. There must be a reason I'm being shown these visions, but very little happens."

"Life isn't in the drama. Life can be found in the small moments that happen every day, all day long. You are part of Ixchel's life. The answers will come. But, Claire Adams, this message about the copper egg is one you must heed. Keep the egg with you at all times."

Claire heaved an elephant-sized sigh. "How on earth could this little thing save anyone's life?"

"Perhaps you will learn that from Ixchel." He placed his hands on the table, clearly signaling the end of the conversation. "I ask two things in payment for my time with you this evening."

"Anything."

"First, take this." He opened a backpack and removed a small vial. He folded her fingers around it. "Another dose of San Pedro might clear your vision."

Instead of refusing, she surprised herself by pocketing the vial.

"Second, trust the spirits. This egg has great power. You must use it when the moment comes." She swallowed hard, frightened. "Part of trusting the spirits is also trusting yourself."

They stood and Claire offered her hand. Julio held it with both of his, gazing deeply into her eyes. He then spoke in Quechua, strange words that flowed up her arms and into her chest. She suddenly felt strong and brave.

"Thank you. And you don't need a feathered headdress or bone rattle to impress me. I see now, through your wisdom, that you are shaman."

She turned back at the door. "One more thing. How do you know Hudson?"

If the man had anything to hide in those eyes, the wink disguised it. "Wednesday night poker game."

Claire was calmer on the drive home. She could do this. She would fully embrace the egg. She would draw its energy toward her. Her confidence seemed more stable, as if a table had been leveled so it no longer rocked.

CHAPTER TWENTY

Claire
Saturday, April 1

The email Claire received the next morning was full of typos, one she would have easily dismissed as a stupid prank except that the writer sounded so very matter-of-fact about cutting off her fingers. She reread it several times, her temper flaring. Holy shit. Who the hell was this guy? She had no doubt he was connected somehow to one of her three stooges, but the tone wasn't arrogant enough to be Higuchi. He would have signed the email and not used a fake address, kingchaco@gmail.com.

This guy thought that threatening her fingers would help her find the tomb faster. Higuchi thought pressuring her would accomplish the same thing. What the hell was wrong with these people? Treasure hunting couldn't be done to a freaking schedule, especially when her only source of clues was her visions.

Claire called her boss, Mac, again.

"Hey, you still in Peru?"

"Yup. Thanks for the advice about being followed. It worked. Now I have another problem. Someone—probably one of the people following me, or at least connected to them—has just threatened to sneak into my hotel room and cut off my fingers if I don't hurry up and find what he wants me to find."

Silence. "Huh. Adams, I gotta say your life is starting to sound like a really bad adventure flick, maybe one starring an ancient Nicholas Cage."

"I know, right? But what would you do? Give up? I hate that idea."

"Can you hire a bodyguard?"

"Hmmm."

"Maybe hook up with some big strong dyke who can pound a man into the ground with one hand while tuning her Harley with the other?"

"I wish, but I don't know anyone like that."

Mac sighed. "I'd offer to come down there myself and do the pounding, but you know, there's my company that's falling apart without you."

"How do *you* protect yourself at night when you sleep?"

"Me, personally? I live in Chevy Chase, Maryland. I sleep like a baby. Also, Roger barks whenever a mouse farts, so he's my alarm system."

"I'm glad for you. But no advice?"

"Yes. Get out of Peru now, before something ugly happens. No hotel door is going to stand up to someone who really wants to get inside."

Claire shivered. "That's not very comforting."

"Wasn't meant to be."

"Okay, well, thanks."

She sat there, unsure of what to do. She needed to call Sochi, but she was afraid. She called her mom but her parents were still rafting, or maybe had gone on to the next adventure. What was wrong with her parents? Why couldn't they remain within cell phone range? Was that too much to ask?

Nancho couldn't drive Claire today, and she didn't want to pay for a taxi to drive her up the coast just so the three jokers following her would have something to do with their day. All she wanted to do was sink further into Ixchel's life and talk to Sochi, but she couldn't yet bring herself to explain that someone—probably Hudson—had switched the letter she'd slid under Sochi's door, that their breakup and three years of heartache had been caused by the man she'd considered her best friend.

Instead, she decided to be a tourist and just walk through downtown. The air felt like spring, not surprising since Trujillo called itself the City of Perpetual Spring. She checked out the other churches—San Francisco, Santa Clara, La Merced, Santo Domingo, and La Compañia.

Claire visited the archaeological museum, actually recognizing some of the finds she'd made. Then on to the zoological museum and its taxidermied animals. By now she was having so much fun leading her posse on that she even went to the toy museum.

While back at the main plaza watching a *marinera* contest, a lovely dance that bugged the hell out of her because tradition held that the male dancers wear shoes and their female partners go barefoot, Claire noticed her three shadows looked tired. Good. The coolest movie characters were those who managed to send a beer or room service to the undercover cops following them, but she wasn't that cool. She wanted these people to be uncomfortable. She wanted them to leave her alone.

That's when Claire headed straight for the Japanese guy. She walked around the crowd and went for him. He looked up in alarm, but the only way he could have avoided her was to start running. She stopped in front of him. "Tell your fucking boss to back off. Leave right now or I'll call to that cop standing over on the corner."

The man sneered. "I am so frightened."

"Maybe he can't arrest you, but don't you think Higuchi will be disappointed in you?"

With a tight jaw, he walked away. Claire turned and headed for the ungrateful woman she'd saved from certain drowning, but she slid into her orange Volvo and took off. By the time Claire started looking for the native guy, he'd melted away into nothing.

She stopped at a shop and bought something to drink, then she called Sochi.

"Yes?" Her voice sounded impatient.

"Hi, I was just calling to ask Mima how she's doing after her ordeal."

"This isn't Mima's phone."

Claire made a face, glad Sochi couldn't see her. "Yes, I understand that."

Sochi sighed. "She's fine. A little dehydrated, and madder than a shorn llama, but otherwise she's, you know, just Mima."

"Could we get together and talk?"

"I said everything I needed to say yesterday."

"I didn't."

"I suppose so."

"Las Dulces, thirty minutes."

❖

Claire arrived first and filled a small plate full of Sochi's favorite treats. When Sochi joined her ten minutes later, her gaze dropped to the plate, then back to Claire.

Sochi wore the same sort of thing she always wore—short, tight skirt and silk blouse that clung to her breasts and ribcage. Her eyes were hidden behind sunglasses, which, thankfully, she pushed back onto her head.

Claire, of course, wore her two tanks and cargo shorts. Despite the years and bad feelings between them, their appearances hadn't really changed. Claire felt as if she were sitting across the table with both a total stranger and her best friend.

"You've lost weight," Claire said. "I thought you could use something sweet and fattening." The first ten minutes were, to say the least, awkward, with Sochi answering her questions with one word or one sentence. But as the plate emptied, they both relaxed. Claire told her about her parents' latest adventure. Sochi discussed a few of their mutual friends.

They remained careful with each other, but the tightness around Sochi's eyes had smoothed out. It felt so good to be sitting there, talking, that Claire almost reached for her hand. Your brain sets down patterns, and despite the three years, Claire's pattern was to tease Sochi and make sexual jokes and touch her as much as possible. Today she could do none of that.

"So, what's new in the world of Peruvian archaeology?" What a stupid question. Where had her courage gone? Oh, yeah. She didn't have any.

Sochi studied her hands. "Did you hear about what some kids found outside of Huanchaquito a few years ago?"

Claire shook her head. Huanchaquito was along the beach between Chan Chan and the airport.

"They were playing in the dunes near the pizzeria and found a pile of bones. The pizzeria owner called an archaeologist. In just a few days they uncovered the bodies of forty-two children, centuries old. And seventy-six llamas—or alpacas—they weren't sure. Enough clothing remained that they identified the kids as Chimú, likely from Chan Chan."

"Sacrifices?"

"Yes. The kids, mostly teens, had been killed over seven hundred years ago with a hatchet blow to the chest, then the ribs pulled apart and the heart removed."

"I'm guessing an El Niño drought made them do it?" Toward the end of the Chimú civilization, El Niño often took up residence over the northern coast and wreaked havoc on all aspects of the people's lives. Year after year, the rain pounded so constantly it became impossible to grow crops. The waters offshore warmed up enough to suffocate algae and phytoplanktons—food for fish, birds, and sea mammals. The animals were forced to migrate or starve. As a result, most of the Chimú's food sources disappeared or died. The rains turned their homes and fields into mud.

Sochi nodded. "Yes, the Chimú were desperate, so they sacrificed children hoping to appease the gods and stop the rain."

"I can't imagine standing there as a parent, watching your child being killed."

Sochi played with the edge of the paper placemat. "Perhaps, but think about it. For a sacrifice to mean something, you have to believe that doing it is the most important thing in the world, that what you are gaining is more important than what you are losing. Perhaps the parents felt honored that their child was going to help save their people. To me, sacrifice isn't frightening. It's something that you do freely because it's right."

Claire sighed. She couldn't put this off any longer, so she handed Sochi a handwritten note. "This is not word for word because I can't remember exactly what I wrote three years ago, but it's close enough. This is the letter I thought I'd slid under your door."

Sochi read the letter, then let it drop onto the table. She covered her face with her hands, breathing deeply.

Claire waited until Sochi looked her in the eye. "Sochi, I'm *really* sorry. When you burned my letter, when you didn't reply, and then the press hit me with all the voices stuff, the only conclusion I could draw was that you'd rejected my apology and talked to the press to punish me." Something stuck in her throat so she looked down at the table until she could swallow again. "I can't undo the damage. I just want you to know that I'm very, very sorry."

Sochi watched a couple walk by, then stared out the window. "I would have accepted your apology if I'd gotten it." She let out a huge breath. "Did Hudson do it?"

"I think so. You know how he was always in and out of my office. He must have replaced my letter with the horrible one."

"That asshole's never getting his backflap now."

Claire relaxed and finally let herself smile. "Sochi, I know that forgiving someone for breaking trust is one of the hardest things to do, so I won't blame you if you can't. But maybe, if we both take Mima's advice about the head and the heart, we could one day be friends again."

Sochi looked at Claire, her eyes swimming. "I accept your apology. As for trust and forgiveness, that I..." She pressed her lips together, then stood. "Thank you for helping me rescue Mima yesterday. I must go."

Claire sighed as Sochi walked away.

CHAPTER TWENTY-ONE

Sochi
Sunday, April 2

When her La Bruja phone chimed early the next morning, Sochi forced herself to check it. A text from Rigo: *We cannot give up. We are close to a jackpot. Even if we can't find Chaco's tomb, the Adams woman will.*

She pulled the covers over her head. She didn't want to get up, even though stacks of files and project reports awaited her at the office. Sunday was the perfect day to work because there'd be no smarmy Manuel yammering on about his drones, no Aurelio pushing her to conduct the NanoTrax sting, even though she was getting closer to making it happen.

She sat up and stretched, knowing she wouldn't sleep even if she stayed in bed. Mima had been put in danger and it was Sochi's fault. How could she keep Mima safe *and* retire as La Bruja? Claire said Higuchi had kidnapped Mima, but Deep Throat was just as capable of harming her. Mima was refusing to stay at her niece's house in Sausa, but instead had come back to her apartment in Trujillo.

After seeing Clare at Las Dulces yesterday, it was as if all the air had leaked out of Sochi's hate balloon, leaving a limp, empty shell. She'd felt angry and hurt for so long that she didn't know what else to feel. It had been nice just sitting there, nibbling on the cookies as if they were friends again. She might, in time, be able to move toward forgiveness, but trust? Too risky. Even though she'd seen Claire's version of the real letter, it was just too hard to let go of the anger she'd nursed like a delicate flower for so many years. With a groan, she finally forced her feet onto the bare floor and stood.

Mid-afternoon she took a break at work, munching on a power bar and guzzling a Coke. She rehearsed what she would say to Rigo tonight. This would be a hard conversation, since she and Rigo had a rich history...

...Sochi had been "dead" twelve months now. She'd died the day Claire left the country. Sochi imagined herself the world's only living, breathing corpse. Her eyes appeared dead when she looked in the mirror, her skin dull as mud. She'd drained all her tears months ago and lacked the will to produce more. Tears meant you cared. Tears meant you had hope and pain and a functioning organ inside your chest, slightly to the left.

She managed to mimic a normal life. She repainted all the rooms in her little house. She'd have a harder time picturing Claire in the bedroom if the walls were now lime green.

She continued to work at the CNTP, so she had no choice when Aurelio sent her to represent him at the Lambayeque event. She dressed in her best suit, too loose now since dead women forgot to eat, and drove to Lambayeque.

As she approached the museum, she remembered how much she and Claire hated this place, not for the artifacts it held, but for what it had begun. A team of lucky looters had stumbled upon the Lord of Sipan's gold-laden tomb in 1987. Before they could steal much, Walter Alva rescued the site and built a museum in Lambayeque to display the treasures. Sadly, the Sipan discovery started a looting frenzy in northern Peru that turned into an epidemic, like the gold rush in America.

The museum was celebrating an anniversary so Aurelio sent her to be a "visible and supportive" presence. But since no one from the CNTP was around, she donned the disguise she'd recently purchased—a heavy, dark brown wig, and a pair of cocoa brown contacts. If she could mingle with others in the field and not be recognized, perhaps she could pull off the assignment from Minister Salazar, who had just convinced her to start looting as a way to put more pressure on Higuchi. She'd fought his request for months, but he finally convinced her. Yet she knew she couldn't do this by herself. She needed help. The likelihood of finding the person she needed here was slim, but as Sochi wandered the museum, she examined each person she passed, not sure what she sought.

She'd been here several times before, but the gold jaguar mask with its sharp incisors, and the delicate pottery figure of a fisherman on his *caballito* still took her breath away. While she stared at a glass-encased suit of ceremonial dress, the curled shoulder pads looking like a collar of waves, a man stepped beside her. "Stunning," he said.

"Yes, it is."

"And a relief that it is still here, within the boundaries of Peru instead of in America or Europe or Japan."

Sochi looked at him, surprised at the passion in his voice. With his wide cheekbones, sharp as anvils, his broad, flat nose and full lips, the man could have been the model for all the gold masks in this museum.

"I share your views," Sochi said.

Together they moved to the next display, a pounded gold panel with images of rulers overseeing crowds of peasants. "Sometimes," the man said, his voice dropping to a hoarse whisper, "I think it would be better if we found all the riches and dug everything up just to make sure that we—the descendants of the Moche and the Chimú and half a dozen other cultures—could keep our people's treasures in Peru."

Sochi gave him a sideways glance, but his gaze continued straight ahead, staring at the gold panels. "There are over twenty international teams of archaeologists working in the country right now," she said, "doing their best to ensure that happens."

"Archaeologists are too slow, too methodical. The treasures must be pulled from the earth quickly before others have time to ship our treasures overseas or pack them over the Andes."

Sochi's nostrils flared. "You are talking of looting your own country."

His black eyes bored into hers. "Yes, I am. The ends justify the means."

Her mouth fell open. Apparently dead people could still be surprised.

He stuck out his hand. "Rigoberto Garcia."

She shook it automatically, searching frantically for an alias. "I'm Juanita Perez. Come with me," she said.

She led him into a smaller room of pottery pieces, one with no visitors at the moment. They sat on the carved wood bench along one side. She kept her voice low. "Since I was a child, I've been concerned about the artifacts buried in nearly every square foot of this country. From age ten to age twenty, I turned at least eighty items in to the CNTP."

Rigoberto nodded. "I, too, have found many things. But I did not turn them in." His grin was wicked. "I sold them to feed my parents and my sisters."

"Are you a drug lord? Murderer? Untrustworthy?" After each question, Rigoberto shook his head vigorously. "I have no idea who you are or what your background is, but you feel solid to me. Reliable."

Now he nodded. "I have done many things in my life, not all of them legal, but I am trustworthy. I do not abandon my friends or my post."

Knowing the risk she took, Sochi plunged ahead. The money from Deep Throat was burning a hole in her mind. "I have a plan," she said, "to create a fearful looting boss called La Bruja sin Corazon, who will loot but keep the artifacts in Peru. But I need help. I cannot lead men every night on digs. I have other responsibilities."

"You seek a partner?"

She inhaled deeply. "I do. Think of all the artifacts you could find. We would sell them to private collectors here in Peru." When he hesitated, she motioned to the treasures surrounding them. "If Walter Alva hadn't swooped in and controlled the Sipan excavation, all these treasures would have been smuggled out of the country. Peruvian schoolchildren wouldn't be able to see for themselves the creations of their brilliant ancestors. Foreigners wouldn't be able to appreciate the wisdom and strength of the pre-Columbian cultures, like learning of their irrigation skills, or their farming practices. Our people had a rich and industrious life before the Spanish descended on the natives as hard as a fist."

The man looked at her, inscrutable, then nodded. "Sounds good, *jefe*. When do we begin?"

They said nothing more until they exited the museum and Rigo shook her hand again, excited now. "Viva La Bruja," he said softly. "We will save this country from foreign exploitation and feed our families at the same time..."

❖

That evening Sochi parked the car on the street behind a large truck, ducked below the dash, and pulled on the wig, tugging impatiently until it settled over her scalp. She inserted the brown contacts, blinking impatiently so they'd settle. She gave the wig one final tug then slid from her car.

The bar's entrance was dark but for a naked light bulb over the solid door and a flashing neon sign of a red martini glass. Smoke assaulted her inside, attaching itself to her drab clothing as she strode past the bar. Half the men swiveled and watched her pass, one man even leaning out far enough she'd either be forced to run into his face with her breasts, or step around him.

She did neither. Instead she stopped right in front of him. Because of her brown contacts, her light blue eyes weren't available to unnerve the man, but she could do a fair amount of damage with the brown ones. His leer began to fade as her gaze bore into him. Then he shrugged and bellied up to the bar again, flushing at the guffaws around him.

She lasered each man until the chuckling stopped. She proceeded to the back booth, passing at least three tables of men drinking beer Peruvian style using only one glass, flinging the last bit of beer in the glass onto the floor, then passing the glass and bottle to the next man. She slid in across from Rigo, his eyes hidden behind sunglasses.

"What a shit hole," she muttered, then nodded her thanks for the beer in front of her. She took a long, long drink.

Rigo shrugged. "True, but it is a safe place." He looked down at his beer, revealing a dark bruise along one cheek.

"Take your sunglasses off," Sochi said.

"No."

Increasingly, she'd begun to wonder who was in charge—La Bruja or Rigo. "Take off your fucking glasses."

Rigo scowled but did as she commanded. She inhaled sharply. Both eyes were bruised, the left one nearly swollen shut. "Not *again*."

He gulped his beer, unconcerned. "Ran into some resistance at the French dig site. Guards were resistant, like the Swedes, but we finally convinced them to leave." He grinned, his teeth gleaming like white corn.

"Gods, Rigo."

He picked up the square coaster for Cumbres beer and began tapping each side sharply against the table. "If the men—guards or looters—do not leave, we have no choice. We have had disappointing finds for months. Tomas thinks Julio needs to bless every site in order to appease the spirits."

"Tomas probably blames me for the bad luck, but we can't afford Julio at every dig."

"You know I don't believe women bring bad luck, but some of the men do. On top of that, now Marcos and some of the others have started bringing guns." He leaned forward. "That Adams woman needs to come through, and soon. I have been following her for days and I don't think she's trying very hard to find the tomb."

She took another sip then wiped her mouth. "I don't know if she is or not. But you're right about the slow month. Between the competition from Higuchi and increased security at the registered digs, we're losing ground." She slid a thick envelope across the table to Rigo.

"What's this?"

"I was given a certain amount of funding to start working as La Bruja. This is what's left. I want you to take some and distribute the rest among the men."

His dark brows drew together. "I don't understand."

This was proving to be harder than she'd expected. "Rigo, I'm done. La Bruja is retiring."

He shook his square head. "No. Not possible."

"Yes, it is. I'm done."

"Why? Just because things are slow? Because I have a black eye? Because we ran up against Higuchi's men?"

She leaned forward. "The instant that wacko Nopa pointed the gun at you, I knew I was done. I *like* you, Rigo."

He blushed violently, making Sochi laugh. "No, not like *that*, you idiot. But when that gun was aimed at your chest, I realized that nothing is worth losing you as a friend. Nothing is worth getting caught, which is only a matter of time thanks to the CNTP drones."

"We will learn to deal with the drones. We can get someone on the inside of the CNTP to make sure the drones stay away."

"I'm still done. If you really must keep going, which I hope you don't, find another woman to serve as La Bruja sin Corazon."

"You *are* La Bruja. You have led us successfully for nearly two years." Rigo's voice fell into a lower register, the sign he was deeply upset.

"It's time. We must stop."

His jaw worked as he struggled to understand. His black eyes narrowed. "If you retire, what will you do with your wig?"

Sochi's eyes widened.

He smiled sadly. "Yes, I know you wear a wig, and that you wear contacts to cover your distinctive blue eyes. For two years I have called you *jefe*, but I know you are Xochiquetzal Castillo."

She pressed her lips together to cut off her gasp.

Rigo's eyes softened. "I did nothing with that information when I learned it, and I will do nothing now."

"How did you find out?"

He shrugged. "I saw a photo of CNTP's Sochi Castillo in the newspaper, and I knew it was you."

"Thank you for keeping my secret."

"I will continue to do so."

"What are you going to do? Will you keep looting?"

Rigo pocketed the envelope of cash. "I do not know, *jefe*. I do not know." With an anguished glance, he slid from the booth and was gone. Sochi waited a few minutes, then ran the gauntlet at the bar one more time. This time everyone behaved. When she reached her car, her phone rang.

"Mima, are you okay?"

"Yes, my dear, I am fine. But you said to tell you if I noticed any strange men hanging around. The two men who tied me up were across from my building this afternoon."

"Call the police, Mima, right away."

"I did that, but they left before the police arrived."

Damn it. Mima still wasn't safe.

CHAPTER TWENTY-TWO

Claire
Monday, April 3

Claire awoke from her dream with a shuddering gasp. She sat up, confused, then realized she was still in her hotel room, alone. She flung herself back onto the bed. Yowza. Hell of a wet dream. The damn thing re-created, almost perfectly, the day after she and Sochi had their first big fight, so big that Claire had slept in her own apartment that night.

Sochi had shown up there the next day, letting herself in with her key.

Claire had just gotten out of bed, naked. When she saw Sochi she grabbed for a towel, but since it was a hand towel, it didn't do much good...

...Sochi took a step forward, breathing heavily as if short of oxygen. "*Jesus Cristo.*" She began murmuring words that Claire recognized as a prayer for strength as she scanned her body.

"You're hyperventilating," Claire said hoarsely. "Go away. I'm still mad at you."

Sochi took another step as she continued to pray. Her eyes glistened, ice melting in the heat. Claire's insides liquefied at the look on Sochi's face. Why was it crazily erotic to know someone wanted you so badly they couldn't control themselves? "Don't come any closer," Claire said with as much fury as she could muster despite her weak knees. "I'm not speaking to you."

Sochi's eyes darkened. "I know. I'm sorry."

"For what? For starting the fight?"

Sochi took a step closer. "No, you started that. I'm sorry for being inappropriate and out of control in the next two minutes."

"We can't," Claire managed to say even though her tongue was stuck to the roof of her mouth.

"Can't what? Do you know it's been nearly twenty-four hours since we've spoken?"

"I wasn't counting. Stay where you are."

Another step forward. "It's been twenty-four hours since we've touched."

"I need more time."

"I know. I should give you that. I should be respectful. I should let you decide what's going to happen next. But here's the thing, I can't wait for that."

"Try." Her heart pounded as she watched Sochi's cat-like advance.

"But I can't. I cannot stop myself, Claire Adams." Sochi now stood inches from her.

The kiss was shy at first, as if they were each as fragile as mist, but Sochi's confidence returned and her arms tightened around Claire.

Without a word they pressed themselves together, sliding thighs between legs. Claire gasped as Sochi pressed her up against the wall, her hands now in possession of her body. The ineffective towel fell to the floor. Claire arched back when Sochi's thumbs grazed roughly over her nipples. She ran a nail up the inside of Sochi's thigh. When she touched her, Sochi let out such an anguished moan that Claire fumbled madly for the hem of her skirt.

"Oh, gods, please," Sochi moaned.

Claire's pulse quickened. Sochi never talked during sex. For her to beg sent lightning bolts straight between Claire's legs.

Then they were on the rug, her clothing moved aside. Then Sochi was moving her mouth lower, wet and hungry and urgent.

Claire's orgasm was fast and red-hot. She cried out, muffling the sound with her hand, feeling as if she'd exploded. Then she pulled Sochi back up and their lips melted together again as Claire's fingers disappeared into Sochi's heat. In less than a minute, Sochi arched, her gasps breaking almost into a sob.

They lay on the rug in a tangle. Claire's toes had gone numb and her legs felt like noodles. Her backbone had melted into the floor, but they weren't done. They rocked their hips together, Sochi gasping almost immediately, Claire following seconds later.

She finally caught her breath. "I think I'm going to like fighting with you."

Sochi's smile sent Claire's chest fluttering. "We're not very good at it," Sochi said. "Personally, I had planned to freeze you with my indifference the next time we met."

Claire chuckled. "What happened to your indifference?"

"It melted." Sochi nuzzled her ear. They kissed again, laughing soft puffs into each other's mouths...

Claire was still trying to shake off the dream when her phone started ringing. It was Sochi. She blew out a huge breath.

"Hey," Claire said, cool and casual. Sochi could not know that in her mind she'd just been stark naked.

"I have a problem. No, I have two problems. I was hoping you might have some ideas of what I could do."

"I'm happy to help. What's up?"

She told her about the CNTP's mad plan to mark some artifacts with a high-tech tracking device as a way to catch Higuchi in the act, or at least find his smuggling route.

"Wait. Are you talking about NanoTrax? My contact told me it didn't work."

"I pushed Hudson harder and he acquired some for me."

"Wow. I didn't know he had those kinds of connections. And he still isn't returning my messages. He knows I'm furious. Still, I like your plan. Higuchi's an asshole. He put Mima's life in danger, so I hope you nail him."

"That's the thing. My boss is sure this will work, and so he's willing to let four artifacts walk out the door, including Hudson's backflap."

Claire whistled.

"But it seems too easy. Higuchi's smart enough to figure out some way to beat this. When he does, we will have lost irreplaceable items."

"How much time do you have?"

"Maybe four or five days."

"Could you make some changes to the list of artifacts?"

"Other than Hudson's backflap, yes. Why?"

Claire thought for a moment. "I know someone who might be able to help. What's the other problem?" She loved that they were talking, but the urge to do more than talk was beginning to overpower her good sense.

"Mima. She won't stay with my aunt. She insists on coming back to her apartment, and she's started seeing Higuchi's men outside."

"That's scary. Okay, I think Denis can help us with both problems. I'll call him. If he's home I'll let you know and we can meet there. However, I also have a problem." She told Sochi about the threatening email. It was gratifying to see that something like this, even if it was threatening her, could rouse such anger in Sochi.

"You need to call the police."

"I'm thinking it's just a prank," Claire said.

"I'm thinking it's not."

❖

The meeting with Denis went quickly. He was willing to help Sochi with her artifact problem, and said he'd be charmed if Mima would be his guest until it was safe. As they waited outside in his garden while he made a few phone calls, the blooming flowers made Claire feel thickheaded and a little high. She stared at Sochi's hand as they sat side-by-side on a padded swing.

Clearly uncomfortable, Sochi began sharing photos of her nephews and Mima. Photos were safer than conversation. "Wait, go back," Claire said. "There." She pulled the phone closer. Damn. It was the woman from the orange Volvo. Should Claire tell Sochi this woman was following her? Did Sochi already know?

"Who's this?" Claire asked.

Sochi pressed her lips together, flushing brightly. "My date. We went surfing at Huanchaco."

If the reference to their own first date meant to hurt, it did. Claire tapped her foot against the flagstones and felt doors slamming all around her. If Sochi had a girlfriend, it might be too late for Claire. Suddenly, she didn't want to talk about Orange Volvo woman. She had nothing to do with what Claire needed to say.

"Sochi, I can't stop thinking about you. I think my mind might be letting go of the pain, just as Mima said. Is that happening to you?"

Sochi's eyebrows raised in alarm. "I don't know."

"Could I hold your hand?"

She stared at Claire's open hand. "No."

Ouch. That hurt. But Claire didn't blame her. She was moving way too fast because she couldn't help it. Claire could finally admit that she missed Sochi terribly. "Why not?"

Sochi stood. "Look, I don't know what you're feeling, but you need to know that whatever it is, *I'm* not feeling it. I'm terrified of you."

"Why?"

"Because you have the power to destroy me. Thank you for finding Mima a safe place to stay. I'll get her now."

"Shit," Claire muttered under her breath. She couldn't blame Sochi for leaving so suddenly, since she'd broken her heart once before. For all either of them knew, she might be capable of breaking it again.

CHAPTER TWENTY-THREE

Claire
Monday, April 3

Bad news gathered around Claire like iron filings on a magnet. Just as Sochi's problems seemed under control, Nancho called Claire, nearly in tears. "It is my cousin, little Mardonio. He went over the mountains as *mochilero* and was killed."

"Nancho, I am so sorry." He continued to struggle so Claire murmured the sorts of things one did in this situation.

"Thank you," he finally choked out. "The *vuelario* is tonight. Would you come?"

"Me? But I didn't know him."

"That is fine. My family would be honored to have you."

Claire doubted that, but agreed because Nancho wanted her there so badly. She found wakes hard anyway, but one for a person killed violently, a person she didn't know? She was going to be uncomfortable the second she walked in. "Thank you, Nancho. I would be honored to be included."

Early evening Claire rode in the front seat with Nancho—he'd insisted—while his wife Carmen and their two children rode in the back. Other than some squirming by the kids, the car was silent for the entire drive up to Chepen.

Mardonio's family lived on the outskirts of town in a one-story blue stucco home. Claire had never attended a *vuelario* before, but had heard about them. Many of the indigenous people practiced a unique religion—part Catholic, part native. Sochi had once explained that instead of abandoning their religion for Catholicism, the native Peruvians had simply braided Catholicism into their traditions and practices.

Claire followed Nancho and his family inside the cool home, breezes blowing through every window. All the large furniture had been removed from the modest living room, which was now packed with folding chairs and people in black. She was relieved she'd packed a pair of black cargo pants and a black shirt. At times it was stressful being so unfashionable. Sochi would have totally rocked a little black dress and some simple silver jewelry. Claire wore the corded amazonite from Mima around her neck.

At the far end of the room, the open casket was surrounded by tall, burning candles. Flowers were piled on the casket and on the floor. The room smelled like a garden. A ceramic statue of Jesus hung on the wall behind the casket, as well as an oversized rosary made of malachite beads.

The buzzing—in both Spanish and Quechua—began the instant Nancho introduced Claire to Mardonio's father. The poor man gripped her hand and shook it vigorously. Women in the room began to whisper behind their hands. Nancho continued introducing her to others with pride. Finally, she leaned in close. "Why is everyone looking at me?"

Nancho ducked his head, as if caught doing something wrong. "You hear the voices of the dead. Everyone is excited to meet you. They are wondering..." He shot her an apologetic look. "They are wondering if you will hear the voice of Mardonio tonight."

"Nancho, I'm so sorry, but it never worked that way."

"That's okay. They are still glad you are here."

The room quickly heated up from all the bodies. The crowd overflowed into the kitchen, hallway, and out the front door. Claire bent her head during the prayers, and the many "amens." When the Catholic rituals were done, Nancho led her to a chair, where his family joined them. Carmen and the children sat on the floor as all the chairs were taken. Then a woman passed through the packed room with a huge basket of coca leaves. Claire watched as the others each took a handful of leaves, stuffed them into their mouths, and began to chew.

The Incas had used coca leaves to fortify themselves during long days of hard work. Today, the natives did the same, as well as to combat altitude sickness in the mountains and to regulate blood pressure. She knew all this, but had never actually tried coca. It wasn't cocaine—the leaves needed to be processed to become the drug, but she was still nervous.

Claire took a few leaves, smiling at the woman with the basket, then popped them into her mouth and began to chew. It tasted like she was, well, chewing leaves. Then a man began circulating the room pouring a clear liquid into a communal shot glass. When it was Claire's turn, she had no choice but to accept the glass and toss back the liquid. She coughed as her eyes watered. The short, stocky man grinned and served Nancho.

"*Cana andino*," Nancho said. Moonshine.

"Very good," Claire rasped. Nancho explained that they believe the soul of the deceased was present at the *vuelario* and might grab on to someone and upset them. The coca and cana were both meant to protect the visitors from this happening. It also helped that most of the people in the room believed that if Mardonio's soul was going to latch on to anyone, it would be Claire.

The multiple conversations around her all concerned Mardonio's death. From the bits she picked up, many believed that Higuchi murdered Mardonio to get back at a business rival. A shiver ran through her. Not to make everything all about her, but Mardonio had made ten successful trips before this one. And now, when Higuchi was lashing out at Claire, the poor boy—connected to her through Nancho—was killed. She hoped it was a coincidence, but then scoffed at her own naiveté.

Claire began to feel lightheaded from the moonshine. To anchor herself, she clutched the copper egg in her pocket, immediately regretting it.

Ixchel's heart ached with deep sadness as she leaned over her uncle. He lay on his pallet, coughing so hard Ixchel could feel it through her feet on the floor. Uncle was smaller now, mostly bone as he wasted away from sickness. "You still have the egg?" he asked.

"Yes."

Uncle coughed harshly.

"Uncle, please save your breath."

"Your father died last year."

Ixchel gasped.

"We did not want to tell you, since you have such hope that he will come one day. He couldn't, you know. They would have followed him. That was why he made the egg for you. He said the egg will save you."

"From what, Uncle? I do not understand."

Uncle and Auntie nodded to each other. "It is time," he said. They explained that Ixchel was to be sacrificed at age five when King Chaco supposedly died from a terrible illness. Atl hid her in a basket and fled. They walked to the city where Uncle and Auntie lived.

But Chaco did not die, and administrators were furious that Ixchel was gone. One of them vowed he would find her and make sure, when the time came, that she was sacrificed. Atl was assigned to build Chaco's great tomb. Not only were his skills in adobe, metalworking, and construction beyond all others, but this way the administrator could keep watch over Atl. This was why Atl never came to visit Ixchel. He could not risk her discovery.

Auntie touched Ixchel's arm. "Chaco is truly dead this time. That administrator was here before. He will come looking for you."

Uncle grabbed her arm, weak as a child. "You must leave."

"But I cannot. You are very ill."

"I'm dying. Nothing you can do about that. You must find a place in which to disappear."

Ixchel clung to Auntie. "I will go to—"

"Do not tell us or that evil administrator may force the truth from our lips. Go, now!"

Ixchel nodded. Tears streamed down her face and burned her eyes. She put on some of Uncle's clothes. She tucked her hair into the neck of the shirt. She would go to Cualli and Tochi. They loved her. They would hide her. All she had to do was get inside their compound, which had only one, well-guarded entrance.

"Mrs. Claire? Mrs. Claire?"

When Claire opened her eyes, everyone in the room was staring at her. A few of the older women made the sign of the cross. She shook her head, still groggy. Where the hell did Ixchel live? She wasn't in

King Chaco's city, but somewhere else. Claire tried to shake off her disappointment for Nancho's sake. "Oh, sorry. I'm fine. Just zoned out for a second."

They all nodded politely, but their faces said *Mardonio had you in his clutches.*

And then the event was over. They all stood and began filing out into the yard. As a space cleared in front of her, Claire looked across it and found herself staring straight at the native man, wearing a black shirt, who'd been following her. She began weaving her way toward him, but he saw her coming and disappeared around the corner of a shed. She moved fast, apologizing as she bumped into mourners.

Two men stood alongside the shed. Claire ignored the guy in the white T-shirt, instead grabbing the black shirt and swinging him back against the wall. "You!" she growled.

She stopped. This wasn't the guy. This man was built just like him, and his face was almost as chiseled as the other man's, but it wasn't him.

She let go of the man's shirt. "I'm sorry. I thought you were someone else."

He smirked. "I can be anyone you want me to be, baby."

"I don't suppose you have a twin brother," she said weakly.

"No, but I have way too many cousins." He shifted his stance, hands on his hips. "But I am the best of all of them. I can show you—"

"Mrs. Claire, please, no." Nancho plucked nervously at her sleeve. "It is time for us to go."

Ignoring the man's leer, Claire turned and followed Nancho toward the car.

"Please, Mrs. Claire, you must stay away from Nopa. He is bad news. Very bad news."

"Let me guess. He's one of your thousands of cousins."

"Unfortunately, yes."

She asked about the other man, the one who'd disappeared. "Is he one of your cousins as well?"

"I do not know who you speak of. Come, children, into the car."

Claire followed, but felt sad. For the first time, Claire's trusted driver and friend had lied to her.

CHAPTER TWENTY-FOUR

Sochi
Tuesday, April 4

Sochi woke with an anguished gasp to find herself twisted up in her damp sheets like a mummy, cupping herself. One touch and she finished what her dream had started, moaning into her pillow.

Gods, what a nightmare. First, Claire came back to Peru, invading her space. Now she was invading her dreams. *Damn it.* Sochi sat up, rubbing her forehead to erase the stupid dream. Life was cruel. She stood but was so swollen that she took two steps and climaxed again. She bent over, palms on her knees. "Claire Adams," she muttered. "May you roast in hell."

Two more steps and she cried out again, this time collapsing against the wall and sliding down to the floor. Her cheek rested against the floor tile, cool against her skin. She closed her eyes. *Quite a life you've carved out for yourself, Xochiquetzal Castillo.*

She'd had a few sexual dreams starring Claire in the past, but since that day when they'd nearly ran into each other in the dark church hallway, she almost hated going to bed at night because that was when Claire had begun stalking her dreams.

She stared at the opposite wall. Sochi loved her compact adobe home with its tiny inner courtyard, uneven tile floors, and brightly painted walls. A reproduction of her favorite artifact—a Tumi knife—hung there, something many Peruvians had in their homes for good luck. Her knife handle was a stout man with a large head wearing a headdress; the blade ended in a sharp semicircle. While the Mochi and Chimú had used Tumi knives, it had been the Paracas who'd used the knife to treat diseases of the brain. They'd cut the cranium with the Tumi knife, let out blood to relieve the "disturbance," then cover the hole with a gold plate. For Sochi, the Tumi knife represented the strange mix of smart and gruesome that characterized Peru's early cultures.

After ten minutes on the floor, Sochi finally rose and staggered into the shower. She would give anything to be able to travel six years back in time and make sure she'd never laid eyes on Claire. They'd spent three years together and three years apart. Three years of heaven. Three years of hell. Since Claire had returned, Sochi was finding it harder to remember the hell.

When Claire appeared in Sochi's office later that morning, Sochi couldn't help the hot flush that crept up her neck and spread across her face. Thank the gods people's dreams weren't available for public viewing.

"Could we talk?"

When Sochi nodded, Claire closed the door behind her and took the chair nearest Sochi's desk. "Because you have, not surprisingly, some trust issues with me, I wanted to tell you everything that's going on with me. I no longer hear voices."

"I'm sure that's a relief."

"It is. But I'd counted on the voices to help me find King Chaco's tomb, so fifteen days ago Hudson and I took San Pedro again."

Sochi felt the beginnings of a headache taking up residence behind her eyes. She massaged her eyebrows. "Interesting choice."

"I know. But it worked, sort of. I no longer hear voices, but I'm having visions."

Attentive now, Sochi listened as Claire explained all about the eggs—how they were sent to her, the visions with the copper egg, her attempts to gather clues from the visions, how she was trying to see the Carina Nebula, how people were following her.

"May I see the eggs?" Sochi asked.

Claire was clearly reluctant, but she handed them over. Sochi rolled them around in her palm. "What are these shallower scratches?"

"I don't know."

Sochi scowled. "Claire, these are ancient artifacts. They belong in a museum, not in the pocket of a nearly-worn out pair of cargo pants."

"I was hoping no one would notice the state of my pants."

Sochi flushed again, uncomfortable to be talking about Claire's pants.

"I'm aware these eggs are valuable," Claire continued, "and that they're not mine. I'm being very careful with them. But please don't ask me to turn them over to the CNTP, at least not yet. I just wanted you to know everything, in the interest of building trust, before you heard the story from someone else."

Sochi knew Claire wanted her to feel safer around her, but she wondered—despite the erotic dream this morning—if the scar tissue from their breakup was just too thick to ever disappear.

Sochi briefly considered turning hard-core CNTP-enforcer and taking possession of the eggs, but what would be the point? Claire wasn't the type to steal. Sochi's gut clenched. She, of course, was. If Claire were ever to find out that Sochi was La Bruja, that would be the end of their fragile trust.

"One more thing," Claire said. "The other day you showed me a photo of you and a woman at Huanchaco Beach."

Sochi nodded. Was Claire jealous?

"That woman is one of the people who've been following me."

Sochi's mouth fell open. "What? That's crazy. Maria Menendez is a regional director for the CNTP. She doesn't have time to follow you around." But then she remembered Maria had been vague about when she might be returning to Lima.

Claire shrugged. "She's the woman." She told her about having to rescue Maria from the surf one evening.

"There must be a good explanation. Perhaps it's someone else."

"Have you taken a good look at her? She's gorgeous. I don't get beautiful women confused."

Sochi's phone chimed a reminder. She stood. "I'm really sorry, but I have a meeting."

Claire gave her a piercing look. "Let's keep talking, okay?"

"Sure, fine." This was damned awkward. After years of despising Claire, Sochi didn't want to keep talking. She wanted to do more than talk, and hated herself because of it.

❖

Sochi glared at Denis when he opened his front door. She refused his offer to join him in the sitting room. "I'm just here to say it's time to put our plan in motion." She handed him a piece of paper. "Photos and information on the four artifacts we'll be using to track Higuchi. I didn't want this online in case someone's watching our emails."

Denis whistled softly. "These look amazing."

"I have your daughter to thank for that. But now I need you to put out the word that La Bruja found Chaco's tomb and that you will soon be taking possession of these four items."

Denis folded the sheet and tucked it into his shirt pocket. "People know that Claire has been searching for the tomb. I will not help you unless you guarantee Claire's safety."

"This sting operation has nothing to do with Claire."

"What if she tangles with La Bruja or her men?"

"She won't. I'm the one who'll pack up the artifacts. I have a driver who'll bring the van here to your house. He'll leave it to come inside, which is when we expect Higuchi's men to steal the artifacts. Then I'll be the one tracking Higuchi."

Denis folded his meaty arms across his broad chest. "You and I both share a passion for the past cultures of this country. We also share a great and deep affection for Claire. I will not help unless La Bruja promises no harm will come—"

"I will see what—"

"No. Now. I want your assurance *now*."

Sochi inhaled then froze, forgetting to breathe. Gods. He knew. Denis *knew*. They exchanged a look that sent a shiver of fear through her. She considered her options and realized there was only one. "No harm will come to Claire Adams from La Bruja or her men. And I, Sochi Castillo, will keep her safe from Higuchi."

Denis's gaze softened, but Sochi still struggled to breathe normally. "Don't let Claire search for the tomb," he said. "Higuchi's men might still be following her."

"I'll keep her safe."

He sent a brief text. A reply chimed back, which he read. He nodded. "Okay, it has begun. The word is out. In a few days, Higuchi will be mad with greed to possess your artifacts."

Sochi licked her lips. "Thank you." She headed to her car on wobbly knees. She'd always been so careful to never contact Denis directly, but only through Rigo.

"Sochi."

She turned. "Yes?"

"Tell La Bruja it's time to retire."

Sochi exhaled loudly. "It's already done."

❖

Claire's sweet almond shampoo filled Sochi's head as she applied the piece of transparent NanoTrax along the backflap handle. The warmed NanoTrax felt like thick pudding as Sochi pressed it against the gold. Claire stood close—too close—watching. All Sochi had to do was turn her head and their lips would touch, but Claire radiated tension. Sochi had been tense herself since her meeting with Denis.

"Careful," Claire said. "It's going on thicker in that spot."

Sochi applied more pressure so the material retreated deeper into the seam along the backflap's handle. "There. Now for the pectoral." Denis had been right. Claire had insisted on being involved. Since Manuel was too busy with his drones, and Aurelio wanted to keep his hands clean, Sochi was grateful for Claire's help.

They agreed on where the NanoTrax would best "disappear," then Sochi repeated the procedure, her confidence growing as the liquid plastic began to feel more familiar beneath her fingertip.

She put the last of the material on the remaining two artifacts.

"What if the items are separated?" Claire asked.

"I was told that when they are close together, the receiver will register them as one dot. If they are separated by more than three meters, they will each have their own dot. Now the stuff must dry for forty-eight hours."

Sochi leaned back, feeling Claire at her shoulder. She turned to say something, then realized Claire was going to kiss her. In a panic, Sochi leapt up and washed her hands at the kitchen sink while she thought. Did she want to kiss Claire?

No. That would be stupid. Claire would be leaving Peru again. Claire would hurt her, yet again.

"So we're on for two nights from now, right?" Claire said. "What time are we leaving?"

"We?"

Claire indicated the two of them. "Us. You and me. I'm coming along."

"Sorry, I already have help for that night, and the fewer people involved, the better."

"But—"

"Thanks for your help." Sochi marched to the front door, opened it, and stood waiting.

"But I can help—"

"—by leaving." Sochi wasn't even close to weakening. Denis wasn't the only one who wanted to keep Claire safe.

Claire's jaw tightened, but she left.

Sochi closed the door and leaned against it. Gods, she was confused.

CHAPTER TWENTY-FIVE

Claire
Wednesday, April 5

A few days after Mardonio's wake, Claire realized that something inside her had shifted. She found herself thinking less and less about King Chaco's tomb—filled with gold and silver and mystery—and more and more about Sochi. Not to get all mushy and overly romantic, but the thought did occur: Sochi was more of a treasure than anything Claire would ever find in Chaco's tomb. How ironic that she—who prided herself on being a fairly competent treasure hunter—had let go of the best treasure ever three years ago. Even though she suspected Hudson had created the rift, Claire had allowed it to widen by refusing to contact Sochi all that time.

That morning she looked at herself in the mirror. She didn't see her green eyes or her frustratingly straight hair. All she saw was an idiot—a stupid idiot.

Why? Because yesterday she didn't kiss Sochi, who was worse than a skittish cat around Claire. She didn't blame her. Kissing was probably the wrong move for both of them.

But a kiss might have shown Sochi that Claire really wasn't a bad person. It might have reminded her of the good times. Most of their three years together had been great.

Claire dragged herself down to Las Dulces, no longer even pretending to be searching for the tomb by combing the countryside with Denis's maps. She suspected that even her three tails had given up, since she didn't see them. They'd probably figured out Claire wasn't going to find the tomb. No, her only goal now was to repair things with Sochi.

What did that mean—*repair* things? Did she want them to be friends? Yes, that was it. She didn't dare hope for more.

"Ms. Adams?"

Claire looked up into the round face of a dark-haired woman wearing ill-fitting slacks and a polyester jacket. She dropped her huge felted bag onto the ground and sat down. She pulled a small notebook from the bag.

Crap. A reporter. Why was she surprised? "Look, I don't talk to reporters."

"I'm Luisa de Salva. I write for *Las Noticias*."

Claire drained the last of her tea. "Going now."

"Wait." She stopped Claire with a touch to her arm. "Is it true that you no longer hear voices, but that you now have visions?"

Her brain spun. Who knew about the visions? Denis did. He would never say anything to the press. The shaman did. And Sochi did. Claire's jaw tightened. No, Sochi wouldn't say anything. She hadn't the first time. She shook her head sadly; apparently, the shaman couldn't be trusted.

"I'm not saying anything."

"Ms. Adams, I'm going to write something. It might as well be the truth—your truth—instead of lies. I feel badly about how my colleagues attacked you when the news of your 'voices' broke. I'm not like that. But you're news. You're in Trujillo looking for Chaco's tomb."

Claire leaned back in her chair and rubbed her face. Maybe it was time to go home. Mac joked about the company falling apart with her gone, but the longer she was gone, the more likely he'd realize he didn't need her. This was the reason vacations taken in the United States had dropped—everyone was terrified of being found redundant.

Claire thought for a minute, then folded her hands on the metal table. "Yes, I am here seeking the tomb. And I may or may not be having some…paranormal experiences. But I can't have this written about while I'm looking. Too many people are breathing down my neck; the less they know about what I'm doing, or *how* I'm doing it, the better." Luisa nodded, her pencil poised above the notebook. "If you wait until I've either found the tomb, or given up, then I'll give you an exclusive to all that's been going on. Write one word about my 'visions,' as you call them, and I'll close up tighter than a clam."

The reporter sat back, dark brown eyes considering Claire. "An exclusive?"

"How about this? Once I've found the tomb, you're the first person I'll call."

Luisa dug out a business card and slid it across the table. "It's a deal. I won't write a word about your visions until you call."

❖

Claire stopped by the CNTP office, but Sochi had taken the day off, so she took a taxi to her house, asked the driver to remain for ten minutes, then she knocked on the bright yellow door.

When Sochi opened the door in baggy shorts, a faded Beatles T-shirt, and mussed-up hair, Claire momentarily forgot how to breathe. God, she was beautiful. "I need to tell you something. It won't take long." She nodded toward the taxi. "He's going to wait for me."

Lips pressed together, Sochi opened the door wider to let her in. She looked worried, as if Claire might try to kiss her again.

"I just spoke with a reporter at Las Dulces. She wanted to know about my visions."

Sochi's eyes widened. "But I didn't say—"

"I know you didn't. That's what I came to tell you. The instant she said that to me, I ran through the list of people who knew about the vision. It's a short list—Denis, the shaman, and you." Claire held both of Sochi's hands. They were cool and smooth. "I wanted you to know that I am changing. I didn't for one minute think it was you, and I shouldn't have jumped to that conclusion before." She squeezed her hands. "You would never, ever do that to me. I know that now."

Sochi struggled, swallowing hard, unable to speak.

"I think you should know that I'm about to hug you, so prepare yourself." Claire carefully slid her arms around her. At first, it was like hugging a tree, but Sochi gradually softened in her arms until Claire had no doubt she was hugging a woman. They rested their heads on each other's shoulders. Sochi's chest heaved as she silently cried against Claire, who fought her own losing battle with tears.

Finally, Claire pulled back and wiped her eyes. "I can learn to trust again. I hope you can, too."

Sochi touched the amazonite teardrop around Claire's neck, then smiled with such tenderness Claire thought she might melt right there. "I wonder if Mima's stone has begun to work." The stone was meant to calm Claire's soul, to give her compassion.

Claire wiped a tear from Sochi's check. "We can only hope."

With another squeeze of Sochi's hands, Claire hurried to the taxi before she changed her mind and kissed her.

Halfway home Claire noticed the blue pickup was following her. The sudden urge to confront someone was strong, so she asked the taxi driver drop her off three blocks from the hotel. Then she walked slowly, anger and frustration bubbling up through her chest. This would force the man to get out of his pickup and follow her on foot.

She turned down the next street, then down an alley. After passing a wall of thick bushes, she turned left and nearly ran into a stucco wall. Heart pounding, Claire pressed herself back into the bushes as the steady footsteps approached. Surprise was her only weapon.

When the man passed her, she leapt out and grabbed him by the jacket, then spun him around and slammed him against the wall.

"Who are you?" This was the man she'd seen at Mardinio's wake, but who'd disappeared before she could confront him.

The guy was built like a Chimú warrior, blocky and strong. His copper face was chiseled into high, flat cheekbones and smooth forehead. He let her press him against the wall, even though he could have easily picked her up and tossed her *over* the wall.

"Why are you following me?" she practically growled.

His black eyes gave nothing away.

"Did you send me the eggs? Is that why you're following me?"

"Eggs?" His eyebrows shot up in alarm.

"Why did you send them to me?"

He shook his head. "My *jefe*...she wants to find Chaco's tomb, that's all."

"Your boss? *She.*" Claire snorted. "You work for La Bruja. No wonder. God, I hate looters." She released the man's jacket. "What will you do when I find the tomb? Cut off my fingers?"

"What?"

"That email must have been sent by another of La Bruja's men, I suppose. Look, tell your *jefe* that once I find the tomb, it will be guarded day and night. She'll never get her greedy, thieving hands on any of the treasure. You got that?"

The man clamped his jaw shut and refused to speak.

Even though Claire blocked his way, he could have knocked her aside as easily as if she'd been papier-mâché. Clearly, he was reluctant to hurt her.

"You give her that message." Claire stepped back. With a curt nod, the man turned into the alley and strode away.

Her quest to find the tomb was beginning to feel out of control.

❖

That night, Claire lay in bed, unable to sleep. What was she still doing here? The treasure hunt was a bust, so she should really go home. She closed her eyes, remembering the feel of Sochi in her arms, and knew exactly why she remained in Peru.

When the floor outside her room creaked, Claire sat up, startled. The door handle rattled. Shit, it had to be the guy coming to cut off her fingers. Asshole. Did he think she'd leave the door unlocked? Heart pounding, Claire slid from the bed and took up her position behind the door, where—the day she'd received the threatening email—she had moved a heavy, narrow plant stand made of wrought iron. She grasped the stand by its legs—even though it made an awkward weapon—and waited. She longed for the baseball bat she kept in her front closet at home for this very purpose.

The handle rattled again, then someone pushed against the door. Now there was a light clinking as the person inserted something into the lock and began moving it around. Not only did Claire wish for her baseball bat, but a chain across the door would have been nice, or maybe a deadbolt. She resolved to speak with Señora Nunez about the hotel's lax security. The legs of the stand slipped in Claire's sweating palms.

The lock clicked. She held her breath as the door slowly crept open. When a man's head appeared, Claire swung the plant stand back and hit that head as hard as she could. He yelled and staggered back so she went on the offensive, bashing the iron stand against any part of him she could see. He fell, scrambled to his feet, and ducked as she just missed his head. He came for her again, but this time she connected with a dull clank. Yelling again, and now clutching the side of his head, the man staggered down the hallway. She followed. "You didn't like that? Want some more?" Aware she wasn't at her smartest when incensed, Claire chased him until he disappeared down the stairs. His footsteps echoed in the empty courtyard as he fled.

Shaking like a dog at the vet's, she returned to her room and closed the door, leaning against the wall until her pulse dropped out of heart attack range. Then she moved the dresser, one table, and the stuffed chair in front of the door. Tomorrow, she would buy two chains and install them herself.

Chapter Twenty-six

Claire
Thursday, April 6

When Claire awoke the next morning, the dresser and table blocking the door convinced her the attack hadn't been a nightmare. She rose, stretching out her aching fingers, then noticed she'd managed to scrape the skin off a few knuckles during the struggle.

Wearily, she pulled on her cargo shorts. Her life had attracted far too much excitement these last few days. Her parents were into wild adventures, not her.

The phone call came as Claire finished dressing. The connection was so garbled it took her a minute to figure out it was Joselyn, her boss's assistant.

"Mac's been shot!"

"What?"

"Some crazy guy came into the office last night and shot him."

"Oh, my God. Is he okay?"

"Two bullets to the chest, both missed his heart and lungs. But the guy stood there, about to shoot him dead for good, when Bob saved the day."

"I'm sorry. Did you say Bob?"

"I know, right? Yes, Bob. But here's the thing you need to know. When the guy was shooting Mac, he yelled that this was a gift from you."

Claire's stomach did that thing it had done the last time she'd had the stomach flu—it flipped, sank, and threatened to eject all its contents. After a quick thank-you to Joselyn, Claire called Mac's cell phone.

His voice was weak. "Hey, Peru."

"Holy shit, Mac. Are you okay?" This was all happening so fast she couldn't process how upset she was.

"Oh, yeah. It's hard to kill me, apparently. But they won't let me out of the hospital yet."

Claire squeezed her eyes shut, horrified. "Mac, Joselyn said the gunman mentioned my name."

"Yeah, that was a surprise. Said the bullets were a gift from you."

"Higuchi, that fucking asshole. He hired the hit on you. Mac, I'm so sorry that my shit put you in the hospital."

The chuckle was faint, but kind. "Well, it would have been the morgue if not for Bob."

"How did that happen?"

"He came by just as the guy was taking aim for the kill shot. I don't remember much, but Bob said I was on the ground, leaking an impressive amount of blood, and the guy had the gun pointed right at my head."

"What did Bob do?"

"He used the only weapon available, the Ming Dynasty vase he was carrying."

"Christ. Seventeenth century?"

"Fifteenth."

"Ouch."

"That's what the gunman said when Bob smashed it over his head."

Claire laughed appreciatively, but her insides had begun to boil. She was going to fucking kill Carlos Higuchi.

"Mac, this wouldn't have happened if I'd taken your advice to get my ass out of Peru."

"Yeah, well, forget that advice." Medical machines beeped in the background.

"Really?"

"Yeah. Stay there and take this motherfucker down."

She inhaled, shaking with emotion. How could she possibly do that? "You got it, boss."

❖

Claire's Internet search revealed two offices for Higuchi International. The main office was in Lima, with a branch in Trujillo. Given what was going on, she knew he had to be in Trujillo. It was a four-block walk to the modern looking, twelve-story Edificio España. Higuchi International was on the top floor. When the elevator opened with a gentle ping, Claire strode toward the reception desk, an impressive short wall of curved wood and glass. "I am here to see Carlos Higuchi," she snapped.

The receptionist calmly asked if she had an appointment, but when Claire said no, the woman's eyes flickered just for a second to her left. That must be the direction of Higuchi's office, so away Claire went.

"Señorita, no. You cannot enter."

Two security men in dark gray suits moved up behind her, but she began to run.

The wide double door with intricate indigenous carvings had to be Higuchi's office. She pushed her way inside.

Higuchi sat at his huge glass desk, talking on the phone. She reached him with the security guys right on her tail. Higuchi held up his hand. "Thank you, gentlemen, but I think I can handle Señorita Adams without help." The bulky men scowled but closed the door as they left.

She stood there, almost panting from her run, while he finished his conversation and hung up. "Claire Adams. A rare pleasure."

"Bite me, Carlos." She leaned over the desk, grabbed his $200 silk tie, and yanked him forward. "You crossed a dangerous line, asshole, having my friend Mac shot." They were so close she could see flecks of gold in his brown eyes. He smelled of Altoids.

He couldn't have looked more delighted. "You received my message, then."

Claire pushed him backward so hard his chair rolled back a foot. "What the hell are you hoping to accomplish by harming my friends? You think that's going to make me find the tomb any faster?"

"As a matter of fact, yes."

"Did you send that man to my room last night?"

"What man?" His confusion was genuine.

"Why is it so damned important that I find the tomb so quickly?"

He laced his fingers together, looking smug. "It's all part of my plan."

"Your plan? To take over the universe by tying a little old lady to a chair and dumping her on the side of a mountain?"

He laughed.

"Maybe it's to take over the universe by tying up a woman on the beach just before high tide? Frankly, your plans make me sick."

Higuchi stood, fingertips on his desk. "I cannot believe I am saying this, Claire Adams, but I really like you. I respect you. No one stands up to me anymore, not even my son." He moved away from his desk to look out his window, a perfect view of downtown Trujillo. "You are a breath of fresh air."

"Seriously, what plans are you talking about? None of this makes any sense." She joined him at the window.

"I'm calling it My Plan of Ultimate Retribution." He sighed happily. "Have you ever met someone capable of destroying an entire country like Peru? You are standing next to one such man."

"Talk about an oversized ego. Are you and Donald Trump related?" She no longer cared that she stood in the office of the most feared man in the entire country. "Peru is your country. Why destroy it?"

He nodded. "You guessed my motivation the last time we talked."

"The internment in the U.S. of Japanese-Peruvians?"

"My grandfather was devastated. The police burst into his home in the middle of the night and arrested everyone—him, my grandmother, my father and aunts, and sent them to a horrible camp in Texas. All in exchange for some tanks, planes, and ammunition."

She sighed. "Look, we've been over this. What my country did to the Japanese-Americans totally sucked. What we did to the Japanese in Peru was equally as horrible."

"My grandfather lost his business—he sold men's clothing in his own upscale shop in Lima. The country never compensated him. In fact, when the war was over, Peru refused to even recognize him as a citizen. It took him five years to save enough money to move his family back here."

"I get that you're still pissed. I don't blame you. But one person can't destroy an entire country."

His grin froze her veins. "I control most of the cocaine exports in this country. What do you think will happen when those exports cease?"

"The poor people growing it and transporting it will be out of a job."

"Yes."

"Punishing the people who are already poor—nice. Really sends a great message."

"Oh, I plan to destroy all levels of the economy. Do you know the major exports of Peru?"

Claire shook her head. Her only C in college had been in Economics.

"Copper, gold, zinc, petroleum, coffee, potatoes, asparagus, textiles, and guinea pigs."

"Guinea pigs? Oh, yeah. Major source of protein."

He waved a hand across the window. "I am the tap root of this country. Cut that tap root and the country will die."

"I don't get it."

"Soon the zinc mining will cease. The coffee plants will die of a mysterious disease. The potatoes and asparagus that your country so greedily consumes will also die."

She rubbed her forehead. "So you're telling me that you plan to ruin the very industries which you own?"

He nodded, happy that she'd figured it out. "Higuchi International owns at least forty-five percent of all the assets connected to those industries, or to the supporting industries like transportation or processing." Claire shivered to think what he had planned for the guinea pigs.

He leaned back against his desk. "Here's proof of how far I'm willing to go. You know of our maca?"

"Vegetable. Looks like a turnip. Tastes god-awful, if you ask me." One day Sochi had made maca juice, however, by boiling the root and blending it with warm milk, fruit, and sugar. Claire had enjoyed that.

"Maca is also an aphrodisiac in China. Peruvian law requires all maca to be processed in Peru so that the country can control the supply. But I've been smuggling seeds out to China for a few years. There are now thousands of acres in China producing maca. Here in Peru, the price has gone from three of your American dollars up to eighty. I'm making a killing here and will be doing the same thing in China. However, Peru will soon learn that world maca production is no longer under its control, and that industry will collapse, as will the price."

"Why are you telling me this? All I have to do is tell someone in the government."

His laugh was deep and harsh. "And what will they do? This country, despite a fair amount of corruption, runs on capitalism. They cannot touch me. I will cease all Higuchi International operations and bring Peru to its knees."

Claire considered his plan. "Carlos, that's sad, that's really sad. Almost everyone involved in the decision to send the Japanese-Peruvians to internment camps is dead. You are trying to punish dead people. That's insane."

His eyes narrowed into steel balls. "This is why I like you. No one else would have the nerve to say such things to me."

She jammed her fists onto her hips. "Well, if you like me so much, stop harassing me."

"I cannot do that, Claire Adams. You are part of my plan. You will find the tomb. I will take possession of its gold and silver treasure, and ship it all to Japan. I will make sure every Peruvian will know what he has lost."

Claire surprised herself by chuckling. "You overestimate the impact of this. Looting national treasures is an accepted part of the culture. You, of all people, should know that. Few people will care."

"But I will. Possessing the treasure gives my Plan of Ultimate Retribution an artistic element, as well as a cultural one. I'm not just a machine of destruction, but am also creative.

"You're sick, Carlos. But why the time pressure?"

"Many of my economic actions have already been put into play and will become known in a matter of days. I think of Chaco's tomb as a brilliant epigraph, those few sentences at a book's beginning that set the tone for all the pages to come. It must come first."

Claire sighed. Her initial anger had turned to exhaustion. "While you may be able to control markets and companies, no one can control a treasure hunt. It ends when it ends, and not before, so fuck off."

She left, feeling worse than when she'd stormed in. Now that she knew what the guy was up to, she also knew there was nothing she could do to stop his plans for retribution. As for her treasure hunt, he would continue to harass her. All she could do was buy two door chains, borrow a screwdriver from Señora Nunez, and improve her security.

CHAPTER TWENTY-SEVEN

Sochi
Thursday-Friday, April 6 and 7

Sochi charged the NanoTrax. Hudson's instructions had been sketchy, but it had worked to take apart a lamp, strip the wires at the lamp's end, attach them to the NanoTrax, then plug in the cord. The receiver chirped happily and showed, with a steady yellow dot, that the four artifacts were located in her house. She was ready.

Unfortunately, she'd lied to both Denis and Claire. She didn't have help for the sting operation. Not one single CNTP employee would help her. Manuel claimed he was too busy with his drone program. She tried seven others, and all were going to be very busy Friday evening. Not even the receptionist, who always complained about her boring job, was willing to ride along. It took Sochi a while, but after seeing the same face on everyone she asked—tight, pale, and frightened—she realized they were all afraid of Higuchi.

She stepped into her boss's office. "Aurelio, how about going on an adventure with me tomorrow night? You can be in on the kill, so to speak, when I put your plan into action."

Aurelio checked his phone. "Sorry, Sochi, I have an important meeting tomorrow night. The regional government, in conjunction with Lima, is putting a great deal of pressure on everyone, including the CNTP, to find some way to nail Higuchi. I need to make a presentation before them."

Sochi rolled her eyes. Claire would appreciate the irony of Aurelio not having time to catch Higuchi because he had to tell the bureaucrats what he was doing to catch Higuchi.

She called Maria, whose warm voice told Sochi she was glad to hear from her. "Maria, I need to ask. Why are you following Claire Adams?"

The gasp reached her over the phone. "You know this?"

"If you'd been following her twenty-four seven, you would have seen us together."

"Sochi, you don't know who she is. This is a bad, bad woman. You shouldn't be seen with her."

"Is that why you didn't talk with her when she rescued you?"

"She told you that? I didn't dare speak with her because she's so dangerous. I was desperate to get away, even though she did save my life."

"Maria, who are you working for? In my position I know most of what's going on, so I won't be surprised at the truth."

And yet, she was. Minister Salazar had contacted Maria, appealing to her sense of patriotism. He said he needed someone unconnected to him or his office to follow Claire Adams, a known terrorist and international thief bent on stealing Peru's greatest treasure once she found it. Sochi sighed as Maria finished explaining that she felt she'd had no choice when asked by the minister to help.

"Maria, if there's anyone dangerous in Peru, it's Minister Salazar. He roped me into helping with another project, and when I tried to quit, he threatened my family. You can't trust this guy, but you can trust me. Stop following Claire. She's one of the good guys. If she finds the tomb, she'll turn it over to the CNTP immediately."

"How dangerous is Salazar?"

"He's terrified of Higuchi, which makes him inconsistent. One minute he wants the man and all his schemes revealed. The next he's afraid to even say Higuchi's name."

"I am to meet with the minister soon."

"Maria, don't. For your own safety, return to Lima."

"But what of us? If I return to Lima we won't be able to spend time together."

Sochi hesitated, amazed at the emotions that shot through her. "Normally, I'd love to do that, but you should know that someone…I don't know what's going to happen, if anything, but she…we—"

"I get it, Sochi. But if it doesn't work out, you'll call me?"

"Absolutely."

❖

Denis's emails worked. Social media sites lit up with discussions about the news. Was it really Chaco's tomb? Where was it located? Who found it? Was the treasure as vast as expected? The rumors Denis started would soon collapse on themselves, but for now everyone seemed to embrace the frenzy. All Sochi needed was for the buzz to last at least until tomorrow night.

CNTP phones rang constantly. Reporters hung around in the hallway pleading for an interview. Aurelio finally agreed. Sochi watched from the back of the room and couldn't have been more pleased. Aurelio was so full of hot air and ego that the reporters lost control of the interview and never regained it.

During a quiet moment, Sochi closed her office door. "Rigo, it's me," Sochi said into her phone.

"It is good to hear from you, *jefe*."

"I need help with something tomorrow night. It's legal, but requires two people. I couldn't convince any of my colleagues to help, basically because they're cowards. I need someone who won't fall apart if we run into Higuchi's men. Besides, I'd rather work with you."

A heavy pause. "I am honored. It's been so long since I've done work that's legal I may have forgotten how to behave, but it would be a pleasant change. No one grows up hoping to be a professional looter."

"Thank you."

"Does it have to do with the rumors that the CNTP has found Chaco's tomb? It couldn't have been the Adams woman who found it. I've been following her."

"Yes, it has to do with Chaco's tomb, but not in the way you think."

"Are we looting it? Shall I call the men?"

"Rigo, slow down. Remember, I said this was legal. No looting involved. Now here's what I need."

The next night, when Rigo drove up to her house in the unmarked white van, Sochi had just finished packing the last of the artifacts into bubble wrap and boxes. They slid them into the back of the van. She stopped him with a touch to his arm. "I really appreciate your help with this."

He smiled ruefully. "I love helping you, but I wish the rumors about Chaco's tomb had been true."

Thirty minutes later, Sochi sat in a dark alley, engine off, watching Denis's dimly lit driveway. She'd asked him to turn off most of the lights to increase the chances that Carlos Higuchi's men would do as she hoped. Clouds obscured the moon.

Rigo drove into Denis's driveway, shut off the van, and approached the front vestibule. She could hear the motor still knocking from her hiding spot. When he disappeared inside, let in by Denis's butler, Sochi held her breath. This had to work. Denis had created a social media frenzy, twisting and confusing the facts until anything seemed possible.

She almost missed it. A long sedan, headlights off, glided to a stop. Four men in black leaped out. One popped open the locked back doors of the van. Each man grabbed a box and melted back into the sedan. In less than thirty seconds, they were gone.

Hands shaking, Sochi texted Rigo: *Bait taken.* She waited the agreed five minutes, then raced to Denis's and picked up Rigo. She handed him the receiver. "Let's do this."

With Rigo giving directions, Sochi worked her way through the outskirts of Trujillo. Higuchi's men were driving east, as if heading for the mountains. But they kept doubling back, nearly driving in circles.

"What the hell are they doing?"

Rigo chuckled. "They are lost. I have spent time up in the foothills and the roads make no sense. The maps are often wrong."

The idiots obviously hadn't done a dry run, one of the most obvious ways to ensure an operation's success.

Sochi and Rigo were silent as she drove. Nostalgia gave this last night with Rigo more meaning. After thirty minutes of wandering, the driver of the sedan finally found a road that took them out of the foothills and around the northern edge of the city. Soon Sochi was on the Pan American heading north. "How far ahead are they?"

Rigo tapped the screen a few times. "Looks like they are about three kilometers away."

"Good. Now that we're on the highway, I'm guessing their escape must be by boat." She let herself feel a flicker of hope that Aurelio's crazy scheme might just work.

"Or they could be heading for Ecuador. There might be roads that snake through the mountains to avoid the border. Or perhaps they are somehow able to hide the artifacts?"

They speculated for a while, each contributing their experience. Then Rigo tapped the screen. "Strange. The blips have stopped. Slow down. We don't want to drive past them."

When the receiver indicated they were one kilometer away from the stationary blip, Sochi pulled over. Even without the moon, she could see the long, slender threads of surf breaking up onto the shore.

"Now there are four blips."

"Hudson said the artifacts will get their own blips when they're more than three meters apart."

They watched, tense, as the blips moved in the same direction. All four blips moved north, but so slowly their motion was nearly imperceptible.

"This is weird," Sochi said. She drove back onto the highway. "There's a road up here that cuts to the left and leads to the beach. We'll take that."

Halfway down the dirt road, she shut off her headlights. Darkness pressed around them. She slowed until the car rose slightly.

"We're at the beach," Rigo said.

Windows down, they listened carefully with the engine off. Nothing but the gentle sliding of the surf up the beach. "Where are they?" Sochi asked, every muscle tense. And why were the artifacts moving up the beach as slowly as sea turtles?

Crouching low, Sochi and Rigo trudged through the sand then dropped behind a slight dune. From there they could see a long stretch of beach. "Nothing," Rigo whispered.

Sochi's stomach began to churn. Rigo was right. No boat lights. No headlights. No float plane. No flashlights. Where had the men gone? "What are those dark shapes there, about halfway down the beach?" she asked.

Damn it. She knew what they were. She climbed over the dune and began running. Cursing softly, Rigo followed.

She reached the first shape. It *was* a sea turtle, ambling through the sand. Sochi flicked on her flashlight. There, on the turtle's shell, was an arrow in red paint. Rigo grabbed the turtle's shell from behind, since turtles could do a great deal of damage when they decided to bite.

Sochi bent closer, focusing the light. At the end of the arrow was a small, clear curl of NanoTrax. Sochi dropped to the sand, stunned. "Shit."

"Not good," Rigo agreed. He gently took her flashlight and ran ahead to the other dark shapes. His soft cursing told her all she needed to know. The NanoTrax from all four artifacts must have been removed and attached to sea turtles.

Rigo quickly returned. He handed her a note. "This was taped to the last turtle."

Sochi sat back, her eyes burning. "Someone tipped Higuchi off."

She opened the note. *Gracias for these treasures. They will look lovely in my Tokyo apartment. I hope we can work together again... Higuchi.*

Sochi sat there, failure burning her throat like cheap whiskey. Even when you expected failure, it still stung. But thanks to Denis, Sochi had not let four priceless pieces of Peruvian culture slip from the country. She'd let four nearly perfect reproductions made by his daughter a few years ago escape the country. "Well, we tried," she said.

Back at her car, Sochi offered her hand. "Rigo, you would be a much better choice to run the CNTP drone program than Manuel."

His broad grin made her smile. "Just let me know when I start." Then, with a wave, he hopped in the van to return it to one of his many cousins.

Chapter Twenty-eight

Claire
Friday, April 7

Claire, too nervous to stay in her hotel room, sat on a bench in the Plaza, enjoying the palms rustling high above her head. People chattered and laughed as they walked through the Plaza on their way to some place interesting.

Claire couldn't stop thinking about her conversation with Higuchi. Could one man really cause the damage he planned? So many people would be harmed, and none of them likely had anything to do with the WWII internment. So pointless.

She checked her watch. The NanoTrax operation was to have started over two hours ago, so Sochi could be anywhere by now—working her way over the Andes to Brazil, or driving down the coast to Chile, or up the coast to Ecuador. Claire's frustration at Sochi for excluding her still burned.

Her phone chirped. Sochi calling with good news? The screen flashed Hudson's photo.

"So, you finally get around to calling me."

"Sorry, I've been really busy these last few days."

"Poor you. Did you switch my letter to Sochi three years ago?"

"Yes." Hudson's voice was conversational, free of guilt.

"And did you put in *Good Riddance* instead?"

"Why, yes, I did."

Claire's chest cramped. "You fucking bastard."

"Why, yes, I am."

"Why?"

"Why am I a bastard?"

Claire swore vehemently.

"Okay, sorry. You had a great job and I wanted it. You had a great relationship. I was tired of living in your shadow. Ever since grad school, I've been your goddamned sidekick, and once I read your touching note to Sochi about you hearing voices, and then realized you and Sochi were having problems, I had this great idea to make sure you left."

"You put getting my job ahead of my happiness. We were best friends."

Sounds of some kind of engine rattled in the background, and Claire could hear the murmurs of men's voices. "I've never really analyzed it in that light," he said, "but I suppose that's as good an explanation as any. And now you're having visions. You, my *best* friend, get all the luck."

"I didn't tell you I was having visions."

"Oh, yeah. Oops. Busted. My shaman friend, Julio, was having a private conversation with another shaman after our poker game. Poor guy doesn't know that I've learned a fair amount of Quechua these last few years."

She tried not to blame Julio. "You told the reporter about the visions."

"Yeah. Thought I'd have fun with you and Sochi again."

"If you hated me so much, why pretend we were still friends? Why text and email me for all these years?"

"I don't hate you. Never did. I just couldn't stand your perfection, your absolute devotion to something. It made me feel like a slacker."

"You *are* a slacker." Her anger drained. Hudson just wasn't worth it. Someone on his end of the phone shouted something. "Where are you?" she asked.

"Yeah, well, that's actually why I'm calling. I thought I should explain the story to someone so I could get full credit for what I've done. Remember I told you that after you left I fell in with a bad crowd?"

"I thought you were kidding."

"Nope. I reconnected with my host family when I was an exchange student in Japan my junior year." She waited, having no idea where he was going with this. "My host family was pretty wealthy, and they were very kind to me. The Higuchis made me feel like part of the family."

"Higuchi."

"Wow. I actually heard the light bulb go off over your head. Yeah, the family started out in Peru, but when the economy tanked in the nineties they thought they'd give Japan a try. Really didn't work, since the Higuchis are Peruvians, not Japanese."

"Hudson, what have you done?"

With each sentence of his explanation, her anguish deepened. Hudson had been desperate to make his mark in her job but failed at every attempt. Mr. Higuchi wanted to help, so he loaned his adopted "son" a backflap he'd found in Peru years ago, long before the intense looting had begun.

"I planted it in Chan Chan, then 'found' it. It brought me the recognition I needed, but then your bitch stole the backflap and locked it up in the vault. Higuchi wanted it back, but I couldn't get it. And if you have something Higuchi wants, you'd better find a way to get it. The whole NanoTrax thing was my solution. On a hunch, I asked Higuchi, and it turns out one of his companies had been the major developer in Japan."

"You got the NanoTrax from him."

"Yes. Then I talked Sochi into using a few more items from the vault as bait."

"Did you steal those artifacts from the van tonight?"

"Guilty. Your girlfriend's plan was so obvious a child could have figured it out. We drove around for a while, then—" Hudson stopped and started chuckling. "Let's just say that by now Sochi has tracked the artifacts to the beach and found the NanoTrax stuck on the backs of four sea turtles."

"Cute."

"Meanwhile, Higuchi picked us up on the beach. I'm on his boat now…What?" A voice, laughing, shouted something in the background. "Oh, sorry, it's a ship, not a boat."

"You must be so satisfied with yourself."

"I admit it, I am. It hasn't been easy these last few weeks. I've been living two separate lives—Hudson, the subdirector of excavation, and Hudson, the looter."

Claire snorted. "And to think I wasted time feeling badly because we'd drifted apart."

"Yeah, I wouldn't spend too much time worrying about that. But I want you to know that on some level, I do feel badly about what I've done, so I'm going to leave you with one gift."

"I'm breathless." Really, she was done with him.

"Higuchi is a smart guy. He watches. He puts things together. He says that if you go into the trunk of Sochi's car, you'll find a black gym bag. Look inside. It turns out that I'm not the only one who's been living two lives."

"Leave Sochi out of this. I don't trust a word you say."

"I probably deserve that. But still, I wish I could have seen her face when she found the turtles."

He'd just handed Claire the perfect line. "I know the feeling. I wish I could see *your* face."

"When?"

She wanted to strangle every drop of self-satisfaction from his voice. "You aren't the only one who can switch things, you know. I wish I could see *your* face when you examine the backflap and the other artifacts and discover they're fakes."

"Ha. Funny. You're a sore loser."

"Look at them closely. I know someone who makes fakes for a hobby, so we put the NanoTrax on the fakes. That's why Sochi changed the list of artifacts at the last minute. These reproductions had already been made."

"You can't make a repo of a backflap." She could hear him running down a corridor.

"You can if you're as good as this person is." A door banged open and there were more noises that must have been Hudson opening the boxes. A low moan gathered strength until it was a horrified shout.

"Fuck!"

"Interesting. It turns out that hearing your despair is just as satisfying as seeing it. You still don't have the backflap, so your buddy Higuchi is not going to be happy with you. Have a nice life, asshole." She hung up.

Damn, that felt good. Her only regret was that Sochi hadn't been part of the conversation. She tucked her feelings for Hudson away into a dark recess of her heart, never to see the light of day again.

Claire needed to share the conversation with Sochi, but didn't want to do it over the phone. It was too late to bother Nancho, so she hailed a cab passing by the Plaza. On the ride over, Claire fingered the vial of San Pedro. Whenever the egg deserted her for a few days, she considered taking it.

Sochi's house was dark but for the front light. Claire slipped around the back and found the spare key hidden under an empty pot, then let herself in to wait. By now Sochi would have found the turtles. Would she come right home, bummed about the failure to track Higuchi but relieved about the artifacts?

Pacing didn't seem to bring Sochi home any faster. Nor did calling her cell every two minutes. Claire finally sat down and fished out the copper egg. This time it was in the mood to show her more.

Ixchel's heart beat with terror. The administrator hunted her. He would kill her.

No, no. Slow down, Ixchel chanted to herself. Calm down. She wove through the homes and fields. Soon she saw the towering walls of Cualli's compound ahead. Cualli would help.

At the entrance, Ixchel stood tall, trying to look like a man, as she was dressed. She hefted her bag of tools to show the guard. "I am here to work."

The lazy guard motioned her in. She hurried through the massive ceremonial plaza, then started down a side street. She had to stop to ask for directions. As she wandered through passageways, her clothing stuck to her back. There was no air circulation this deep into the palace, even with the fishnet walls. Again, she asked for directions. She grew calmer as she neared Cualli and Tochi's home. Soon she would be surrounded by safety and love.

She entered the house and heard their voices.

She stepped into the room. "Cualli, it has happened."

Cualli gasped in horror, but not at her words. Tochi reached out as if to stop someone.

Hard hands grabbed her from behind. She struggled, but was unable to free herself.

The administrator leaned in. Smug. "I knew you would come. All I had to do was wait. Your timing is perfect because your king requires your attendance on his final journey."

Tochi restrained a wailing Cualli. His eyes gleamed with pain, having great affection for both Cualli and Ixchel. "I am nephew to this city's ruler," he said. "You cannot take Ixchel."

"Watch me." Two men bound her arms and began dragging her toward the door. The house servants stopped to stare.

Ixchel's breath came in gulps. "You are taking me back to my city?" There was still hope. She could escape during the long journey.

The administrator glowed with smugness but did not answer her question. "My only regret is that your father is no longer alive to witness my triumph. Come along."

Cualli's screams followed them out the door.

CHAPTER TWENTY-NINE

Claire
Friday, April 7

When Claire came out of the vision, Sochi was shaking her by the shoulders. "I'm okay," Claire said weakly. She rubbed her burning eyes, reliving the vision. Her treasure hunt was a bust. She was never going to figure this out. Ixchel had been from Chaco's city, but she'd fled that as a child, and now she was being taken back there. Identifying the location seemed impossible.

Sochi retrieved a bottle of water, then pulled up a chair and sat down. "Where the hell *were* you?"

Claire opened up her palm to reveal the copper egg, glistening with her sweat. "That one was intense. Harder to come back from." She guzzled the water gratefully. Ixchel's life was in danger. For all Claire knew, this might be the last vision she would have. How far did Ixchel have to travel before she reached the tomb and was then murdered by the administrator?

The vision raised questions. Ixchel had the copper egg, Cualli had a silver egg, but how did all three eggs end up in the tomb? Were they on Ixchel's body? Had they been placed there by different people? Claire drained the bottle and handed it to Sochi. "Refill, please?"

She drank the second bottle as quickly as the first. These later visions were taking more out of her than the earlier ones. "I know what happened with the NanoTrax artifacts."

Sochi drew back. "How could you know?"

"Hudson called me."

After Claire shared her conversation with Hudson, Sochi cursed. "I knew someone had tipped Higuchi's men off. I shouldn't be surprised it was Hudson." She shook her head, her short hair wild and stiff from her adventure on the beach. "I wish I could see his face when he realizes the artifacts are fakes."

Claire snickered. "I know we'd agreed to keep that fact quiet, but he was being such a smug son of a bitch that I couldn't resist."

A slow smile spread across Sochi's perfect, caramel-smooth face. "He freaked?"

"Total meltdown."

"Good."

Claire leaned back and stretched overhead, aching from holding still during her vision. "But he never stops trying to mess us up. He started ranting about you living two lives and having a secret in your car, some sort of black bag." She yawned so widely that her eyes closed. When she opened them, Sochi had gone from amused to angry. Her eyes had darkened to navy blue, never a good sign. "What's wrong?"

"What else did he tell you?"

"That you were keeping something secret in your car, but he's just trying to drive a wedge between us. How could you be living a secret life? You don't have the time. Besides, two lives implies that one of them involves something illegal. You'd never do that."

"Oh, really? Are we going to do this now?" Her lips trembled with anger, leaving Claire more confused.

"Do what now?"

"It's only a matter of time, and you've been so sweet and kind these last few days, talking about trust and openness. Well, I'll give you openness, and I guarantee you'll no longer trust me. You'll be disgusted and indignant and then you'll leave all over again."

"What are you talking about?"

"Wait here." She stomped out to her car and quickly returned with a black bag. "There's the black bag. Might as well look inside."

"Soch, I don't understand why you're so angry with me. What have I done?"

"It's not what you've done, it's what you're going to do. Open it."

Claire unzipped the bag and pulled out a soil probe and small shovel, then some hand brushes and rags. She pulled out a dig kit. "This is your dig kit and tools for excavating. What's so shocking about that?"

"Keep going."

A plastic bag came out next. Inside was a Styrofoam head holding a long, brown wig. The last item in the bag was a small pouch. Inside was a contact case holding brown contacts. Claire tried to laugh, but it turned into a cough. "I don't understand. Dig tools, brown wig, brown contacts—"

She stopped, reviewing the description of La Bruja. Brown hair, brown eyes. Claire's heart leapt into her throat. "No, that can't be."

Sochi narrowed her eyes. "Yes, it can be. The native who's been following you? That's my man, Rigoberto."

"Your *man*?" Claire jumped to her feet and backed away from the table as if the items were radioactive. "He told me he worked for La Bruja."

Sochi waited, the muscles along her jaw rippling.

"Oh, no. Sochi, no. The Sochi *I* know would never loot!"

"So now you know the truth. Time for you to judge me, to reject me. It turns out I'm just as bad as you thought I was three years ago, only for a different reason. Rigo's been following you so that when you found the tomb, we could raid it."

Claire felt as if she were sliding down a cliff, struggling for a handhold to stop this freefall. "I don't understand. Explain it to me."

"What for? You won't listen. You never listen. I knew getting close to you again was a bad idea."

"Hey, calm down. I'm not the looter here."

"You left three years ago because of something you *thought* I'd done. You're going to leave again because of what you now *know* I've done. Let's just skip ahead to the end of the story, okay? Get out."

"But I—"

"Out!" She grabbed Claire's arm and shoved her at the door. "You can catch a taxi two blocks down on Universidad."

Claire turned the knob, so stunned that her brain refused to work. "But—"

"Go. We're done."

In a fog, Claire walked the two blocks, raised her hand for a passing taxi, and was soon back at La Casa del Sol.

❖

The next morning, Claire awoke with a start, then moaned at her stiff neck. She wiped her mouth, horrified that the woven blanket which she'd wrapped around herself last night was damp near her shoulder. Great. Drowning by drool. She sat up, stretching her back. The rattan chair, the only piece of furniture on the little balcony, squeaked in alarm as she shifted her weight forward and hung down from the waist. What a night. God, why couldn't she have been drinking? At least then she'd have the hangover as an excuse for feeling so rotten this morning.

But no. She couldn't blame it on the Cabernet. An entire menu of incredibly unwonderful feelings swirled inside her like a blender that just wouldn't shut off.

Claire tucked the blanket around her legs. It was still early. Sounds of a neighborhood starting another business day echoed off the walls—car doors slamming, delivery trucks backing up, two dogs barking at each other from different blocks. Her balcony looked out over the property line, which was overgrown with climbing vines and a thicket of trees.

She didn't want to get up, officially. She didn't want to leave the balcony. Why couldn't she just hide out here for a few weeks? She could have food brought in and spend hours watching the little birds fly in and out of the greenery.

The minute Claire left the balcony, she'd have to figure out what to do next. That meant thinking about all the Sochis she knew: Sochi as her lover for three years; Sochi as the woman she'd wanted to spend her life with; Sochi as the woman Claire had thought had betrayed her to the press; Sochi as the dedicated CNTP employee; Sochi as La Bruja sin Corazon. Sochi as the real reason Claire had come to Peru without knowing it.

She tried to imagine the mental gymnastics Sochi would've had to perform in order to spend the nights looting, then showing up at the CNTP the next day to protect the very resources she vandalized at night.

Claire sighed. It was time to end this treasure hunt. She'd never figure out either the location of Chaco's city or the city where Ixchel had lived with Uncle and Auntie. She slid down farther into the blanket.

When she woke up again, the sun poured into her lap. She called the airport. The next open flight to Lima left at six p.m., and she would be on it. She finally stood, shaking out a foot that had fallen asleep, then staggered into her room.

Claire took one last walk to Las Dulces and ordered her five favorite pastries, pretending to the clerk that she had friends waiting at a table outside. Then she sat in the cool shade and ate them all herself. That's when she realized her three shadows were truly gone. No more tails.

Claire loved watching people in Trujillo. A pod of bikers flashed by, all Lycra and calf muscles. Across the street, two men were repainting a building from orange to lime green. The other buildings were hot pink, teal, and pale yellow. These people were not afraid of color. She could hear, but couldn't see, someone drumming on a street corner.

A native woman walked by in her wide, colorful skirts and brown bowler. Down the street, another woman was doing a brisk business selling vegetables.

An odd feeling clutched at her, and she teared up, suddenly so grateful for the color and music and smells. She loved these hardy people who continued to overcome all that had been imposed upon them by their Spanish conquerors. They'd been enslaved, tortured, killed by disease, forced to mine silver until they died on their feet, and yet, here they were, driving electric blue Volkswagen beetles and smiling at her as they passed her table.

Claire called Mac, who was home from the hospital, and bored to distraction. "You catch that bad guy yet?" he asked.

"No, Mac, and I don't think I will. He's stuck his evil hand in nearly every Peruvian industry and plans to bring the whole country down. First, I doubt he'll succeed—it's a crazy scheme, and second, I can't do anything to stop him."

"Huh. The asshole had me shot."

"I know. But I'm thinking that you need me back there."

Silence. "Well, that is true. Someone needs to explain to the British Museum about the Ming vase Bob broke over the gunman's head." More silence. "But I gotta say, giving up doesn't really sound like you."

She told him about her fight with Sochi and how she wouldn't even explain why she'd been La Bruja, or let Claire talk, but that she'd just shut her down. "I'm done, you know? I'm done with Higuchi and the egg and the visions."

"Visions?"

"Long story. And I've gained another ten pounds eating at this café every day. I want to come home."

"Why won't Sochi talk to you?"

"I don't know. I suppose because she knows I'm horrified she's been looting."

"Yeah, I get that. She expects you to reject her again like you did before."

Claire looked longingly at a plate full of *orejitas* on the table next to her. Yes, she had rejected Sochi and her proposal, but she'd tried to apologize…but only once. She never contacted Sochi after leaving Peru. Suddenly, she wasn't sure if she could blame all this on Hudson. "I suppose she might have a good reason for being La Bruja."

"And if she doesn't? Then you'll love her less?"

Her chest started to ache. "You're confusing me."

"Seems like you have a choice, kid. You told me you made a mistake leaving three years ago. You either make that same mistake again, or you fix the problem." Mac had begun to speak softer and more slowly, clearing growing tired.

"Mima always said if your life wasn't going right, to stop and fix it."

"Wise advice. But my pain meds are kicking in. I can barely keep my eyes open."

"Mac, one more thing. For the last three years, I've been feeling sorry for myself because I didn't think I had any friends. But you're my friend, and a good one."

"Thanks, kid, but don't tell anyone, okay? Then everyone will want to be my friend."

She snorted. "Maybe everyone will want to be *my* friend."

They paused. "Nah," they said simultaneously.

As Claire watched the throngs of people passing by Las Dulces, she fingered the amazonite teardrop around her neck. What was the stone for again? To help her see the other side, to see through someone else's eyes.

This time the vision she received wasn't one from the copper egg, or about Ixchel; it was about her and Sochi. If anyone was going to fix this, it would have to be Claire.

CHAPTER THIRTY

Sochi
Saturday, April 8

Sochi wasn't sure where she was going, but it was away from Trujillo. Perhaps she'd drive up to Ecuador and go surfing or shelling. As she packed late Saturday afternoon, she struggled to ignore that sick feeling she had whenever something in her life went desperately wrong. Hopelessness and regret mingled together, along with the harsh truth that much of our lives were outside of our control. She'd let Aurelio down, failing to catch Higuchi in the act. She'd let Rigo down by retiring La Bruja. In a way, she'd let Claire down by becoming La Bruja in the first place. At least Mima was safe.

Sochi dropped onto the bed, head in her hands. Claire. What had Sochi been thinking this last week? They'd begun to talk, to reconnect, even laugh a little. Sochi should have known it was only a matter of time before she gave Claire another reason to leave. It didn't get more offensive than La Bruja.

She checked her phone. Still no response from Aurelio. She'd texted him that she'd lost Higuchi's trail, but balanced that with the good news that the backflap and other artifacts were still safe in the CNTP vault. She also texted that she needed to take some time off. She ran the risk of demonstrating that the organization could function just fine without her, but she no longer cared. Her obsession with keeping Peru in Peru had helped destroy her relationship with Claire, and had made her more vulnerable to Minister Salazar's pressure to become La Bruja.

She jumped at a determined knock on her door. It must be Rigo, come to talk her out of quitting. But when she opened the door, it wasn't Rigo's square, chiseled cheekbones that faced her.

Claire's long hair, pulled back into a ponytail, shone like polished brass in the sunlight. "We need to talk," she said.

Sochi blocked the open doorway with her body. "I told you. We're done."

Claire took a step forward until their chests nearly touched. "Not until we've talked." She moved so close that Sochi had no choice but to step back into the room.

Claire wore what she always did, and looked as hot as she always did. The extra pounds took away the bony, hard look she'd had three years ago. Now she looked strong, but soft at the same time. She unslung her leather bag, which looked as if it were about to fall apart, and dropped it onto the floor. "We could get comfortable," Claire said. "Perhaps share some tea."

"Say what you have to say, then leave." Sochi folded her arms protectively.

Claire inhaled, then slowly exhaled. "Three years ago, I jumped to conclusions. I left without talking to you. I saw you burn my letter so I assumed you had rejected me. This time I'm not going to do that. We need to talk. I want to know what's going on with you."

"What's the point?"

Claire's face looked pained, her brows gently furrowed. "I've been thinking about why I left with just the letter instead of talking to you. I think I was ashamed to love someone who could betray me the way I thought you'd betrayed me. But I've decided that shame is the biggest waste of time on the freaking planet. It helps no one. So I'm going to stop being ashamed. I don't care what you tell me about La Bruja. I don't care why you did it. I'm not going to be ashamed to love someone who's broken the law."

Sochi's pulse quickened. "You just said you love me."

Claire's cheek lifted in a quick smile. "I do love you. Desperately. It turns out that I've never stopped loving you." She looked at the floor. "I know you probably can't love me back because hearts heal at different rates, but that's okay. I'm not sure I actually deserve it anyway. But I want you to know that even though I didn't find

Chaco's tomb, and am going to stop looking, I found something even more important, and that was the truth: That you will always, always, be the love of my life. I just let my shame and my ambition blind me to that fact."

Sochi sighed heavily, placing one hand over her heart, then she backed up and sat down on her plush sofa. "You don't care that I was La Bruja?"

"I only care because it must have been incredibly difficult for you to live two such opposite lives. Have you had *anyone* to talk to about this?"

Sochi found it hard to swallow. "No. I've had Mima, but I couldn't tell her about La Bruja." She wiped her eyes. "But I would like to tell you." She began at the beginning, which was the time when she still felt dead inside after Claire had left. Minister Salazar had taken her aside after a huge CNTP conference and proposed she become La Bruja in order to harass Higuchi, in hopes of getting him off balance enough that he'd make a mistake. She explained about Rigo, and how well they worked together, and that Rigo had known her true identity from the beginning, but had said nothing to her. He could have destroyed her a dozen times over, but didn't do it.

By the time she'd finished, Claire was holding both her hands. Blinking, she looked up into Claire's soft green eyes. "You're still here."

"I told you. I'm not leaving, no matter what you did. But I don't think you had any choice. I might have done the same thing if I'd been in your situation. Higuchi is one crazy dude, so I get why Salazar and the others are so afraid of him. But using people like you—"

"And Maria Menendez, the woman who followed you."

"She was working for Salazar too?"

Sochi nodded.

"What a coward. He puts women in danger to fight his battles for him."

A calm descended over Sochi. What did it mean that she felt so comfortable sitting here with Claire, and so relieved? It was as if a long, dark nightmare had finally ended. Claire gently stroked her cheek.

"Do you remember when we had our first fight and we separated for twenty-four hours?"

A bolt of desire shot through Sochi's body and settled between her legs. "Yes, I remember."

"Just before you kissed me, you apologized for not being able to wait until I'd had more time to recover from our fight."

"I remember."

Claire moved closer, shifting one arm around Sochi's waist. "I'm in that position now. I know you need more time, but I can't give it to you." Her gaze dropped to Sochi's lips. "I think you should know, Xochiquetzal Castillo, that I'm going to kiss you. So if you need to run away or scream for help, you have about four seconds... three seconds..."

Desire flared in Claire's eyes.

"Two," they whispered together, then, "one."

They came together in a kiss that was charged with renewal and excitement and regret for lost time and the deep, deep love they'd both hidden from themselves. She pulled Claire closer, and they fell back against the sofa, lost in each other's touch.

Claire finally took a breath. "If we were stuck in some romance novel, this is the scene where we'd strip each other naked and make creatively-varied love all night long." She left a string of kisses along Sochi's jaw. "But I'm too happy. I just want to look at you."

Sochi nodded. "How many couples get the chance to rediscover one another? I'm so overwhelmed that all I can think about is holding you."

"When I was a teenager," Claire said, "my dad brought home a kitten he'd found in the middle of a country road. I named him Emmett and we became inseparable. When he was really little, he'd snuggle up next to my face, put his entire nose into my nostril, then we'd just stay that way, quietly breathing each other in." Claire pulled Sochi down on top of her. "That's what I want to do. Just breathe you in." Within minutes, curled into each other, they fell asleep. Sochi's last thought was that Mima was so right—when the mind let go of the negative crap, the heart could heal just fine.

CHAPTER THIRTY-ONE

Claire
Sunday, April 9

When Claire woke up and felt Sochi's breath against her neck, she nearly cried. Everything in her life had felt wrong and off-kilter for three endless years. And now, with Sochi in her arms again, all that faded. Sochi was warm and soft and hers. And she wouldn't let anything come between them ever again.

Except a full bladder. Carefully, Claire extricated herself from Sochi's smooth limbs and used the bathroom. On the way back, her blinking cell phone caught her eye. It was a photo sent around midnight, an hour ago.

Claire gasped. Mima, this time bloodied and unconscious, was tied up, on the ground. Next to her was Denis, in the same shape, blood staining his white jacket. She clenched her teeth so tightly they ground together. Then the text: *You have until daybreak.*

She clutched at her hair. When was this idiot going to get it—she couldn't find a treasure on command. Claire began pacing. She should wake Sochi up, but what could she do? What could Claire do? There were no GPS coordinates with this photo, so the message was clear—no treasure, no saving Mima and Denis.

Claire pulled the copper egg from her pocket and held it tight.

Nothing. God *damn* it. Nothing.

Her bag still rested on the floor. There was only one thing left to do, only one way to increase her chances of a vision. She pawed through the bag until she found the vial of San Pedro the shaman had given her.

She didn't want to do this. The drug made her feel lost and out of touch. Using her pocketknife, she cut the piece in half, returned one half to the vial, and swallowed the rest.

Then she sat on the floor beside the sofa, comforted by Sochi's warm presence, and held the copper egg. It only took about a minute.

Ixchel stumbled between the two guards as they left the compound. The administrator led them east, skirting the artisan homes, then he turned north past the next compound. Soon they left the city behind and trudged up and down land dotted with scrub brush and yellow-tipped grasses. The administrator chattered on about how honored Ixchel should be that he had dedicated years to tracking her down.

Ixchel's mouth was dry. Uncle and Auntie had spent their lives keeping her safe. This wasn't their fault. It was hers, but what could she have done differently? She thought of Cualli and their love. She thought of Tochi and their affection for each other. She would go to her death with these good feelings in her heart. This man could never take those away from her.

"Here. Stop."

They stood before a long wall of sand. Another dune. But there was an opening, a doorway reinforced with bamboo. She saw now it wasn't a dune, but a building, most of it buried in sand. At the far end, men still shoveled the sand to hide the adobe walls.

"Here?" she asked, pulse racing. She would have no opportunity to escape.

"Our wise king knew his tomb would be better protected if he built it not near our own small city, but near a much larger city instead. Come, the others have already been sacrificed inside the tomb, so there is no time to waste."

This was it. This was the tomb. She swung toward the ocean, seeking help. Nothing but blue water falling off the edge of the world. She swung toward the mountains. Nothing but the distinctive outline against the cloudless sky: four peaks ascending to the right, a plateau, then a sharp drop. No help in that direction. She closed her eyes. At least she still had the egg.

"No!" Cualli shouted behind her. Ixchel was knocked to the sand as Cualli swarmed over her, hands tearing at her, clawing at the pouch at her waist. Cualli shouted, "No! A mistake, a mistake!" Ixchel tried to calm her as Tochi ran toward them. Cualli yanked the pouch so hard the thin string broke.

Cualli leapt to her feet, holding up the pouch in triumph. "I am Ixchel. See?" She poured the egg into her palm. "I have the copper egg. You have made a mistake. I am the daughter of Atl."

The administrator looked confused. Tochi approached, arms waving.

Ixchel was horrified. "Cualli, do not do this. You cannot sacrifice yourself for me."

Cualli ignored her, thumping the man on the chest. "I am Ixchel. Do not anger the gods by sacrificing the wrong female or you will never join our great king. He will bar the gates to you."

His face hardened. He nodded to the guards and they took Cualli by the arms. Ixchel grabbed at their clothing. "Cualli, use the egg! The egg will save you! Use the egg." Cualli gave Ixchel a look of deep love, then was dragged toward the tomb.

When Cualli disappeared inside the tomb, Ixchel threw herself at the guards blocking the entrance.

Tochi joined her, but four guards beat them until they were bloody. Tochi pulled Ixchel from the tomb entrance and they crawled over the next dune. He held her as she cried.

Stunned, Claire stared at the egg. She had recognized the horizon the second Ixchel's gaze took it in: four peaks ascending to the right, a plateau, then a sharp drop. But that was the horizon directly to the east of Chan Chan. That would mean Chaco's tomb was practically on top of Chan Chan. The administrator said the tomb was close to Ixchel's home, but Claire struggled to believe it. The room spun as the drug hijacked her system.

Panicked now, she reached over and gently shook Sochi awake. When she showed her the photo, Sochi moaned in fear.

Claire held out the copper egg. "I just had a vision, but it didn't help. It looked like it was near Chan Chan, but that just can't be right. Chaco's tomb wouldn't have been right next to Chan Chan. My visions must be faulty." Her head rolled back. "Or the San Pedro was bad. I don't really know where the tomb is."

Sochi took her hands, cursing softly about the San Pedro. The touch and the warmth calmed Claire a little, but she was sure the world had tipped on its side...only Sochi's hands kept her from falling over. "Claire, calm down. You can do this. You observe. That's what you do, even if you're unaware of it. Your mom once told me how you'd be in the grocery store and predict that you'd run into the minister, and you would. Then you'd tell her that the school principal was there, and she was. It's because you saw everything, including license plates, and recognized them in the parking lot. So we're going to go through each vision, and you're going to just relax and observe, okay?"

Claire inhaled, shaky. "Okay. Still really high."

"Close your eyes. Focus, Claire. Ignore how the drug is making you feel. This last vision you saw something that reminded you of Chan Chan?"

"The horizon to the east, the outline of the mountains."

"Okay, anything else?"

"It was daylight so there were no stars." Despite her addled state, she managed to tell Sochi of her plan to use three stars in the Carina Nebula to help locate the tomb. "The vertical line of the three brightest clusters in the nebula tipped just slightly to the left at 50 km north, and just slightly right at 50 km south. If I could see the nebula, it might help me locate the tomb in relation to Trujillo."

"Good. Now let's go back to the vision before that."

Claire pressed her lips together, still feeling Ixchel's terror as the administrator took her prisoner. "Nothing helpful."

"The vision before that?"

"Nothing. She was inside with her dying uncle."

Gently, slowly, she relived each vision. Being high on San Pedro made the visions feel like a comfortable place in which to stay, but Sochi's voice and strong hands kept pulling her back.

Claire reached the vision where Ixchel had been on the ground, looking up at the sky, when Cualli had kissed her. Claire still couldn't see the nebula.

Sochi took her all the way back to the first vision, the evening when she'd taken San Pedro with Hudson, hoping to restart the voices in her head.

It was dark. Claire could smell the sea. Smell warm llamas.

Ixchel was back home now; she passed through a room into an inner courtyard.

"Come here, Ixchel," said Uncle.

Uncle and Auntie gave her a present. To celebrate. "You are ten cycles."

She was thrilled. She'd never been given a gift before. There just wasn't enough for extra things like gifts. She opened the small bag and pulled out a small copper egg.

"It's from your papa," her uncle said.

Ixchel jumped up. "Papa? You've seen him? Is he here?"

Uncle and Auntie exchanged a glance. "No, your papa isn't here," Auntie said, "and he won't likely come to visit. But he managed to get this egg to Uncle. It's for you."

Sadness coursed through her. Ixchel missed her papa. He had left five years ago, but she didn't know when—or if—he was ever coming back for her. She looked up into the sky, as if it could tell her where her father might be. The night sky was bright. Clusters glowed.

Claire's eyes flew open. "Holy crap. I saw the Carina Nebula. The three bright clusters were lined up in a perfect vertical line. This means Ixchel *was* near Chan Chan. And the tomb was close to Uncle and Auntie's house."

Sochi squeezed her hands. "Excellent."

"But where do we look? Most of the area around Chan Chan has been developed."

They stared at each other, as if their eyes held the answers. Sochi cocked her head. "May I see the eggs again?"

She rearranged them in her hand. "These shallow scratches still bother me. They're light, as if added later. Perhaps by the person who removed them from the tomb? And here, what I thought were two half-circles...couldn't that be two Cs, standing for Chan Chan?" She lined the three eggs up side by side and began following a line. When it disappeared on one egg, it appeared on the next.

Heads touching, they studied the scratching. Then Sochi laughed. "It's a freaking map! Look. The double Cs are here, near this small square. Then there are eight more squares."

"The nine compounds of Chan Chan?"

"Yes, then if you follow the scratch, it passes through Chan Chan, then turns north. The line stops at this hatch mark. If the map is to scale, then the hatch mark is directly on top of..."

They looked at each other. Claire's chest opened up. Could it be? Could she and Sochi, with all their picnic lunches and talks, have been sitting right on top of the damn tomb all along?

"It's our hill," Claire whispered, the excitement dispelling some of the drug in her system.

Sochi did a quick search online and found the GPS coordinates for Chan Chan. "Adjust the coordinates just a bit because the hill is north of Chan Chan."

Claire texted Higuchi: *Have coordinates for tomb. Send coord for hostages.*

A set of GPS coordinates appeared on her screen. "Thank the gods," Sochi breathed as Claire sent them to her phone. Then Claire sent a set of GPS coordinates to Higuchi.

Sochi grabbed her keys. "You stay here until the San Pedro wears off. I'll go find Mima and Denis."

After Sochi left, the house was silent. Claire stood, feeling shaky but not as badly as before. Could she do this? Only taking half of the piece must have helped. She called the twenty-four-hour taxi service and had the man drop her off at La Casa del Sol, where she managed to reach her room, retrieve the metal detector, then take Señora Nunez's car keys from the back of the small office.

She hadn't given Higuchi the exact coordinates. This way if Sochi came up empty-handed in her search for Mima and Denis, Claire had one more card to play. But the truth was that someone had sent *her* the three eggs. This was *her* treasure hunt, and she would be FTF if it killed her.

CHAPTER THIRTY-TWO

Claire

Driving at night while under the influence of San Pedro was just as bad, if not worse, than driving drunk. The streetlights became white suns with glowing haloes. Traffic lights were moving blobs of color. But Claire managed to find the narrow road that ran north of Chan Chan without hitting anything or anyone. She parked the car close to the row of towering bushes that separated Chan Chan from the sugarcane field north of it. She didn't see anyone following her.

The warm night air felt cool on her moist skin so she just stood there for a minute, collecting herself. Past the sugarcane field the sandy ridge rose, outlined against the midnight blue sky. Overhead the three star clusters of the Carina Nebula lined up, one on top of each other, like a stop light.

With her bag over her shoulder, and the metal detector, Claire pushed through the bushes and took the trail that wrapped around the sugarcane field. She set her flashlight app on low.

She finally reached the long, narrow hill that ran east and west. It began high on the east end, then gradually sloped westward to a last bit of flat land planted in sugarcane, before reaching the beach. She and Sochi would come here to escape. They'd sit up there, removed from the world, and talk. Few others came here because it was hard to reach, and it was dry and barren. Only the two of them seemed to appreciate its stark beauty.

Taking a few deep breaths, Claire turned to her right, facing the foothills of the Andes. Four dark peaks ascending to the right, a plateau, then a sharp drop. There it was: the exact image from Ixchel's vision. The tomb had to be buried in the hill in front of her. The problem was, how deep? By this time, the caverns of the tomb would have collapsed upon themselves. It would be an archaeological team's job to slowly remove the layers, creating a clear image of what the tomb once looked like, and who was buried inside it. All Claire needed to do was dig up a few treasures to satisfy Higuchi, then she'd call the CNTP. She suppressed a few giggles as she puzzled things out, still high enough to find the whole thing amusing.

If Señora Facala's boyfriend, NP, had entered and exited the tomb, there must be some sort of door. When she waved the detector along the side of the hill, it began to chirp weakly. Working methodically, she moved from right to left, climbing the hill. With each step the detector's beeping grew stronger. She walked along the top of the hill, the detector now very, very excited. Her mouth went dry with treasure hunting fever. There had to be a huge amount of something metallic beneath her feet.

The detector slipped from her sweating hands. Thunk.

Claire stopped. That sounded like wood, which made no sense because the Chimú didn't have much wood available to them. She tapped the ground with the detector and heard the same clunk. Then she jumped up and down. This, in retrospect, might not have been the wisest move, but she was still under the influence of San Pedro. The ground gave way beneath her, and she plummeted straight down into a cloud of dust and cracking wood.

Claire yelped as she slammed against the side of whatever she fell into, then hit a pile of something and rolled over and over until she landed with an "oomph" at the bottom. Sand swirled up her nostrils and into her mouth. She lay there, stunned, heart pounding, coughing so hard her eyes watered. Finally, she caught her breath and was able to test her arms, then her legs. Nothing broken, but she felt banged up. Her arm burned from a cut, and she was covered with scrapes. Everything hurt.

Above her, faint moonlight filtered down through the dust. She coughed and wiped her eyes again. Half way down, she'd hit a pile of dirt and debris that luckily broke her fall; otherwise she would have fallen at least three meters.

Claire's hip burned. When she shifted, she discovered she'd landed on her phone and smashed it to bits. She cursed. How could Higuchi call her for the true coordinates? Had she put her friends in even more danger? Not being truthful with Higuchi might have been another miscalculation, thanks to her treasure hunter's fever.

Claire dug a spare flashlight from her bag. When she switched it on, at first she couldn't see anything because of the dust she'd created. She waited patiently, thinking that this couldn't be Chaco's tomb. No way could its chambers have remained intact all these centuries. But the air smelled old, as if it hadn't been refreshed in years. Finally, enough dust settled that Claire could see the wall next to her.

She gasped and leapt to her feet, wincing at the pain. A niche in the wall held a warrior's mask. Empty eyes stared back at her. Golden spikes radiated out from the face, each set with a dark red jewel. But was it really gold? It was so dull. She ran her fingers along the mask. Gold gleamed in the marks left by her fingers.

Heart really racing now, she swung the flashlight along the walls. She was in a chamber about three meters by ten meters. A forest of slender bamboo poles supported planks holding up the ceiling. The plank and pole had given way where she'd fallen through.

The walls were a dull surface that reflected more light than adobe should. She wiped the wall again, feeling cool metal under her fingertips. She wiped more surface with her sleeve.

Claire gasped. The walls were covered in pounded gold.

This was it. This had to be King Chacochutl's tomb.

She ran her flashlight along the floor and stepped back in alarm. Dozens of skeletons lay stretched out down the middle of the chamber. She focused the flashlight upward. There was no ladder in the corner, no door. No way to get back out. Suddenly cold, she hugged herself, trying to calm her breathing, feeling blood trickling down her forehead and arm.

She was used to *uncovering* skeletons in the ground, not sharing a dark chamber with them.

CHAPTER THIRTY-THREE

Claire

Triage first. She ripped off the bottom of one tank and did her best to wrap it around a gash on her arm, which had splattered blood all over her. She wiped the blood off her lip, dabbed the cut on her forehead until it stopped bleeding, then examined the cut on her knee. The arm gash would need stitches, and perhaps the one on her knee as well, but scars didn't bother her. Scars were the stories our bodies had to tell.

When Claire felt she could walk without shaking, she took a few steps. Directly across from her was a table with buckets and rags and brushes. She tucked a rag and a brush into her back pockets. Two large white buckets rested on the floor beside the table. The flashlight revealed the buckets were half-full of a black sludge. She leaned closer and sniffed. Oil.

A quick scan of the walls showed what she'd missed the first time: torches, wrapped with cloth, mounted along the walls every two meters or so. She dunked one of the torches into the oil, replaced it, then lit it with a very old book of matches from the table. It ignited with a terrifying whoosh. Smelling of oil, the torch threw off a golden light, and a little black smoke as well. She didn't dare light all of them without more ventilation, but the torch helped dispel the gloom. Weaving carefully through the forest of bamboo poles, she lit two more torches in the chamber.

Then she turned her attention to the skeletons on the dirt floor. The ones nearest where she'd fallen were a bit jumbled, but still recognizable as llamas or alpacas. She counted twenty skulls. The next skeletons were human, likely female. Twenty of them. Some still had small shreds of cloth nestled against a shoulder blade or tucked in around a waist, but most of the fabric had turned to gray powder. She walked slowly, aching to know what had happened. Had Cualli figured out how to use the egg? Or was one of these women Cualli?

About halfway down the row of skeletons, Claire stopped. One skeleton had the remains of an orange and brown sash wrapped around its waist, with a small woven pouch attached. She let out a long breath. In the last vision, Cualli had worn an orange and brown sash, and she'd taken Ixchel's woven pouch.

Cualli hadn't survived. She hadn't figured out how to use the copper egg. She'd sacrificed her life to save the woman she loved.

Saddened, Claire reached the end of the chamber, which turned to the left into darkness. Another chamber. She retrieved a bucket of oil, then used her flashlight to illuminate the way as the path snaked 180 degrees to the left. This chamber was about the same size, with the same forest of bamboo poles holding up planks overhead. But almost the entire floor was piled full of items she couldn't identify. She lit three more torches, then bent down and brushed a hand over the nearest item. Gold flashed in the flickering light.

"Holy shit." Claire's voice echoed in the narrow chamber. Gold. The entire chamber was filled with gold masks, gold chains, gold bowls, gold vessels, anything that King Chaco might need in his new home. She shivered at the sight, and leaned against the gold-plated wall for support. A treasure hunter's dream.

There was more gold here than all the gold items recovered in Peru during the last twenty years. No wonder the person who'd sent her the eggs wanted to find this tomb. The walls were covered in pounded gold, with the same niches as in the first chamber. Each niche held special items. One was a pair of gold hands, the fingers reaching toward the ceiling. Others held conus shells that came from the more tropical seas of Ecuador. One held a ceremonial Tumi knife, its silver handle inlaid with gold and copper. She turned the knife over in her hands, then touched the edge of the semi-circular blade. A thin line of blood beaded on her finger.

Claire replaced the Tumi knife, then marveled at all the craftsmanship surrounding her. Using the rag, she wiped down the walls, then lightly brushed at the top items on the pile on the floor, which was just enough to send sparkles of light flashing around the room. If only her phone had worked so she could take photos. The tomb would never look this undisturbed again.

That it was still standing, still intact, was beyond amazing. Obviously, people had successfully cared for this tomb for centuries, bringing in the bamboo and planks to keep the ceiling from collapsing.

The darkness at the end of the chamber curled to the right this time. She shone her light around the corner. The room was empty but for the bamboo poles and two large objects. Claire lit two more torches, then approached what looked like a long cabinet. The item's surface was coated with too much dust to see clearly, so she brushed it off and inhaled sharply. A ferocious Chimú warrior had been carved into a slab of light brown soapstone.

Holy shit. This was an altar, a sacrificial altar. She used the cloth to wipe more dust from the carved warrior. He wore a large, spiked headdress that ran to the top and side edges of the altar, each spike ending in a small, delicate oval. The ovals formed a pattern that ran around the altar's top edge.

The body of the warrior was squat and wearing a ceremonial reed skirt that flared out from stubby legs. One bit of skirt flared out far enough to reach the right side and end in another oval. All the rest of the skirt's reeds flew out to the left and bottom edges.

She gently stroked this carved masterpiece. Ixchel's father had been one of the craftsmen to work on this tomb. Uncle had said Atl could create wonders with any material. Did he build this masterpiece? The thick side edges of the carved top were lined with a deep groove. The base of the altar was built of mortared adobe bricks.

Claire moved toward the second item, which was a platform with a body wrapped in cloth.

Chaco's body. The top layers of cloth had succumbed to time, but those closer to the body remained more or less intact and were decorated with copper discs. An exquisite gold and copper burial mask gazed fiercely at the ceiling, the eyes made of emeralds and amber. Arranged next to Chaco on the platform were war clubs, shields, a copper spear, and dozens of ceramic vessels. There was also a curious pile of rope sandals and the remains of clothing.

She shone her light at the wall. This was where the tomb ended. A wooden door, mostly in splinters, bulged out into the room. The caretakers must have entered through a tunnel leading to that door. The tunnel had obviously collapsed.

She returned to the altar and continued cleaning its surface. The carving was breathtaking. But her head shot up at a metallic clunk in another chamber. She stopped breathing to listen hard. More clanking.

A ladder. Someone had just lowered a ladder down into the tomb.

CHAPTER THIRTY-FOUR

Claire

By the time Claire reached the first chamber, someone was coming down a yellow metal ladder leaning against the hole she'd made. She laughed with relief to recognize Sochi's legs.

"Did you find Denis and Mima? Are they okay?"

Sochi's head was bleeding, and her eyes blazed. "They're okay. They were in Denis's garden." She jerked her head toward the legs now descending the ladder. "So were these guys."

The person down the ladder, armed with a gun, was the man Claire had accosted at Mardonio's wake.

"This asshole is Nopa," Sochi said sourly as she gently probed the cut along her hairline. Her white-blond hair was stained red on the right side of her head.

"We've met," Claire said.

Nopa had a bruise of his own, just about where Claire had hit the man who'd tried to break into her room. "Nopa," she snapped. "How's your face?"

But he paid them no attention. Instead, tears streamed down his face as he gazed reverently around the chamber, as if he'd entered a church. He whooped then began cursing with joy in Quechua.

The next man down the ladder wore sharply creased wool trousers. Higuchi.

Claire's jaw dropped. "But I thought you left the country with Hudson and the artifacts."

"That was my son, Antonio. He and Hudson went to high school together for a year in Japan." He dusted off his slacks. "Thank you, Claire Adams, for cooperating with my timeline, although you have cut things quite short. I only have tomorrow in which to publicize this Chaco victory." He gazed around the chamber. "However, I don't see anything but old bones."

"How did you find me?"

Higuchi tugged at his cuffs, looking uncomfortable. Good. She hoped he was claustrophobic. "I knew you'd given me the wrong coordinates. It's what I would have done. So when Ms. Castillo arrived, I persuaded her to tell me exactly where to find the tomb. I knew you'd already be here."

"Aren't you smart." Claire winced at Sochi's wound. "Are you okay?"

She nodded.

Higuchi spoke up the ladder. "You can deliver that package now. We'll need her in a few minutes." He turned to Claire. "Give us a tour, won't you?"

One of the guards descended carefully with a bound woman over his shoulder.

"Maria," Sochi cried.

Her hands were bound, but her mouth was free. She glared at Higuchi. "I should have listened to you. Salazar led me into a trap so this jerk could snatch me."

Higuchi perspired slightly in the hot, dry air. "The minister is a fool who finally realized that it is better to work for me than to work against me. Let's go on that tour."

Sochi reached for Maria, but Nopa raised his gun. "Higuchi," Sochi said. "Let Maria go. She's not part of this."

"I need her," Nopa growled, done rhapsodizing over the tomb. "I need three."

"Three what?" Claire asked.

Higuchi waved impatiently. "Later. First, a tour."

"Wait." She glared at Nopa. "Before we go any farther, I want to know if you sent me the eggs."

Nopa's face still glowed with joy, but he managed to focus enough to answer her. "My family has cared for this tomb for centuries because one of our ancestors—a skilled administrator named Nopaltzin—believed Chaco to be the most important man ever to be born. And because Nopaltzin was chosen by Chaco for the Great Miracle, the family began tending the tomb to honor Nopaltzin. When it was my grandfather's turn, he took the eggs, but then he was killed before telling his eldest son—my father—of the location."

"Your grandfather scratched a map to the tomb on the eggs," Sochi said. "Too bad no one in your family was smart enough to figure that out."

Nopa turned red, grabbed Sochi by the hair, and jammed the gun against her cheek. She shot him her most arctic glaze, the one that could subdue even Claire. "Shut the fuck up!" he yelled. "Where are my eggs, by the way?" He looked at Claire.

She shook her head, suddenly terrified because she actually didn't know where they were. "I don't have them."

Sochi batted Nopa's gun arm away and he let her go.

Claire felt sick. Julio the shaman said she needed to keep the copper egg with her. She surreptitiously moved her hand against her pocket. Nothing! The last time she'd seen the eggs, she and Sochi were studying them in order to read the map. Uneasiness crept through her limbs. She didn't have the copper egg.

She whirled on Higuchi. "I don't understand how you fit into this."

"Nopa is my employee. One day I was about to kill him for his incompetence when he told me of the eggs and how he'd sent them to you. That's when I saw how Chaco's tomb could fit into my Plan of Retribution."

"You're both insane," Claire said.

Nopa waved the gun at her. She should have been afraid, but she suspected he had other plans for her.

"I have the tomb now," Nopa said, "so I guess I don't need the eggs. This is the most important day of my life, and of this country's existence. Generations of my family have kept the roof from collapsing, kept the torches working, cleaned and oiled the altar, all to honor both the great king and his administrator, Nopaltzin. I have many cousins, but it is *my* branch which was honored with this task." He stroked one of the bamboo support poles. "My grandfather, Nopaltzin, let Chacochutl down."

Claire realized that Nopa's grandfather, Nopaltzin, could be Señora Facala's NP.

"I am finally able to continue what centuries of my ancestors have done—honor Chacochutl. And I will do what no one has yet tried—bring Chacochutl back to life."

Claire's eyes met Sochi's. What did they have to do with his plan?

"Plenty of time for that," Higuchi snapped. "Let's see the treasure."

CHAPTER THIRTY-FIVE

Claire

When Higuchi nodded to Claire, she led them into the second chamber, where even Sochi gasped at the treasure. Nopa began chanting something in Quechua that she didn't understand. The gold was even more impressive with all the torches lit.

Higuchi stood in the chamber with his hands on his hips. "And so my plan begins. Nopa, I will call your cousin." He punched the screen a few times, then waited. "Yes, bring men and backpacks for transporting the stuff. Walk in, since the four-wheelers might draw too much attention at this time of night. You have several hours of work here. Photograph everything before you move it, then photograph each individual item. I want Peru to know exactly what it's lost." He ended the call.

"Why?" Sochi asked.

He nodded at Claire. "She understands. I am going to punish Peru for its treatment of Japanese-Peruvian citizens during World War II. The best way to do this is to steal its greatest treasure." He opened his arms toward the pile. "Which I have now discovered."

"I'm FTF," Claire snapped.

"Ohh. So competitive. Is there more to the tomb?"

She led them around the corner to the altar room.

"Yes!" Nopa shouted. "It is here, just as my father said it would be." After forcing Claire, Maria, and Sochi into the far corner, both Nopa and Higuchi ran their fingers over the carved warrior on the altar.

"Amazing," Nopa breathed. "Thank you for cleaning this," he said to her. "This entire tomb has gone untended for over forty years, thanks to my grandfather." He happily traced part of the warrior's reed skirt.

Nopa finally noticed the raised platform behind them. With a cry, he dashed toward it and dropped to his knees. The chamber was silent as he gazed reverentially at the wrapped skeleton. Claire hoped he wouldn't unwrap the cloth—that would surely destroy it.

Finally, Nopa stood.

She cleared her throat. "Higuchi, I found the tomb for you. It's time to let us go."

Higuchi smiled one of those creepy, sweet smiles. He turned to Nopa. "I told you we'd find your family's tomb. If you want to do that whole 'Chaco back to life' thing, now is the time."

"What do you mean?" Claire asked.

Nopa cocked his head, as if listening to a secret voice. "I intend to bring King Chaco back from the dead to live again. He will honor me by inhabiting my body."

"That's bullshit," Sochi snapped. "No one believes that crap."

"Our family was the chosen one, thanks to the Great Miracle." His expression didn't change. "Our king had llamas and women to accompany him on his journey to the heavens. He will need the same on his return to Earth. It is time."

He pushed them back to the first chamber. "First, I must sacrifice llamas to help carry Chaco's food and belongings for the return journey. I realized it might be difficult to transport the llamas quickly when the time came, so we have sacrificed them already." He hefted the bag over his shoulder. "I have the llama blood here."

They watched while Nopa removed a plastic bag of blood and poured it over the llama skeletons. The harsh smell of iron and death filled the chamber. He folded the plastic and tucked it into his bag. Then he turned to Claire. "Now I need attendants for the king. The eggs gave me the idea. Gold, silver, and copper. I will offer three female sacrifices—gold, silver, and copper."

Her stomach dropped. He couldn't be serious. That explained why Maria was here. Three female sacrifices: Maria, Sochi, and Claire.

Sochi leapt for Nopa's throat, but he deflected her hands and flung her against the gold-lined wall. The wall trembled but held. "No, you can't do this," Sochi growled.

Higuchi shook his head. "Nopa, tie them up." Higuchi held the gun on them while Nopa fastened their hands behind their backs with plastic ties. When the hard tie cut deeply into Claire's wrists, she hissed in pain, but forced her mind into problem-solving mode. What could she do? And how had she gone from being a nosy archaeologist, snooping around for a fabled tomb, to someone about to be sacrificed? She waited for it to seem funny, but nothing came.

"All three of you, sit down there in the corner."

They dropped to their knees, then awkwardly lowered themselves, hard to do with your hands behind your back. Nopa and Higuchi were busy conferring.

"Sochi," Claire whispered. They were sitting back to back, with Maria farther down the wall. Sochi shifted, obviously trying to relieve some of the pressure across her shoulders. "It would be stupid and unfair for us to die now."

"I know," she replied.

Their fingers managed to touch, and the reality of the situation came crashing down on Claire. No one else knew they were here. No one was going to rescue them. Her throat closed up so it took her a minute to get the words out. "I would have liked to get a dog." Unfamiliar despair seeped into her soul as she realized how much of her life she'd wasted running from Sochi.

"I will get you a dog. We will name her Suyana."

"Hope?"

Her fingers squeezed Claire's. "We're not dead yet, my love."

CHAPTER THIRTY-SIX

Sochi

Sochi refused to accept that this was it. After years of living a double life, and staying safe, was she going to have her throat slit open on an elaborate altar within shouting distance of Chan Chan? No. *No.* Her parents would soldier on, but Sochi's death would kill Mima. Her eyes began to sting. And Claire's death? Couldn't happen. If Sochi could sacrifice her own life to save Claire's, she would. She'd never felt so certain of anything.

Higuchi was done conferring with someone on the phone so they returned to the women's corner. "Who goes first?" he asked Nopa.

Nopa was fumbling with a small bottle of capsules. San Pedro. He popped three into his mouth. He'd be higher than Machu Picchu within minutes. "I have given great thought to this. Do you know the name of a father and son who were both president of America?"

"Bush," Higuchi said.

"Yes, but also Adams! I researched this. Claire Adams is descended from her country's rulers, so she will be my gold sacrifice. She will be the first to die."

Sochi felt as if she'd been kicked in the gut.

"And this Menendez bitch is my silver sacrifice because her family owns all the silver mines in the country that *you* don't own."

Maria began to struggle. She sat up and yelled. "I'm not part of this. Let me go! You can't do this!" When she started to scream, Nopa hit her with the butt of his pistol and she collapsed. Then he slapped a length of duct tape across her mouth. He glared at Sochi and Claire. "One scream out of you and you get the tape as well."

He prodded Sochi with his toe. "And this one comes from goat herders, and is as common as they come. She will be my copper sacrifice."

His pupils had already begun to dilate.

"Higuchi," Sochi said. "You don't believe in this reincarnation crap. I can see it on your face. So why kill more people than you have to? Give Claire and Maria some San Pedro and let them go. They'll be so high no one will believe them. You'll have time to empty the tomb and be long gone before anyone comes looking for you." She strained against her bindings, ignoring the pain.

"How self-sacrificing of you," Higuchi said, "but no. Nopa has worked hard to make this happen, and I promised him this ceremony."

Claire shifted against the wall. "You know perfectly well that killing us won't harm either Peru or the U.S."

"No, but it will rid me of La Bruja, and it will also be satisfying to see the three of you dead. As for harming Peru, my plan for retribution begins later this morning. Thank you again for finding the tomb." His broad smile made Sochi shiver. "When the sun rises in a few hours, I will begin bringing Peru to its knees. As for the Americans, I will use Peru's downfall to educate the world about the internment camps. Few people know that America did this. I have articles ready to send to the *New York Times*, NPR, the BBC, and other radio and TV stations all across the world. People will learn what was done to my people, to my grandfather."

"Higuchi," Claire said. "I agree that it was horrible. I'm ashamed of what the United States did. Not only did we lock up our own Japanese citizens, but we went trolling for more and bribed your government to turn over all its Japanese citizens. But be reasonable! Our deaths will mean nothing to the world."

"Ah, but they will mean the world to Nopa."

"Enough talk," Nopa said. He was high now, but not in the way Sochi had expected. His gaze was clear, his voice hard. He was totally committed to killing them all. He pulled them to their feet. Maria whimpered but stood. Then, prodding their backs with his gun, he forced them back to the altar chamber. Smoke from the torches burned in Sochi's throat and nostrils. Think, Sochi, *think*. She had to find a way to save Claire.

CHAPTER THIRTY-SEVEN

Claire

Higuchi had returned to the first chamber and was talking to his men. Clanking metal told Claire that they'd begun packing up the treasure. Normally, she would have been upset they were destroying valuable evidence about an ancient culture, but with herself and Sochi about to be sacrificed to King Chacochutl's reincarnation, all Claire's brain cells were busy. Sweat ran down her neck and back. Her knees burned and her arms had gone numb from shoulders to fingertips.

Nopa had begun to chant and gently sway. Sochi and Claire looked at each other with the same thought. He was distracted now, so perhaps they could somehow get the gun away from him. Maria's eyes were glazed with terror; luckily, her mouth was taped, since Claire was frightened enough without Maria sharing her own fears.

Claire looked at Sochi, then back at Nopa's gun, which he held loosely in one hand as he swayed. "I'm not ready to die," she said to Sochi.

"Me neither."

But before they could get any further in their plot, male voices from the other chambers rose in alarm, with cries of "Stop!"

Two men crowded through the entrance to the altar chamber. "Nopa! Stop this madness."

Claire's heart rose like a euphoric butterfly. Nancho! The man behind Nancho was the guy who'd been following her, the one she'd accosted in the alley.

"Rigo, thank the gods," Sochi whispered.

The two men filled the doorway, and only now that they stood together could Claire see the resemblance between all three men—Nancho, Rigo, and Nopa.

"Nancho," she said. "Nopa thinks he's going to sacrifice us on this altar."

"Mrs. Claire, I am so sorry about my evil cousin."

Sochi actually laughed. "The three of you could be brothers."

"I'm sorry, *jefe*," Rigo said. "Nopa is my evil cousin as well."

"Go away," Nopa said to the men. "I do not want you here."

Claire looked between Nancho and Rigo. "So you two are cousins then." They nodded. "You were the man I saw at Mardonio's wake."

"Yes, that was me."

She glared at Nancho. "You knew your cousin followed us every day."

Nancho shrugged.

"Well, forget that for now. You've come just in time," Claire said. "How did you know we were here?"

"Higuchi called our cousin Miguelito, so Miguelito called us to come help move the treasure. But when we heard about the treasure, we feared you were in danger."

"You feared right," Sochi said.

Nancho took a step toward Nopa. "You cannot do this. It is one thing for your branch of the family to tend to the tomb, even though most of us didn't believe it existed. But now, for you to think you can bring Chaco back to life?" He took another step. "The whole family knew you were crazy, but we never realized you were actually insane."

The first bullet hit Nancho so hard in the shoulder he spun around and collapsed face down in the dirt. The second bullet hit Rigo in the chest. He flew back against the wall, then slid down, legs bent beneath him, unconscious. Claire's ears rang with the gunshots and everything sounded very far away. Blood had spattered against the dull gold walls, and began pooling in the dirt at their feet. Maria whimpered, and Sochi's face was white as the moon. Claire's eyes teared up, but her hands weren't free to wipe them. Her vision blurred.

Nopa stood facing his fallen cousins. "You stupid idiots! You made me shoot you. This is all your fault. You know how important Chaco is to my family."

Neither man moved. Claire stared hard, praying to see some sign of life in either man. Finally, Nancho's foot moved slightly. Rigo's chest rose and fell, but just barely. They were still alive, but they were no longer in any condition to help.

Sochi and Claire exchanged a quick glance. This was really going to happen now. The last two people who might have stopped Nopa were unconscious and possibly dying.

Higuchi appeared in the doorway. "Nopa, you seem to have shot your cousins."

"They were going to stop me."

"Their fault then. The raiding of the tomb is underway, so I have time. How may I assist you?"

Nopa waved the gun at Claire. "We will do the gold sacrifice first."

Sochi rose to her feet as she barked a harsh laugh. "You know nothing about this ritual, do you?"

He whirled on her, waving the gun in her face. "Shut up."

"That's backward," she snapped. "You start with the humble and proceed to the great. Copper is humble, gold is great."

"Sochi, no," Claire cried. She was on her feet now as well.

Nopa cocked his head, his eyes blank as he considered her suggestion. "Yes, I see that you are correct."

Claire threw herself at Sochi, whispering, "I don't have the copper egg. You can't do this without the egg."

Sochi leaned in as the two men began pulling them apart. "I have it. How do I use it?"

Fear and frustration ripped through Claire as she pressed her cheek against Sochi's for the last time. "I have no idea."

Higuchi pushed Claire back against the wall hard enough that she tripped and fell. He tied her feet and stretched duct tape across her mouth so tightly her skin stung. Then he helped Nopa carry a writhing, cursing, kicking Sochi toward the altar.

Claire rolled on her side, terrified and powerless. One of the visions she'd seen through the copper egg had come to life: Ixchel had watched Cualli being dragged to her death, and now Claire was watching the same thing happen to Sochi.

CHAPTER THIRTY-EIGHT

Sochi

As she was dragged toward the altar, Sochi frantically scanned it for clues. What the hell was she supposed to do with the copper egg? She would not get a second chance. If she didn't figure it out, all three of them were dead.

Nopa half-pulled, half-lifted Sochi up onto the altar. The stone was cool; the carved design of the warrior cut into her shoulder and thighs. Wrists still cuffed, she lay twisted on the slab.

"I am ready for the knife," Nopa said.

Sochi swallowed. Gods, this wasn't really the way she'd pictured going out, not that she'd spent much time thinking about her death. She sent a silent apology to Mima.

Higuchi pulled a long, wicked-looking knife from the bag at his feet.

Nopa hesitated. "No, I no longer want that one. We must use the Tumi knife from the treasure chamber."

While the two of them returned to the other chamber, Sochi raised her hips high enough to shift her shorts until her right pocket rotated nearly over her butt. She managed to slide a few fingers inside, wincing at the burning around her wrists. It took her three tries, but she scooped up all three eggs. She put two in one hand, then lifted the third for Claire to see.

"Copper?" she whispered over her shoulder.

Claire's mouth was covered, but she could still make a negative sound in her throat.

Sochi held up a second egg.

Claire made the negative sound again.

Sochi held up the third, worried she might have gotten them mixed up as she passed them from hand to hand.

Claire hummed a "yes."

Sochi let herself fall back onto her shoulder. Her arms were going numb. She was never going to be able to do this with her hands tied.

She'd had a split second to scan the altar surface before Nopa thrust her onto it. Lying there, she tried to put herself in Atl's place. He had wanted to protect his daughter. The copper egg played a role. He had to find some easy way for this to happen since he couldn't explain it to her.

The carved warrior's reed skirt spun out around him. From the perspective of where she lay, many of the reed spikes reached the left side of the altar, ending in multiple oval, egg-shaped depressions. But only one reed spike touched the right side of the altar, ending in one egg-shaped depression. Assuming Ixchel was right-handed, this was the only logical place for the egg. But had she been right-handed? And would that hole line up with Sochi's hand when she could lie flat on her back?

The men returned. Nopa moved toward the altar. "We will use this knife," he announced, waving the sharp Tumi knife. "Gold, silver, and copper. Perfectly symbolic."

"Nopa, you're going to have to untie me. It's not a true sacrifice if the person is restrained." She was spouting bullshit, but he was high enough he might fall for it.

He cut the ties and she moaned, hugging herself with aching arms. The copper egg was tucked into her right palm. She was able to see Claire between the two men. Instead of looking horrified or sad or frightened, the look Claire gave her was calm and confident. Sochi drew courage from Claire's clear gaze. It was classic Claire—don't wallow in your fear. Just do what needed to be done. Sochi nodded her thanks.

Nopa moved to the right side of the altar, Higuchi to the left. Higuchi held her down by her shoulders. Sochi couldn't stop trembling. All three of them breathed rapidly, as if the tomb's oxygen was nearly gone.

Maria had begun to moan, protesting through the tape across her mouth. Claire's gaze was steady.

Sochi forced herself to breathe slowly through her nose. She rested her hand over the altar surface, feeling for the depression. She found it and gently placed the copper egg inside. It fit perfectly.

Nopa began chanting in Quechua, calling forth the spirit of Chacochutl. The chamber echoed with the melodic sounds of the two silver rattles Nopa shook. Then he dropped the rattles. With one hand, he grabbed her hair in his fist. With the other, he picked up the knife.

Higuchi's face was drenched in sweat. Sochi's scalp pinched where Nopa held her. She waited. Gods, the egg hadn't done anything.

But as Nopa moved the knife toward Sochi's throat, she thought of Claire and Mima and her parents and her friends and all the things left to do in her life. She pushed down hard on the egg. The egg dropped. Something underneath her clicked. There was an odd whirring sound. Nopa and Higuchi heard it and exchanged a confused look.

The altar rattled beneath her. Whoosh! Something spun out horizontally from the edges of the altar. Nopa and Higuchi dropped from her sight. Maria let out a muffled but terrified scream. Claire was yelling beneath her tape.

Sochi was afraid to move. The smell of blood and flesh rose up around her, sickly and suffocating. She turned her head. Claire's eyes were filled with tears, but she nodded once. *You did it*, the proud nod said.

Sochi took a few deep breaths until her heart stopped racing. Slowly, her muscles protesting, she sat up. That's when she saw Nopa and Higuchi, both nearly cut in two, splayed out on the ground in pools of blood. Two long blades, dripping with blood, jutted out from the left and right sides of the altar.

Suddenly wobbly, Sochi lay back down. She held up one finger and Maria quieted. They needed to be freed, but her knees wouldn't work just yet.

A few minutes later, she slid off the end of the altar and stood. She managed to take one step on her liquefied knees, then another, careful to avoid the carnage at her feet. She used the knife Nopa had dropped to cut Claire and Maria free.

Claire and Sochi collapsed into each other, pulling Maria into their quick hug. Then they crawled over to Nancho and Rigo.

The men were still alive.

CHAPTER THIRTY-NINE

Claire

Claire shook Nancho until he moaned and opened his eyes. She used another few inches of one of her tank tops to staunch the blood. He was weak, but insisted on talking through lips caked with dirt. "I am so sorry, Mrs. Claire. We have known that Nopa is crazy. We just didn't know what to do about it."

Rigo's condition was more serious. While Sochi tried to stop the bleeding, Maria sprang into action, calling the police emergency number. Then she retrieved Nopa's handgun and marched back through the chambers. Now that she wasn't tied up, Maria had lost her fear. She yelled horrible threats to the men stealing the treasure, and then she was back.

"The looters are gone. All of the treasure is still either in the chamber or stacked outside by the ladder." She lightly touched Claire's arm. "I am sorry I was so ungrateful the day you rescued me. I thought you were a terrorist."

Claire gave her a quick hug. "Don't worry about it."

Within minutes, sirens blared outside. Between Claire and Maria, Nancho was able to walk to the ladder, where the emergency personnel took over.

After stopping the bleeding, the emergency crew then strapped Rigo to a stretcher and managed to get him up the ladder as well. One of the men wanted to look at the bandaged wound on Claire's arm, but she waved him off.

Claire and Sochi were both anxious to follow the ambulances, but the police insisted on interviewing them. After about thirty minutes of questions, Claire remembered her promise to the reporter, so she used Sochi's cell to call her. Luisa soon arrived, bleary-eyed but armed with her notebook. Claire wanted to make sure the tomb hit the news so Aurelio and the CNTP couldn't keep it to themselves.

Claire knew the cops kept asking questions because her story sounded pretty freaky. And to ensure that none of them were charged with murder, Claire showed them the blades in the altar. She tried explaining about Ixchel and her father Atl, and how he designed the egg and the altar so that his daughter could escape sacrifice, but the cops, older guys with gray hair and skeptical eyes, kept shaking their heads. Another set of police had been dispatched to Denis's house, and both Mima and Denis had been released. Denis had a concussion, but Mima refused to go to the hospital. Sochi called cousins to make sure Mima was surrounded by family.

Finally, finally, Claire was able to climb the ladder, Sochi right behind her. The sky had begun to lighten above the Andes to the east, and Claire was suddenly more tired than she'd ever been in her life. Sochi slipped her hand into Claire's. "I need to sit for a while," Sochi said. "I need to let all of this sink in before the day starts."

She led them to the far western edge of the hill, where Claire welcomed the sound of the surf—loud and boisterous—after the muted voices in the chamber. The slight breeze refreshed her sore and tired body.

They both lay down in the sand, looking up at the sky. The Carina Nebula had almost totally faded as day approached. "Treasure hunts are exhausting," Claire said.

"So is being nearly sacrificed."

They held hands. "You did it," Claire said. "You figured out how to use the egg."

"It helped that you didn't panic. You seemed certain I could do it."

"It's weird, but I found myself trusting Atl, of all people. I never saw him in the visions, and have no idea what he was like as a man, but if Atl's message to Ixchel was that the copper egg would save her life, I trusted that Atl had figured out a way to make that happen." Claire squeezed Sochi's hand. "Thank you for not dying."

Her answering smile was bright in the dim light. "So was the treasure worth all that's happened?"

Claire rose up on her elbows and leaned close. "I could give a rip about the treasure in the tomb below us."

Her face must have softened because Sochi groaned. "You're not going to get all mushy and say that the only treasure you care about is me, are you?"

Claire lowered her lips and showed her exactly how mushy she was feeling.

"Mmmm," was Sochi's reply.

"Seriously, you are the treasure worth hunting for, and now that I have you again—I do have you, right?"

Sochi laughed and nodded.

"Now that I have you again, I'm not going to lose you."

Sochi nestled against her shoulder. "I just wish we knew how Ixchel's story ended."

Claire sat up. "Could I see the egg for a minute?"

Sochi reached for her pocket, then stopped. "I don't know. This thing has become really important to me."

"I'll trade you." Claire reached into her cargo pocket and withdrew the moon shell she'd taken from the cache in the mountains, the one Sochi had left there to show how unimportant their relationship had been to her. "I thought you might want it back."

With a happy sigh and a few more kisses, Sochi traded the copper egg for the shell.

Claire held the egg in her palm. Nothing. "Crap. And I'll bet Aurelio is going to want the eggs today, isn't he?"

At that moment, Sochi's boss, Aurelio, emerged from the tomb, snapping instructions to someone below. He approached Claire, his hand outstretched. "I just wanted to thank you, Ms. Adams, for your fine work. This is an incredible day for Peru, and for all lovers of Peruvian culture."

She stood and shook his hand.

"We have already done a quick survey and have discovered the skeletons belong to nineteen women and one man, since one of the skeletons has the narrower sciatic notch and pelvic inlet."

"A man?" She raised an eyebrow at Sochi. With a wave, Aurelio and his staff headed down the hill, sliding in the sand.

They looked at the copper egg in Claire's hand. Clearly, it was not going to give her what she wanted.

"Oh, what the hell." Claire dug out the vial containing the half-piece of San Pedro. "Will you watch over me and make sure I get home? Make sure no one takes advantage of me?"

Sochi pulled her into an embrace, their hips nestling happily together. "I want you to be fully awake when I take advantage of you." After another kiss that left her weak-kneed, Claire swallowed the San Pedro.

Ixchel sat on the dune with Tochi. He gave her the gold egg. "Cualli had this made for me. You should have it."

Then he pulled out the silver egg. "She gave this to me just before she ran after you and the administrator. You should have it as well."

Ixchel's vision blurred. She rubbed her eyes. She must stop crying. "What will you do now?"

Tochi hugged her. "There is someone for me. Cualli always knew I married her for my family. Now I act for myself. But first, I will provide a distraction for you," Tochi said. He quietly slipped away down the dune.

Ixchel's heart was heavier than rock. She must see Cualli. She must say good-bye.

She watched the guards and heard shouts from the shore. Tochi was yelling something threatening. Guards ran to check on the disturbance, leaving the entrance to the tomb unguarded.

Ixchel slid down the dune and through the open tomb door. She ran down a narrow tunnel that twisted and turned. She ended up in a chamber full of gold. She cared nothing for this. The smell of death called to her so she hurried to the next chamber. Dead bodies of women and llamas ran down the center of the chamber. Ixchel covered her nose.

There, in the middle, was Cualli, her neck bloodied, her face pale. With an anguished cry, Ixchel fell to her knees and rested her head on Cualli's chest. The chest rose and fell.

"What?" Ixchel looked up.

Cualli's eyes were open and she was smiling. "I knew you would come for me. I've been afraid to move until then."

Ixchel's heart expanded until it no longer fit inside her. "How? How?"

Cualli sat up. "Your egg. It saved me. But it killed Nopaltzin. I was frightened people would blame me, so I drew a line of blood across my neck and lay down with the other sacrifices and played dead. Someone will come soon, however, so we must go."

They rose. Ixchel saw that without Cualli, there were not enough bodies in the row. The administrators would find another girl or woman to kill. Ixchel asked, "Where is Nopaltzin?"

Cualli led her deeper into the tomb, into a chamber with another exit. Ixchel's stomach turned at the sight of Nopaltzin's body nearly cut in half.

"First, we must hide the blades," Ixchel said. They lifted off the top of the altar and peered into its workings. She swelled with pride. When the egg depressed a lever, the lever released the pins and the blades flew. She carefully moved the blades back into the altar and reset the pins, then sent a thank you to her father for his gift.

"Next, take off your clothes," Ixchel told Cualli.

While Cualli did this, Ixchel undressed Nopaltzin. She was soon sticky and hot with the administrator's blood.

They moved his body to the sacrifice chamber, dressed it in Cualli's clothes, and rearranged the hair of the women on either side so it looked like women's hair around Nopaltzin's head.

Cualli was worried. "People will wonder where Nopatlzin has gone."

Ixchel smiled. She left a pile of clothing near King Chaco's head—Nopaltzin's sandals, pouch, and any clothing not soaked in blood. "They will see the pile of Nopaltzin's clothing next to Chaco's body and believe that he accompanied Chaco on his journey. It will be considered a great miracle."

Cualli opened her hand. "What do I do with the copper egg?"

Ixchel had the other two eggs as well. "We will leave them behind. Start a new life. Someone else may need the eggs some day." They slipped the eggs into Ixchel's pouch and she tied the pouch around what was left of Nopaltzin's waist.

Ixchel removed a fine woven blanket from the pile of treasures and wrapped it around Cualli. They left the tomb by the rear tunnel.

"Where are we going?"

Ixchel held her hand. "We will stop to see how Uncle fares. We will get you clothes. Then we will leave Chan Chan and shed the past like a snake sheds its skin. We will build a new future together."

Claire snapped out of the vision to find herself still in Sochi's arms, their bodies still pressed together, which was good because Claire's world tipped crazily. The activity near the tomb looked like splotches of color instead of like people. Traffic had begun to move up and down the Pan American. Her mouth felt like it was lined with cotton balls. God, she was hungry. Who knew San Pedro could make you so hungry?

She sighed and gave Sochi back the egg. "You may give this to Aurelio now." She threw her arms around Sochi. "I love you so much."

"You're high."

"I still love you."

"This is good, since I love you. Now what about Ixchel?"

Claire nuzzled into Sochi's neck, breathing in the scent of her future, a scent she would never tire of for centuries to come. "I'm so famished. Maybe some *orejitas*, and a really good burger. Do you know that I really, really love you?"

Sochi laughed, pulling her down the hill. "And Ixchel?"

Claire sighed again, feeling as if she floated over the sand. She hoped she came down soon, but was warmed by the knowledge that Sochi would be there to catch her.

"Ixchel and Cualli did the same thing we're going to do."

"What's that?"

"Leave Chan Chan. Shed the past like a snake sheds its skin. Build a new future together."

"Where will we live?"

"I don't care."

"Claire, I don't care either. I'm letting go. I can't save every artifact still buried in Peru, and it was crazy to try. We can live anywhere you want."

Claire stumbled then leaned on Sochi's arm for support, whispering, "Did you know I like how dog feet smell?"

"Oh, baby, you are so high."

"I think they smell like toast. Will Suyana's feet smell like toast?" Claire had never felt so happy, even though the sugarcane plants ahead looked like skinny elves dancing to the breeze off the ocean.

"We won't adopt her unless they do."

Hand in hand, they slid down the last of the hill and headed for Chan Chan.

Claire sighed happily. Searching for a dog with great-smelling feet would be another treasure hunt, but this hunt would be the very best kind—one she didn't have to do alone.

About the Author

Catherine Friend has won four Golden Crown Literary awards, as well as an Alice B. award for her body of work. Several of her books have been finalists for a Lambda Literary Award, including her memoir, *Sheepish: Two Women, Fifty Sheep, and Enough Wool to Save the Planet.* She and her wife, Melissa, raise sheep on their southeastern Minnesota farm. She writes fiction, memoir, nonfiction, and children's books. She's won a Minnesota Book Award and the Loft/McKnight Fellowship in Children's Literature. She loves to snowshoe around her farm in the winter, and hang out with the sheep in the summer. She knits, swims, and is perfectly happy leaving the wild adventures to her characters.

Learn more about Catherine at www.catherinefriend.com.

Books Available from Bold Strokes Books

A Touch of Temptation by Julie Blair. Recent law school graduate Kate Dawson's ordained path to the perfect life gets thrown off course when handsome butch top Chris Brent initiates her to sexual pleasure. (978-1-62639-488-9)

Beneath the Waves by Ali Vali. Kai Merlin and Vivien Palmer love the water and the secrets trapped in the depths, but if Kai gives in to her feelings, it might come at a cost to her entire realm. (978-1-62639-609-8)

Girls on Campus edited by Sandy Lowe and Stacia Seaman. College: four years when rules are made to be broken. This collection is required reading for anyone looking to earn an A in sex ed. (978-1-62639-733-0)

Heart of the Pack by Jenny Frame. Human Selena Miller falls for the domineering Caden Wolfgang, but will their love survive Selena learning the Wolfgangs are werewolves? (978-1-62639-566-4)

Miss Match by Fiona Riley. Matchmaker Samantha Monteiro makes the impossible possible for everyone but herself. Is mysterious dancer Lucinda Moss her own perfect match? (978-1-62639-574-9)

Paladins of the Storm Lord by Barbara Ann Wright. Lieutenant Cordelia Ross must choose between duty and honor when a man with godlike powers forces her soldiers to provoke an alien threat. (978-1-62639-604-3)

Taking a Gamble by P.J. Trebelhorn. Storage auction buyer Cassidy Holmes and postal worker Erica Jacobs want different things out of life, but taking a gamble on love might prove lucky for them both. (978-1-62639-542-8)

The Copper Egg by Catherine Friend. Archeologist Claire Adams wants to find the buried treasure in Peru. Her ex, Sochi Castillo, wants to steal it. The last thing either of them wants is to still be in love. (978-1-62639-613-5)

The Iron Phoenix by Rebecca Harwell. Seventeen-year-old Nadya must master her unusual powers to stop a killer, prevent civil war, and rescue the girl she loves, while storms ravage her island city. (978-1-62639-744-6)

A Reunion to Remember by TJ Thomas. Reunited after a decade, Jo Adams and Rhonda Black must navigate a significant age difference, family dynamics, and their own desires and fears to explore an opportunity for love. (978-1-62639-534-3)

Built to Last by Aurora Rey. When Professor Olivia Bennett hires contractor Joss Bauer to restore her dilapidated farmhouse, she learns her heart, as much as her house, is in need of a renovation. (978-1-62639-552-7)

Capsized by Julie Cannon.What happens when a woman turns your life completely upside down? (978-1-62639-479-7)

Girls With Guns by Ali Vali, Carsen Taite, and Michelle Grubb. Three stories by three talented crime writers—Carsen Taite, Ali Vali, and Michelle Grubb—each packing her own special brand of heat. (978-1-62639-585-5)

Heartscapes by MJ Williamz. Will Odette ever recover her memory or is Jesse condemned to remember their love alone? (978-1-62639-532-9)

Murder on the Rocks by Clara Nipper. Detective Jill Rogers lives with two things on her mind: sex and murder. While an ice storm cripples Tulsa, two things stand in Jill's way: her lover and the DA. (978-1-62639-600-5)

Necromantia by Sheri Lewis Wohl. When seeing dead people is more than a movie tagline. (978-1-62639-611-1)

Salvation by I. Beacham. Claire's long-term partner now hates her, for all the wrong reasons, and she sees no future until she meets Regan, who challenges her to face the truth and find love. (978-1-62639-548-0)

Trigger by Jessica Webb. Dr. Kate Morrison races to discover how to defuse human bombs while learning to trust her increasingly strong feelings for the lead investigator, Sergeant Andy Wyles. (978-1-62639-669-2)

24/7 by Yolanda Wallace. When the trip of a lifetime becomes a pitched battle between life and death, will anyone survive? (978-1-62639-619-7)

A Return to Arms by Sheree Greer. When a police shooting makes national headlines, activists Folami and Toya struggle to balance their relationship and political allegiances, a struggle intensified after a fiery young artist enters their lives. (978-1-62639-681-4)

After the Fire by Emily Smith. Paramedic Connor Haus is convinced her time for love has come and gone, but when firefighter Logan Curtis comes into town, she learns it may not be too late after all. (978-1-62639-652-4)

Dian's Ghost by Justine Saracen. The road to genocide is paved with good intentions. (978-1-62639-594-7)

Fortunate Sum by M. Ullrich. Financial advisor Catherine Carter lives a calculated life, but after a collision with spunky Imogene Harris (her latest client) and unsolicited predictions, Catherine finds herself facing an unexpected variable: Love. (978-1-62639-530-5)

Soul to Keep by Rebekah Weatherspoon. What *won't* a vampire do for love… (978-1-62639-616-6)

When I Knew You by KE Payne. Eight letters, three friends, two lovers, one secret. Can the past ever be forgiven? (978-1-62639-562-6)

Wild Shores by Radclyffe. Can two women on opposite sides of an oil spill find a way to save both a wildlife sanctuary and their hearts? (978-1-62639-645-6)

Love on Tap by Karis Walsh. Beer and romance are brewing for Tace Lomond when archaeologist Berit Katsaros comes into her life. (987-1-62639-564-0)

Love on the Red Rocks by Lisa Moreau. An unexpected romance at a lesbian resort forces Malley to face her greatest fears where she must choose between playing it safe or taking a chance at true happiness. (987-1-62639-660-9)

Tracker and the Spy by D. Jackson Leigh. There are lessons for all when Captain Tanisha is assigned untried pyro Kyle and a lovesick dragon horse for a mission to track the leader of a dangerous cult. (987-1-62639-448-3)

Whirlwind Romance by Kris Bryant. Will chasing the girl break Tristan's heart or give her something she's never had before? (987-1-62639-581-7)

Whiskey Sunrise by Missouri Vaun. Culture and religion collide when Lovey Porter, daughter of a local Baptist minister, falls for the handsome thrill-seeking moonshine runner, Royal Duval. (987-1-62639-519-0)

Dyre: By Moon's Light by Rachel E. Bailey. A young werewolf, Des, guards the aging leader of all the Packs: the Dyre. Stable employment—nice work, if you can get it…at least until silver bullets start to fly. (978-1-62639-662-3)

Fragile Wings by Rebecca S. Buck. In Roaring Twenties London, can Evelyn Hopkins find love with Jos Singleton or will the scars of the Great War crush her dreams? (978-1-62639-546-6)

Live and Love Again by Jan Gayle. Jessica Whitney could be Sarah Jarret's second chance at love, but their differences and Sarah's grief continue to come between their budding relationship. (978-1-62639-517-6)

Starstruck by Lesley Davis. Actress Cassidy Hayes and writer Aiden Darrow find out the hard way not all life-threatening drama is confined to the TV screen or the pages of a manuscript. (978-1-62639-523-7)

Stealing Sunshine by Tina Michele. Under the Central Florida sun, two women struggle between fear and love as a dangerous plot of deception and revenge threatens to steal priceless art and lives. (978-1-62639-445-2)

The Fifth Gospel by Michelle Grubb. Hiding a Vatican secret is dangerous—sharing the secret suicidal—can Felicity survive a perilous book tour, and will her PR specialist, Anna, be there when it's all over? (978-1-62639-447-6)

Cold to the Touch by Cari Hunter. A drug addict's murder is the start of a dangerous investigation for Detective Sanne Jensen and Dr. Meg Fielding, as they try to stop a killer with no conscience. (978-1-62639-526-8)

Forsaken by Laydin Michaels. The hunt for a killer teaches one woman that she must overcome her fear in order to love, and another that success is meaningless without happiness. (978-1-62639-481-0)

Infiltration by Jackie D. When a CIA breach is imminent, a Marine instructor must stop the attack while protecting her heart from being disarmed by a recruit. (978-1-62639-521-3)

Midnight at the Orpheus by Alyssa Linn Palmer. Two women desperate to make their way in the world, a man hell-bent on revenge, and a cop risking his career: all in a day's work in Capone's Chicago. (978-1-62639-607-4)

Spirit of the Dance by Mardi Alexander. Major Sorla Reardon's return to her family farm to heal threatens Riley Johnson's safe life when small-town secrets are revealed, and love may not conquer all. (978-1-62639-583-1)